Praise for **ST.**

"*St. Christopher on Pluto* is good word medicine. I belly laughed and was so touched so many times, I had to keep tissues on hand. I will stock up and give this book to any friend overwhelmed by life."

—Beverly Donofrio,
author of *Riding in Cars with Boys*

"Set amidst Pennsylvania small-town life, the linked stories in *St. Christopher on Pluto* tackle big subjects: war, faith, AIDS, female friendship, race, and aging. Gravitas and comedy are not an easy combination, but Nancy McKinley masterfully mixes the two in a moving, memorable, and inspiring collection."

—Steven Schwartz,
author of *Madagascar: New and Selected Stories*

"A dazzling collection, recounted in multiple colloquial voices and acute imagery that conveys a palpable and cinematic sense of place."

—J. Michael Lennon,
author of *Norman Mailer: A Double Life*

"This book is the real hillbilly elegy, this tour through an Appalachia whose female warriors mess up and flounder but somehow survive. Nancy McKinley's stories are both sad and hilarious, and punctuated by unexpected wonder."

—John Vernon, author of *The Last Canyon*

NANCY McKINLEY

ST. CHRISTOPHER ON PLUTO

WEST VIRGINIA UNIVERSITY PRESS
MORGANTOWN

First edition published 2020 by West Virginia University Press
Printed in the United States of America

This is a work of fiction. Names, characters, places, and incidents are the products of the author's imagination or are used fictitiously. Any resemblance to actual events, locales, or persons, living or dead, is entirely coincidental.

ISBN
Paper 978-1-949199-26-0
Ebook 978-1-949199-27-7

Library of Congress Cataloging-in-Publication Data
is available from the Library of Congress

Book and cover design by Than Saffel / WVU Press

Stories in *St. Christopher on Pluto* appeared in slightly different form in the following publications:
"Cara Dog," *To Unsnare Time's Warp Anthology: A 2016 Main Street Rag Short Fiction Anthology*; "Navidad," *Cortland Review,* issue 53, 2011; "Signed Sealed Delivered," *Tattoos: A 2012 Main Street Rag Short Fiction Anthology*; "Sweet the Sound," *Blue Lake Review,* February 2013; "Less Said," *Punkin House Digest: Family Edition,* volume 1, edition 2, 2011; "Yellow Tape," *Coming Home: A 2010 Main Street Rag Short Fiction Anthology*; "Love, Masque & Folly," *Porches: A 2013 Main Street Rag Short Fiction Anthology*; "Hand Against the Horn," *Timberline Review,* Issue 7, 2018; "Ramp," in *Blue Penny Quarterly,* Spring 2014.

To My Family
Mike, Darcy, Kelsi, Hali

I think it is a good thing that important events which quite accidentally have never seen the light of day should be made public and not buried in the grave of oblivion.

—*Lazarillo de Tormes,* sixteenth-century novel

CONTENTS

ST. CHRISTOPHER
ON PLUTO

THE MOMENT I steer Big Blue from Anthracite Expressway onto a dirt road, I regret following Colleen to the mechanic. She asked me for a ride so she can leave her Honda. The '81 silver hatchback, dented like an old beer can, belches smoke and needs a head gasket. Colleen said the repairs cost more than blue book value. But what choice does she have? She can't get a loan for a new car due to a bad credit rating, the result of a marriage that ended way back. Why she keeps full insurance on the wreck is beyond me.

Her Honda slows, and I read her newest bumper sticker: *The Suburbs—Where They Chop Down Trees and Name Streets After Them*. Doesn't Colleen realize farmers cut the trees a hundred years ago? Housing developments ravage corn fields, not forests. I'll have to mention that when she gets in Big Blue.

She sticks her hand out of her open window and gives a thumbs-up. Why? I wonder, trying to fathom our route. We're on a service access built by the railroad to transport crops that once grew along the Mighty Susquehanna. Nobody drives these unpaved tracks other than hunters. It's October, too early for deer season, so tires haven't deepened the ruts, but a rock jabs Big Blue. The shocks protest. Big Blue doesn't like rough conditions. Me neither. If the surface gets worse, I'll pull over and tell Colleen she needs to get a ride from a four-wheel drive. How can a mechanic operate a business this far from Wilkes-Barre?

We descend a switchback flanked by pin oak, their limbs gnarled and gray, warning of the river below. Deceivingly shallow, the water rarely rises, but when it floods, there's no stopping it. That's why industry hasn't built here. Homeowners won't take the risk either. Yet as Big Blue rounds a curve, I witness how civilization stakes its claim: tires, box springs, refrigerators, lots of cans and bottles heaped like ancient prayer mounds. Next thing, Colleen will lobby for trash removal. She's an activist for any cause that's happening, especially those with bragging rights. I couldn't shut her up after she organized the First Annual Mall Parking Lot Cleanup Day. "See what one woman can accomplish. Me. Impressive, huh? Can't sit around doing nothing."

Her Honda stalls. Colleen waves, fingers waggling to communicate since our cell phones don't get coverage out here.

I blast my horn, "What?"

Her door opens, and Colleen heaves upright. She wears all black: tunic sweater, maxi skirt, and square toe flats with buckles like Pilgrim shoes. "Black is slimming," she has assured me.

We're both sensitive about our weight, and during our breaks, we get low-fat items at the food court. That's where we reconnected. While standing in line at the Java Bean, we each called out the same order: "Small coffee with Splenda." While waiting for my order, I turned to see a big, red-haired woman, wearing a T-shirt emblazoned with fluorescent green—SAVE PLUTO—and below the words, not an image of the cartoon character or the underworld's mythic god, but a picture of the little planet. Pluto had been in the news ever since astronomers ousted it from the solar system, saying it was too small to be officially recognized. The demotion sparked protests around the globe. Who in their right mind rallies for a dwarf planet?

"ME! Don't you recognize me?" called the large woman.

My memory clicked: "Colleen," I said. We had attended Our Lady of Perpetual Help Elementary School, but back then, she was lean, her hair pinned above her collar as required by the nuns. How different it looked, fanning out in a peculiar red, obviously bottle enhanced.

Colleen grinned and yammered like we still sat in the same row. No matter that we lost touch when we went off to different high schools—Colleen to Vo Tech and me to St. Rose Prep. Life had put us into different orbits for decades. Then our jobs landed us at the mall. "I work at the Hallmark store," announced Colleen.

"I'm at Waldenbooks," I added. That was before they got bought out by Borders.

She raised her eyebrows, tweezed with the curve of question marks, "What would Thoreau say if he saw that name in neon at a Pennsylvania mall?"

Her humor was a relief from my semiretired coworkers. Most brought bag lunches and thermoses supposedly filled with coffee. I pretended not to smell the difference. Nobody fell down drunk. They just sipped and smiled at customers who came in to buy self-help books.

Colleen steps away from her Honda and thrusts out her chest like a bow on a ship. Wind fills her skirt and she sails toward Big Blue. She pokes her head in my open window. "The engine's overheating. I've got to let it rest."

"Where are we?" I keep my voice level, so she can't tease me about my anxiety. "How did you find this place?"

She rounds her mouth. Her lipstick is the same mud color as

the road. She leans in closer, and I sniff cucumber melon lotion. Her tone becomes confidential, "I've finished the next part of the novel."

Colleen claims I'm her favorite editor. How she determines this is a mystery, for none of her book has made it onto the page. She writes in her head. Ten months ago, she took a one-night writing class at Boscov's department store, and ever since, she bubbles over with what she calls "The Novel of the Century." She thinks my job at the bookstore will give her a connection to get it published, yet I've reminded her, "I work in the music section, selling the stuff people listen to on public radio."

She purses her lips, expecting me to ask about her material, but we don't have the right atmosphere. Typically, we go to the Riverbed Tavern for the Thursday special: two Yuengling drafts for the price of one, and until we counted calories, cheese filled potato skins. Colleen gabs about characters scraping by at a mall, not so different from us. The women, well-meaning and still sexy at midlife, try their best to help others, and along the way, they find love, too. I can't let Colleen start blathering out here. "This place is creepy."

"I figured you'd say that, Mary Katherine."

I press my upper teeth to my lowers. Colleen knows I haven't used that name since I was a kid. What's she up to?

"I mean MK," she corrects, kind of smarmy.

Maybe she's got a thing for the mechanic? Why else act so weird? A new man in her life might be good, yet I can't help thinking something is wrong. I hope this guy isn't a loser or that Colleen has made a deal she'll regret. Sun filters through the rear window, lowering on the back of my neck, a reminder of limited daylight. "Let's go. Your engine should be cooled."

"Got any food?"

"What about our diet?"

Her nostrils quiver. "I have to eat. For my low blood sugar. I can't help it if I inherited large genes."

Here she goes again.

"My family's Irish. Everyone's large."

Colleen's declaration undoubtedly covers up Polish or German heritage from immigrants who settled long before the Irish, but her red hair, what she considers alluring, forges her link to the Emerald Isle. "How could your relatives get big with a history of potato famine?" I ask.

She shakes her red mane, just like she always does when I call her on a whopper. "Celtic warriors," she rails and stomps off to her car. The Honda starts so suddenly, it lurches ahead, funneling dust.

I roll up my window. Big Blue wheezes, reminiscent of my grandmother who willed me this Buick. I can practically hear her warn how I'll need a tow truck if I'm not careful. Most vehicles past the age of forty head for demolition derby, but Big Blue, pampered like a virgin queen, took few excursions beyond my grandmother's five-mile loop: Weis Markets, Golden Touch Beauty Shop, and Our Lady of Perpetual Help Church.

A pothole nips at Big Blue's rear tire, and we shake like we're on a roller coaster, causing the St. Christopher statue on the dash to list to one side. Originally put there by my grandmother, I press the figure's plastic base onto blue vinyl, making a mental note to glue it later.

The four-inch glow-in-the-dark statue, not much bigger than a clothespin, depicts a bearded man wearing a toga. He clutches a staff, and on his shoulder, sits the child Jesus. But the story goes that St. Christopher didn't know who the child was, heavy with the weight of the world, as he carried the boy across the swollen river. Not until they reached the opposite bank did he learn the child's identity and how Jesus was with him all the time. That's why St. Christopher gets championed for safeguarding drivers. Good thing, for this road has narrowed to one lane, and no one can pass. Perhaps I should try a three-point turn and head back to town, but I fear careening over the side. The shoulder has crumbly soil—ideal cave-in conditions for Big Blue to drop with a deadly plunge.

Colleen speeds up, and smoke mushrooms from her tailpipe. Despite my closed windows, I cough from the exhaust and debate whether it's worse to inhale the noxious air through nose or mouth. We gravitate closer to the river. Sumac bushes scrape the hub caps. Could the mechanic operate a meth lab too? *The Riverside Gazette* has stories about drug dens: the further off the beaten track, the better. I should have asked Colleen for more details, but I'm doing a good deed, and I thought it wouldn't be far.

Boulders, the height of kegs, create a horseshoe formation to block the road. Can't Colleen see the rocks ahead are a barrier? She weaves past them and disappears, emitting so much smoke the Environmental Protection Agency will marshal forces.

I press the brake, shift into park, and venture out. The exhaust mixes with the rotting leaves underfoot, making me gag. I consider the risks of trekking in after Colleen. There's no roar of her Honda, no seizing engine, just a bunch of angry jays.

Big Blue idles. The Buick Regal looks as stately as the first time I saw it, the summer of Granddad's funeral.

Sadness and uncertainty weighed on my brain, for I also heard my mother on the phone, scheduling her own doctor's appointment with a specialist at Geisinger Medical Center in Danville. When I asked her why, she got a pinched look on her face and stared across the kitchen. Then she straightened her shoulders and said what we needed was a day at Knoebels Amusement Park. We'd bring my grandmother, too.

Eager for the flume ride, I trotted to the porch swing. When the phone rang, I didn't rush to answer, figuring it was Aunt

Rosemary. My hunch was confirmed as my mother's voice carried outside. Yet again, she and Aunt Rosemary worried about my grandmother: *Pop drove her everywhere. How will she get by?*

I turned up the volume of my boom box. "Let It Be" filled the sticky air. Then, a big daddy car screamed into the driveway. The front end had a cross-hatched patterned grill and glistened as sunlight blazed over side-by-side round headlights. On the hood stood an ornament like a mini Academy Award. The driver's door opened, and out stepped my grandmother. I didn't even know she had a license, but there she stood, wearing a blue pants suit, the same color as the car, like she planned it.

I leapt from the stairs, waving my hands until she grabbed them for our promenade around the sky bright majesty. She whispered, "Remember, Mary Katherine, when I'm gone, Big Blue is yours." The car was named, and even better, promised to me.

How we grinned, but not my mother and Aunt Rosemary. They carried on like she got a new husband. *She rushed into this. It's too soon. What was she thinking, paying that price for a used car?*

But the deed was done, and I loved everything about Big Blue: shiny chrome trim, blue velour upholstery, radio with cassette player, and despite coming from the preowned lot, the smell of new.

Birds squawk, calling me to the here and now. From above, I see wings flutter in my direction. Below them marches Colleen. Her skirt poufs like a parachute, and she rubs her palms together.

By the time she grabs the passenger door handle, she breathes hard. Her lips peel back from her teeth. "Don't stand there. Let's go before somebody sees us."

I rump bump into the driver's seat and whack my knees on the steering column. Quickly, I set my hands at the 10:00 and 2:00 position, same as my daughter, Jenna, when she got her learner's permit. It's the best handhold for control, yet I expect Colleen to mock my pose. "What about the Honda?" I ask.

"A goner for sure."

"What?" Her comment stabs at my brain. "What do you mean?"

She blinks with a clownish smile.

Is she telling me she dumped her car? "I'm not sure I follow you."

Her grin widens, and she blinks rapid fire.

Too shocked to speak clearly, I stutter, "You're just leaving your car? Haven't you heard of a junk yard?"

"Bye-bye insurance," says Colleen.

"There's no insurance for dumping a car."

"Duh—I know."

On the verge of hyperventilating, I feather the gas. Big Blue chugs along while I try and register what's what. How could Colleen do such a thing? Why didn't I realize what she was up to? Even worse, she used me. Some environmentalist she is. "There's big fines for littering in the Chesapeake Bay watershed."

"Not if the car is stolen."

I hit the brakes. We're going less than ten miles an hour, but Colleen bangs against the dash. The glove box opens. St. Christopher goes belly up. I grunt one word: "Fraud."

Colleen is unrepentant: "I paid full coverage for years. I'm owed a payback."

"Where's your conscience? I can't believe you got me involved with this." I consider pulling over and kicking her out the door. Serve her right to spend hours walking home. But then I worry: What if hunters come scouting and find a fleshy redhead all by her lonesome?

Colleen fiddles with the radio knob, undoubtedly seeking a distraction.

"No reception," I remind her. "This is the boonies."

"The perfect place. When I collect, I'll have enough money for a decent car."

I flex fingers on the steering wheel. "People get incarcerated for insurance fraud. That means prison."

"You always overreact, same as when we were kids." She stares out of the passenger window.

My voice accelerates: "Behind bars might be good. You'll have the time to actually write your book."

"Ever think about the fact you're an accessory?" Her words reverberate with a disturbing impact. Big Blue stops fast in its tracks. I lean across Colleen and force open her door, "Get out right now."

She stiffens, "Wait. Do you hear that?"

My ears strain as the rumble of a vehicle can be heard coming our way.

"Start driving," she whispers, and gently shuts the door.

My palms sweat against the wheel. The road can't hold two vehicles, and with Big Blue on the outside, anything barreling around a curve will edge us into the river below. I attempt a cleansing breath. Colleen fidgets. She slides off the seat and wedges down in a fetal position, butt to floor hump, head riveted to air vent. I'm reminded of gargantuan pumpkins featured on the cover of *Harvest Magazine*, popular at the bookstore this time of year. "What're you doing?"

"Keep your eyes on the road."

I know that sound can travel across water. Maybe the motor noises came from the other side of the river? I roll down my window and listen, but the landscape is mute.

"Speed up when you pass. They can't make a connection if they don't see me."

My brain comprehends the obvious: Big Blue, plus my face,

equals not good. I twist my hips and drive sidesaddle, offering a profile view. Big Blue jerks a bit, but I hold steady, tipping my head just enough to squint through the windshield.

"Why are you sitting that way? Do you have to pee?"

"No," I snap, praying the other vehicle has parked, swallowed by willows, and the driver is doing whatever. I don't care, just so long as the person doesn't get a good look at me or Big Blue.

Colleen rubs her forehead, embossed by the grid of the interior vent. "I'm so squished. I can hardly breathe."

"Sshh." Twenty yards from the road, about the length of a public pool, I see the car nosed into the naked limbs of raspberry bushes. Boxy and wide, the gas-guzzling SUV is topped by a black luggage rack. The rear passenger doors are open like wings while the front doors remain closed.

A man and woman walk with their backs to us. They aren't hunters, no orange vests or camouflage clothing, and it's too cold for a picnic. He has on brown pants, like a UPS guy, but his jacket is leather and goes below his hips. She wears a pink sweater, short denim skirt, and fishnets. The ground, thick with fern, covers their shoes, so I don't know if they're moving slowly because of the uneven terrain or the weight of the rolled-up carpet that they lug between them. It has a bulge in the middle. "I think they're dumping a rug with something in it."

"A rug?"

"It's a mess," I say. Colleen furnishes her apartment with items left at curbside, and I don't want her to get ideas about bringing home the rug.

I eyeball the carpet droppers, surprised more people haven't tossed stuff out here. The county commissioners instituted a policy whereby residents must buy stickers for their garbage bags, so haulers will pick them up. The commissioners figured people would generate less trash and recycle when they had to pay for each bag, but letters to *The Riverside Gazette* suggest no one likes the policy. Some people boycott the stickers completely. At the mall, when I take trash to the dumpster, I find mountains of crap. The manager, Ralph, his arms folded over the tan sweater he wears like a uniform, wants to put a lock on the dumpster, so freeloaders can't use it. Colleen says a lock is not the solution: "Sales tax should absorb the cost of trash pick-up." Yet elected officials fear the word *tax* like a plague, and the irony of Colleen wanting to raise taxes hasn't been lost on me, any more than her ire at the rug dumpers.

"What are they doing?" she asks. Then like a water buffalo hiding girth below surface, she stretches her neck just enough to rest eyes along the window base. "Couple of lowlifes. Backup and get their license plate number."

"Have you forgotten why we're here?"

"You didn't tell me the rug is so stained."

"Yeah, like blood," I say without thinking. Then, I dry swallow. Could the rug hold a body?

The guy turns, and we lock eyes. Time becomes slow motion like I'm looking through the nickelodeon at the Steamtown Museum. My instincts yelp to hit the gas and floor it, but I'm trapped in the high beams of his gaze. Get a grip, says my brain while I try to note his eye color. He's too far away, yet I'd wager brown, same as his hair and droopy moustache.

Colleen ducks down. "Some mug. He's probably wanted."

Her indictment prompts me to gun the gas with race-car fury. Not until the tires roll across the paved road do I breathe freely. I glance at the dashboard clock and am amazed Big Blue managed our escape in less than fifteen minutes. Colleen shifts her elbows onto the seat, pressing hard to hoist up. "What do you bet that dude shaves by the end of the night?"

The more she laughs, the straighter I sit. Am I a complete idiot to have missed what she was up to? How did I fail to realize she was dumping her car? My throat constricts. I want to strangle her, but I can't. I'm not a violent person. I don't even yell. Instead, I listen for rumbles, the sounds of a damaged muffler. Hearing none, I say, "Watch out for deer." The sky, marbled gray, has shifted to dusk. It's cruising time for deer in the rut, and all we need is for an amorous Bambi to buck-up against the hood of Big Blue.

Colleen turns on the radio. Froggy 101 blares out the oldie "Down by the River." She pounds on the dashboard like she requested the song. Seeing my dismay, she says, "Sorry this took so long."

Does she expect me to say it's not a big deal? A highway reflector stake flashes, resembling deer eyeballs. I honk the horn. We pass an abandoned coal breaker. The windows are broken, and the siding, long gone from the two-story structure, exposes a cagework of struts on the verge of collapse.

"You're so tense," says Colleen. She rummages in her shoulder purse, shaped like a toaster, and offers me a piece of gum.

I shake my head no. My breath comes in short bursts, "Those people saw me. What if they're murderers?"

"You have such an imagination—way better than mine."

"They might come looking for me."

"Now that would make a good scene in my book." Colleen chomps her Juicy Fruit. She marches her fingers across the dashboard to the fallen St. Christopher statue, takes the gum from her mouth, sticks it onto the base, and returns St. Christopher to his standing position. "No need to thank me. It was my last piece, you know."

My tongue presses against the back of my teeth.

"How could the church take away his feast day? It's the same as declaring him a bogus saint. A sacrilege, don't you think?" she says, baiting me to talk.

Rather than respond, I stare through the windshield, glad my grandmother never witnessed St. Christopher's demise. How she invoked his prayer, murmuring thanks after each car trip. I'd pray too, but I've parted with the church. Besides, what prayer gets said for stupidly helping a friend dump her car?

Colleen taps the head of St. Christopher, just like my grandmother used to do. Maybe my grandmother would smile at Colleen's ingenuity—using gum to glue the statue. But not at abandoning the Honda. Colleen chirps, "Remember how Sister Paracleta made us memorize the St. Christopher Prayer? I can't recall the words exactly, but it went something like this, right? Oh, Patron of Travelers, help me stay focused with my hands steady on the wheel, so no one gets hurt as I pass by."

I don't think the prayer was anything like her version, but I remain silent.

Undeterred, she continues. "The next part makes me think of you: Oh, St. Christopher, as we journey, let me use my car to assist others."

Colleen is up to no good. I should throttle her, but we're on a curve, and there's no guardrail.

She blurts, "And never speed so fast, we fail to see beauty in the world."

Big Blue whooshes, forcing me to ease off the gas pedal.

Colleen twists her hair around her index finger. "The last line, what is it? Come on MK, help me, I know you can remember it."

I sniffle, recalling our girlhood and how we sat on the playground during recess and memorized catechism lessons. Colleen pretended to need a review of our homework, but her ruse was meant to help me. My brain was a snarled mess after my mom went to the hospital and I had to stay with my grandmother. Unable to sleep, I spent most nights with a pillow over my face. At class, I couldn't recite the homework, much less say the words *cancer* or *breast*. How can Colleen resurrect those dark times? "You put me in terrible danger, dumping your car."

"Is that what you think? Let me guess, you imagine the car rotting by the river until a flood carries it off and the water gets polluted?"

I nod.

She snorts. "No way. I parked there temporarily. I don't like it, but desperate times call for—"

"Listen to you," I scold.

Colleen raises her elbows and finger types on the windshield. "Haven't you learned anything from my book? I'll make right on what happened. It's the storyline for my next chapter."

"Give me a break."

"Where's your faith?" she challenges. "When I took my writing class, the teacher said to write from the place we know."

The sooner I get rid of this conniving car dumper, the better. I coax Big Blue over the speed limit, but then slow down, fearful of deer.

Colleen lowers her hands from the windshield. She expects me to say something nice. Hopefully the quiet will prod her conscience and summon her much-needed remorse.

We travel a mile. She vents, "How can I be creative when you sit there judging me?"

You're reprehensible, says my glare. Then I sigh.

"Let it out, girl."

"Colleen," I snap.

"You'll thank me when Oprah features the book. She'll put both of us in her magazine. You're more than an editor, you're crucial for what happens."

I slump close to the steering wheel. From my angle near the dash, St. Christopher looks different. The child Jesus on his shoulder has grown larger, and they smile. I don't mention anything to Colleen.

She'll allege to have seen their grins, too, adding how they're giving us a positive sign.

"I remember the end of St. Christopher's prayer," she gushes. "Oh, patron of travelers, please protect and guide us to our destiny." All exultant, she taps his head. The statue tips over. "Damn sugarless gum."

I stretch my right arm and set the figure upright. Both St. Christopher and Jesus wink at me. I glance toward the road before looking back at them. Again, they wink. Have I witnessed what scientists call an optical illusion?

"Why are you biting your lip?" asks Colleen.

I shrug, but laughter bubbles up. The absurdity prompts me to tell her what I think I saw: "Can you believe it?"

"Sure, took you long enough," says Colleen. "They wink at me all the time. You just have to be willing to see them."

"What I have to see is the road." I turn on the headlights. Their beams, in need of alignment, project a haze over the river as if I'm looking through a wax-paper shroud. The effect proves oddly comforting. I smile at Colleen, and she smiles back at me. Big Blue purrs. I press gently on the gas pedal, and we motor along like all is well and good.

The absence of chatter makes me think a change has taken place. But why should I feel that way?

Colleen takes a deep breath. I expect she'll tell me, whether or not I ask her.

CARA DOG

ON THAT warm October afternoon, Tiffany rolled down her car window, yet within minutes, she was shivering. Where had the brown dog come from? Why did it charge at her car? Tiffany's foot still hurt from pressing hard on the brake. She hadn't been going fast. Anthracite Expressway had too many curves for that but not much along it other than an abandoned coal breaker, the siding gone from its two-story frame, its beams listing like a toppled cage. Tiffany had seen few houses until she rounded the bend by the tan farmette. Then *Thud*. The sound would stay in her ears forever.

"Shit!" Ron yelled from the passenger seat.

The dog got up, leg spurting blood like an oil rig. Tiffany watched in disbelief as the dog limped toward the house. A gray-haired man, hovering on the porch, knelt and hugged the dog. Time sped up and slowed down all at once. Tiffany had never even hit a squirrel. How had this happened?

Herky-jerky, she pulled off the road and cut the ignition to her SUV, a fourteen-year-old clunker, purchased from her mom's ex-boyfriend. The front end shimmied, clearly in need of a tune-up, but Tiffany had no money for a mechanic. She unbuckled her seatbelt, yanked the handle, and elbowed open the door. Stepping onto the berm, her heels slid on the gravel, forcing her to grasp the side mirror for balance.

Mouth open, she listened as the rumble of cars approached from the same direction she'd driven. Until now, Tiffany hadn't seen any other vehicles along their route. She turned and spied a dented, silver hatchback, so beat up it looked like a wreck from demolition derby. The driver, a woman with red-hair, raised her index finger. Tiffany knew it was a local's gesture for hello, but she felt it pointed at her accusingly: *You hit the dog.* Right behind the hatchback motored a big blue sedan; it edged so close to the berm that Tiffany could see a St. Christopher statue on the dash. What was the deal with those weird statues? Mostly old people put them in their cars, but some kids at her high school had them, too. Tiffany sighed: Why didn't that blue car hit the dog?

"Let's get out of here," hissed Ron.

"I have to check on the dog."

"No, you don't. The guy took it inside."

He's such an asshole, thought Tiffany. What had made her think Ron was nice? Sure, she liked playing pool with him at the Corner Pocket. He paid for their games after she got laid off from Kuhner's Gas & Videos. She wasn't let go for being a crappy worker. Customers just left when Sheetz opened, lured by low fuel prices and Redbox.

Severance pay? Ha. Tiffany got nothing more than free time, opting to go out at night rather than stay home. Ron, a talker, bought them Yuengling on draft. No matter she was a senior at Ridge High.

"You're years ahead of them kids," he said.

When Tiffany announced her plan to leave Northeast Pennsylvania after graduation, he added, "You're smart to think ahead."

"I want to get a job at the Jersey Shore."

But to move, Tiffany needed money.

Ron said the Mohegan Sun, a ritzy casino in the Poconos, was hiring for weekend shifts. "With your personality and looks, you'll make a perfect blackjack dealer."

Tiffany had smiled when he had suggested driving with her to the casino so she could apply for the job. Ron's license had been suspended after he got stopped at a Labor Day checkpoint near Hazleton and refused to take the breathalyzer. "I had a couple beers. I wasn't weaving or anything. Entrapment, that's what happened to me." But not taking the breath test meant no license until he pleaded his case, and the Luzerne County court was backed up for months.

Ron had recommended this winding road even though it lacked signs. He claimed it was better than I-81, fewer miles, so she could save on gas. He paid for her full tank. Ron was thoughtful, not an ass-grabber like the other guys who played pool. She had wondered if he could be gay, but his brown jeans and leather jacket said straight—a straight throwback to the nineties.

Throat dry, Tiffany shuffled away from the car. Her brain replayed the dog's yelps as it hobbled out from the tire. She turned toward the house. Paint peeled from the window frames, kind of scary looking. She wanted to get back in the car and leave, but she had to do the right thing. Could she help the dog?

With small steps, she trod the flagstone walkway, recalling how she had considered becoming a vet tech. Then she learned about euthanizing procedures. Tiffany's neck veins throbbed. She walked up the porch steps, paused by the open door, and glanced out to the roadside. Perhaps it was a good thing she had put the key in her pocket so Ron couldn't drive off with her car. She knocked on the siding.

"Come in," the old man rasped.

Tiffany crossed the threshold. She wrinkled her nose against the musty smell, like the windows hadn't been opened for months, and looked down. Rust-colored paw prints marked the wood floor. She had figured the man had carried the dog inside. But no, the dog had walked. Maybe that was a good sign?

"We're in the den."

Blood swirled like spin art on the white walls, proof of her misdeed. The realization weighted each footstep until she spied the old man kneeling beside the dog, its legs splayed out.

"Cara's gone."

Tiffany's tongue swelled in her mouth. She wanted to tell him how when she had slammed on the brakes her car had stopped so fast, her chest banged against the steering wheel.

"At least I was with her at the end," he sighed.

The scent of blood and dog stink made Tiffany woozy. She cupped her hand over her nose and mouth. The man shifted back on his heels. His flannel shirt seemed askew, one arm longer than the other. But no, his left sleeve was tucked over the empty space of his missing forearm. He petted the dog with his only hand.

Knees weak, Tiffany dropped like a plumb bob and sat beside him. Neither spoke. She tugged down on the hem of her denim skirt, worn with fishnets, so she'd get hired for the casino job. The man reached behind her to the couch and grabbed a crocheted blanket. The black knit was embossed with yellow Steelers football helmets. Tiffany thought he wanted to give her the blanket to cover her thighs, but he placed it over the dog, a big retriever mix.

"Not your fault." He pressed his palm to the braided rug.

Coughs echoed from the hallway. Tiffany smelled Ron's cologne before he entered the room. He stared at her, his dark mustache twitching. His eyes had a molasses tinge that said he felt badly.

Relief powered through Tiffany. Ron wanted to help.

From his leather jacket, he pulled out his wallet and extracted three twenties. "Will this take care of things?"

"Money? I don't want your money," snapped the man.

"Stop!" cried Tiffany. Her urgency startled her.

Both men glared. Not at each other. At her.

She placed her hand over her heart. "So sorry."

"Me too," said the man.

Ron remained silent and put his wallet back in his pocket.

Tiffany sputtered, "I think he figured you could use the money for a burial. At that place near Wilkes-Barre where they bury pets. My mom put Bowzer there." What made Tiffany say such things? She had no idea what Ron thought, most likely that they should get in the car and hope the man wouldn't call the cops.

"I'd never put Cara there. She didn't like cities. Cara liked fishing with me by the river."

"Right," whispered Tiffany, wondering how he fished with just one hand.

"Cara found sticks along the bank."

"I didn't mean to be abrupt," said Ron. "I guess I'm in shock. Like all of us."

The man snorted as Tiffany lifted her chin, uncertain if she should trust Ron's words.

"Thing is, I'm a practical guy," continued Ron. "I grew up on a farm near Shamokin. We had sheep, some cows, too. Animals teach you the immediacy of life and death."

Was he for real? Tiffany remembered him saying he'd grown up near Charmin, the paper mill in Mehoopany. He'd driven a forklift at the plant until he hurt his back. Now he got worker's comp.

The man smoothed the blanket over the dog. "My wife named her Cara, short for caramel, saying her fur was candy color."

"Sweet name," said Tiffany, her voice high and earnest. "I'm Tiffany Kowal."

"Jarek Hajduk."

"And this is—"

Ron cut her off. "Let me explain about the money. It's for the rug. To help you clean it, or get a new one, if that's what you want."

The man crossed his good arm over the stump. "Cara loved sleeping on that rug."

"Nice," mumbled Tiffany.

Eyes rheumy, he gazed at her. "I found Cara by the river when she was a pup. You think that's where I should bury her?"

Breath caught in Tiffany's throat. The Susquehanna River had long, deserted stretches where burlap bags of puppies got thrown in the water all the time.

"I knew Cara's eyesight was going."

Tiffany couldn't think about the burlap bags. Instead she considered the puppies that clawed free and swam to shore.

"Cara charged off before I clipped on her leash."

"So sorry."

"There's a stand of hemlocks near the river," said Ron. "It's high enough above the water it won't flood, a nice place to bury her."

Tiffany squinted. How did Ron know of such a place?

"I could use some help. I'm not really good with a shovel." The man wagged his stump at them.

"You stay here and rest," said Ron. "We'll take care of everything."

"What about your bad back?" started Tiffany. Ron squeezed her shoulder as the man cleared his throat.

"Might be best if I stayed put. My heart's not so good."

"Should we call your wife?" offered Tiffany.

Ron flared his nostrils.

The man shook his head. "She passed three years ago. Tad, my son, lives out West."

"Oh," whispered Tiffany.

"There's a tarp in the back of the car," said Ron. "We can wrap her in it."

"No." The man slapped his hand against the floor. "That would never do."

Tiffany was glad he said no. The tarp belonged to Sal, her mom's new boyfriend. It probably cost twenty bucks, and she'd have to pay him back.

Ron shifted from foot to foot. Tiffany listened to the ticking of the clock on the mantle above the stone fireplace. A stack of *Penny Savers*, the free weekly, were piled in front of the mesh screen. The man must have kept them for months. Same with the magazines on the lamp table near the easy chair. The TV was one of those consoles with bunny ears. Tiffany realized people way out here in the boonies didn't get cable.

The man barked authoritatively. "The rug stays with Cara. It's her favorite place to sleep. My wife made it, you know."

Ron nodded and strode to the far end of the room. He knelt, hunched his shoulders, grabbed the edge of the rug, and by sliding on his knees, rolled it toward them.

Tiffany stood and whispered, "Maybe you should wait in the other room while we do this?"

The man pushed up from the floor, then bent at the waist and petted Cara. When he straightened, he blinked repeatedly.

Tiffany blinked, too. She leaned toward the man, hoping to comfort him, and patted his stump.

"Give it some muscle," ordered Ron. He stood on the porch with the rear of the rolled-up carpet balanced on his shoulder. Tiffany descended the stairs and hugged the front of the load against her hip. The angle meant Tiffany got the bulk of the weight, forcing her to take baby steps. The dead dog had to be about sixty pounds, maybe more. Tiffany's breath came in short bursts. She padded onto the stone walkway, fearful she might slip.

Ron did little to offset her burden as he came down the stairs. "Not much further to the car," he said.

Tiffany knew without turning around that the man watched them. She was both relieved and surprised that he let them take the dog. She'd read how loss had a way of paralyzing people. Was Cara his only companion?

"Let's put the rug on the hood while I open the rear doors," said Tiffany.

"It's better to swing sideways. Give me the key, and I'll open the tailgate. We can use the cargo area."

"The tailgate doesn't work anymore."

"I'm trying to help," said Ron.

"We have to be careful." She envisioned him dropping the load, the poor animal rolling out onto the ground. What then?

"You're getting dirt on you. You can't look bad at the casino."

Tiffany must have brushed against the muddy fender. Thing is, she felt sick, hardly in the mood to continue with their plan. But she needed a job. The money. After they got the dog in the car, she'd use the old man's bathroom and clean up.

Ron grunted as she hoisted her end into the back seat. She tried to slide it forward, but the rug created friction against the interior. Would nothing go right?

"Push harder," said Ron.

Tiffany panted and gave her all. The load skidded onto the seat, burning her palms. She stepped away, blowing on her hands, and walked toward the house.

"What're you doing?" said Ron.

She ignored him.

"We've got to go."

Tiffany met the old man's gaze as she walked up the stairs. "Mind if I use your bathroom?"

He ushered her inside and waited in the den until she finished.

"I have a job interview."

He raised his eyelids. "I appreciate you taking Cara. Maybe I should come and help?"

She smiled gently. "Don't even think about it. It's the least we can do. We can still make the Mohegan Sun before 5:00."

"The casino?"

"Yeah," said Tiffany, brightening. "They're hiring blackjack dealers. Ron says I'm perfect. He goes there all the time." Tiffany kneaded her right thumb against her other palm.

"You're not old enough."

She shook her head. "I'm seventeen. I worked at Kuhner's until it shut down."

"You can't enter the casino if you're under twenty-one. He knows that. They won't let you in the place." He puffed his cheeks, lips tight like bailing wire.

She heard the car's horn. The man was mistaken. Old people frequently got confused. "I need a job," she said, surprised by the sound of desperation in her voice.

"Not there."

"It's good pay."

Ron honked the horn again. Long continuous bleats. The man talked over the noise. "I'll tell you where they're hiring. The mall. At the food court."

Tiffany listened as Ron pressed non-stop on the horn.

The man wagged his stump, "I've seen help wanted signs at the Java Bean."

Why hadn't she considered the mall? It was way closer to her house than the casino. The horn shifted to sharp, staccato beats.

"Guess he wants you to hurry."

She shrugged. "You really saw help wanted signs?"

"The senior bus picks me up every Wednesday. We walk the mall loop and get lunch there."

"I better go," she said. "But I'll come back and tell you where we put Cara. In case you want to visit."

The man's eyes got teary. "Not your fault," he reminded her.

Tiffany wished she could believe him. And Ron? Soon as they buried the dog, she'd tell him a thing or two.

Tiffany buckled her seat belt and scowled at Ron.

"Why are you looking at me like that?"

Her stomach tightened. She checked the rearview mirror and noted the rolled-up rug. With a deep sigh, she shifted into drive.

Ron rapped his knuckles against the dash. "I told you we should've kept going. Now, it's getting late."

"Where's that place for the dog?"

"I've been thinking," said Ron, his voice dripping honey. "We can deal with the dog after the casino. I got people waiting on me for cards."

"It'll be dark by then. The dog could start smelling."

Ron patted her shoulder. "Listen, I know you're upset. Shit happens. The accident wasn't your fault."

Tiffany sniffed. Her thoughts seemed foggy.

"We can put the rug in the next dumpster we see. That way you don't have to worry about any smell."

Tiffany made an *O* with her mouth. She shook her head.

"We'll stop back for it later, if you want. Then bury it."

Tiffany was so outraged she had difficulty speaking. A muscle spasmed in her right eye. "You told him you knew a good place to bury the dog."

"I'm telling you, our luck is about to change."

Tiffany gripped the steering wheel. Her knuckles whitened. "That old man said I can't get in the casino if I'm under twenty-one."

Ron sputtered, "What does he know?"

"I think you're playing me." Tiffany stared through the windshield at the river, meandering far below them.

"With my winnings, I'll buy you a nice dinner. And if it's late, I'll get us a room, right at the casino. When you win big, they comp you a room." Ron rubbed his palms against his thighs.

Tiffany thrust out her jaw. "You lied about that place by the river. But I'll find a spot to bury this dog."

"You sound like a kid," said Ron.

Tiffany careened through a curve, her foot pressed hard on the gas until she saw reflectors, signaling a turn-off. She spun the steering wheel so abruptly, the muffler smacked bottom when going from paved to dirt road.

"Don't wreck the car," said Ron.

She fought the urge to bulldoze his passenger side into a tree, but drove on, searching for a burial place. They were on an access road, probably left over from railroad days when farmers needed to transport grain. The farms were long gone, and these dirt ways rarely got used except during hunting season. Or when people dumped something.

After a mile, the road narrowed. Sumac bushes scraped the sides of the car. Then Tiffany saw a stand of hemlocks. Was this what Ron had described to the old man? Had Ron been telling the truth? She steered toward the trees. Soon as she braked and cut the ignition, she pushed open the door and got out.

Ron got out, too. He opened the rear passenger door. "Where's the shovel? We should dig the hole before we move the dog."

Shovel? Oh, crap. Tiffany stifled the urge to cry. "Can we use the jack?"

Ron didn't yell at her. "Let's look around. There's got to be some natural depressions. We can put the dog in one, and then cover it with rocks."

"Some branches, too," said Tiffany.

They walked in a wide circle, the size of a horse arena, and found a spot behind the tallest hemlock. The opening resembled a bathtub that had been pressed into the earth. "We'll have to fold the ends of the rug," said Tiffany.

Ron said that wouldn't be a problem. They returned to the car and wrestled out the rug. Walking proved difficult, owing to unsure footing. The ground was masked by thick fern that had a sweet smell. Tiffany wondered if she should say a little prayer when they lowered the dog into the resting place. But getting to the spot was the problem. The load was so heavy, Tiffany's arms ached.

"Do you hear something?" asked Ron.

The sound of an engine pierced the air. Tiffany squinted and saw a big blue car motoring up from the river. She stopped, holding fast to her end of the rug. For some reason, the sedan looked familiar, but from the distance, she couldn't make out the people inside.

"Better hurry before they see us and think we're druggies," said Ron.

"Should we leave? Find a different place?"

"Just joking," he rasped. "Haven't you noticed how peaceful this is?"

Tiffany rotated her head from left to right. Oak saplings, having shed some of their leaves, stood like dwarf sentry and guarded the expanse. Their size couldn't compare with the hemlocks, but they added to the area's protection. Same with the fern. Then she noticed wild raspberries. The snarl of thorny limbs would bear fruit in the summer. She could return next year and bring berries to the old man.

"You okay?" asked Ron.

"Yeah," whispered Tiffany. "But I want to drive home after we finish."

Ron nodded.

Tiffany was relieved he didn't argue. Her jaw relaxed. She stepped over a gray rock, shaped like a tackle box. Maybe she could use it as a headstone?

NAVIDAD

COLLEEN yanks open the passenger door of Big Blue, rattling me and the car as she hoists herself onto the seat. Instead of her usual black attire, chosen for its supposed slimming effect, she wears a red sweater matched by a voluminous skirt that cascades over her knees.

"Ho! Ho! You like?" she asks. Her fingers tug at silver garland edging the hem. "My skirt was half price at Salvo."

I smile, knowing how Colleen takes pride in snagging deals at the Salvation Army thrift store.

"It's handmade, but the seams aren't finished. No clasp at the waist, so I used duct tape."

And that's when I realize she's wearing one of those round, felt covers people put under Christmas trees. I decide not to say anything. She's been a grump ever since she couldn't collect insurance for her car.

"Where's your holiday spirit, MK? Couldn't you put on something nicer than jeans and a green turtleneck?"

I point to my necklace. The strand of miniature, plastic tree lights is quite festive if you ask me, but Colleen is on a roll.

"Are you depressed?" She raises her eyebrows, arched like the curved tops of candy canes. "Lots of people get depressed this time of year."

I'm grateful she didn't say "divorced people," or mention how my daughter, now grown and working in Chicago, had phoned me last week, pleased that she had bought her own plane ticket to Florida where she'd spend Christmas with my ex. "It's Dad's year," reminded Jenna, as if I'd forgotten the arrangement for rotating holiday visits.

Sighing, I shift Big Blue from park to drive. The front end shakes as we lurch away from the curb. Big Blue scolds me, for, yet again, agreeing to give Colleen a ride. We're taking Anthracite Expressway to the community outreach center at Our Lady of Perpetual Help Church. Colleen and I no longer belong to the parish, but we went there as kids, and recently she joined their volunteer services. Today is the gift party for children from low-income families. Colleen's not sure exactly how many kids will attend, because the church doesn't require parents to fill out forms like they do at Giving Tree or Toys for Tots. She said that putting names on paper means high risk for people lacking W-2s or green cards. A date with Santa could translate into deportation or jail time. This troubling realization, heightened by visions of poor children being denied presents, prompted me to drive.

She pats my arm, "What you need is more meaning in your life. That's why we help those less fortunate."

Whenever Colleen spews like a self-improvement book, I refuse to respond. Plus, she knows I'm thinking of moving and believes volunteering will make me want to stay where I have roots. I stay put because I don't know where else to go.

Big Blue wheezes up the steep rise. I peer through the windshield. The sky, razor-blade gray, has been dismal all week. Snow might soften the barren hills, especially as we've reached December 22nd without a single flake, but there's none in the forecast. I grip the wheel and coax us past potholes and other hazards. This area is known for black ice. Below us, the Susquehanna River weaves through Northeast Pennsylvania like a vital force. Only it's not. I can hear my grandmother, who willed me this Buick eons ago: *We have the longest nonnavigable river in the United States, but it's not safe.* Each winter, at least one vehicle turns too fast and plummets into the waters of the ever-after. How easily Colleen and I could join the departed. I picture headlines rife with irony: "Two Women Checkout While Doing a Good Deed." Quickly I purse my lips. If Colleen sees me smile, I'll have to explain why. Then she'll gush with more of her Let's Give to Others theme.

Colleen is the real reason we're doing Santa Fest. Undoubtedly, she thinks her charitable work will erase the not-so-little fabrication of her missing car. Each time I think about what happened, I cringe from the bad karma, and worse, how she involved me. I can't believe I was so clueless, figuring she was going to a mechanic and needed a return lift to the mall where we work. No way did I think she'd dump her car on the floodplain and claim it as stolen. Hers was the malfeasance of a deadbeat, not a middle-aged woman who works at the Hallmark store and organizes the mall parking lot clean-up day.

I worried about being put on the witness stand, picturing myself in an ivory pantsuit, a paragon of veracity, as I placed my hand on the Bible to testify: *I merely drove. I was not an accessory.*

Then a teenage boy had discovered the car. What he was doing by the river is anyone's guess, but he hot-wired the wreck and got it onto the road, careening down Mill Street until a cop saw him run a stop sign. Sirens blared, and supposedly a chase ensued, though I find that hard to believe since the Honda ran on three spark plugs and couldn't go more than 25 miles per hour. The boy and the cop burned rubber past the empty granary and the old Texaco Station.

Then, at the curve by Golden Touch Beauty Shop—*Smash!*—right into the fire hydrant. No geyser erupted, but the Honda folded up like an accordion. Thankfully nobody got hurt.

When Colleen heard the news, she pulled her hair away from her scalp, all tight, and fluttered her eyelids: "No fault insurance! There goes my money."

"Be glad the car got towed to the dump where it always belonged," I said.

But here's the glitch: the culprit was David Green, the high school kid who mows the lawn and shovels snow at Colleen's apartment complex. He does a good job and always says hello whenever I pick up or drop off Colleen.

"I have to do something to help him," fretted Colleen. "That judge locks up juveniles over the slightest infraction."

That's why she emailed the judge, saying David was a nice boy and worked hard at an afterschool job. She promised not to press charges or request payment for the car. Who knows if the judge read it, but he put David on probation and ordered community service.

Is it any coincidence that Colleen signed on to the Our Lady of Perpetual Help Outreach Center? Clearly her action reflects a need for penance, but rather than admit her guilt, she told me, "I can use this as material for my book."

Ha! Colleen writes the novel in her head. She hasn't put a word to paper yet and claims to draft a new chapter each time I give her a ride in Big Blue.

"Your silence is deafening," says Colleen, pounding her fist on the dashboard. "Why won't you talk to me? You'll stifle my creativity."

Reluctant to encourage her so-called novel-in-the-making, I fumble with the radio knob. We have discussed more plot scenarios than I can count, but whenever I suggest that she take notes,

she dismisses me, saying the act of putting pen to paper is prema-
ture. Her writing needs mental stimulation. Mental is right.

Froggy 101 blares out the song "Grandma Got Run Over by a
Reindeer."

Colleen elbows me in the side, hoping I'll sway like she does.
She knows I don't like these dopey songs, but she laughs, "Get with
the season. Don't you love how people decorate?"

Big Blue rumbles down the hill. Are we looking at the same
place? Houses stand close, leaning side-by-side for balance. If
one drops, they'll all collapse—swoosh—like dominoes. Styro-
foam candy canes dangle from porch rails where paint peels like
curled ribbon. Artificial wreaths are tacked to doors, and the few
windows without plastic insulating them against the cold yield
stick-on snowflakes. Icicle lights droop from roof gutters. Maybe
they'll sparkle when lit, but the wires resemble wet spaghetti.
Several yards have signs with red, white, and blue lettering: *We
Support Our Troops*. Then I spy the deflated blow-ups. Those dec-
orations are pricey; I can't imagine how people can afford them.
When filled with hot air from whirring motors, they expand into
a toy shop, snow globe, or gargantuan Santa. But flattened against
dirt yards, they remind me of condoms littering the mall parking
lot after a Saturday night.

"Check out Rudolph," smirks Colleen. Four reindeer line up
in procession. Each has a mechanized head. The one in front
flashes a red nose as the next deer sways its snout, seeming to sniff
Rudolph's butt.

I pretend not to notice. Last year, at the mall's employee party,
Colleen made a meal of red and green Jell-O shots. Afterward, I
gave her a ride, and she yelled, "Pull over." I thought she was going
to hurl, but as I stopped Big Blue, she hopped out, lumbered across
the lawn, grabbed a couple of reindeer, and repositioned them in
a Yuletide hump.

We turn onto River Street and pass a stout, plastic snowman, the kind my grandmother displayed back in the seventies. It's probably a collector's item from when Coal was King and the farms thrived. Now people celebrate with acrylic stars atop molded nativity sets. I'd like to think the real straw in mangers flanked by cows and donkeys offers reassurance. But for what?

"We're here," says Colleen, donning a Santa hat.

The outreach center, formerly called Church Hall, looks like a train car with narrow windows zippered into gray siding. Above the doorway, red and white lights, the size of fishing bobbers, flicker with incandescence as the sun fades. I ease Big Blue curbside, under a street lamp. "We'll want light after we finish."

Colleen plucks garland from her hem and crowns the St. Christopher statue on the dash. "Keep us safe, St. Chris."

Soon as I lock Big Blue and place the keys in my pocket, I notice a guy standing near the alley adjacent to the building. He's thin and wearing baggy jeans weighted by a chain on his belt loop. The pants sag below his hips, showing the top of boxers. His hair, flat along the sides, is buffeted up on his skull like the peak of a conquistador's helmet. He waves his right arm behind his back, signaling to someone. Out marches a little girl in a pink fuzzy jacket, so big it hangs to the ankles of her white tights. She taps her scuffed shoes, followed by four more preschool-age kids, and then a cluster of ten bigger kids.

Colleen walks, jangling bells on her skirt. The kids point her way.

"*Mira. Mira*," says the guy, and I figure that means *look at her*.

He's in his twenties, half Colleen's age, but she gets all flirty. She rolls her shoulders and grins. "Ho, Ho," she says.

The kids laugh at her emphasis on the second Ho. A boy

wearing blue mittens waves to us. Then more little bodies bunch into the pack.

These kids with dark eyes and straight black hair do not look anything like homegrown towheads. "Where are they coming from?"

"Sshh," says Colleen.

Then I remember her gag order: no asking where they live or moved from.

Last summer, *The Riverside Gazette* featured headlines about the mayor in Hazleton, forty miles away. He blamed Spanish speakers for the bad economy and instituted an ordinance to fine landlords for renting to undocumented immigrants. Next thing, all Latinos got blamed for every one of the city's many woes. Rocks got thrown at their windows. Tires got slashed. Families left, no one asked where they went.

It wouldn't take much to track their path. Our school district has want ads for teachers of English as a Second Language, and Weis Markets stocks a shelf with Goya foods. Yet *less said* is the dictum at the outreach center. That's why *The Riverside Gazette* won't cover the event for its lifestyle section, and there will be no human-interest clips on TV-28.

"Too much attention and they're gone. Then what do these kids have?"

Colleen says Perpetual Help is doing the right thing by providing them assistance—legal or not.

Leave it to Colleen to involve me in a covert Christmas party.

I pull open the front door and smell kettle corn, hot chocolate, and peppermint. Father Ryan stands in the entrance, his face is as white as his collar. "I expected twenty kids, same as always, but there's way more. They arrived early. I don't know what to do. We won't have enough for them."

Colleen jokes, "Multiply loaves and fishes?"

He doesn't laugh. Father Ryan, frail and wrinkled, seemed ready for retirement when he came to the church as a temporary appointment in the eighties, yet here he stays. Maybe the parish can't find a replacement? Priests are in short supply, what with sex abuse crimes, and few men want to join.

"Woohoo—this place is packed," says Colleen, pushing me until I am pressed thigh to thigh with Father Ryan, an awkward moment.

I sidestep and glance at the children. Father Ryan rasps, "Santa can't make it. He got called to the pileup on I-81. There's fatalities."

Bob Jenkins, the county coroner, plays Santa every year. What now? The group must tally over a hundred. Children shuffle with anticipation, forming one huge amoeba. Three boys with buzz cuts raise shoulders and giggle. They squish closer, clearing a passage for us.

I turn, looking for a coat rack, and see the girl in the pink jacket step across the threshold. She stops due to the crowd. I worry the kids left standing outside won't be able to fit in the room. "Señora Santa," she calls. As Colleen spins around, I wrack my brain for ideas. I stare over heads to the rear wall and spy a folding table with cookie trays. A few women hold babies. Beside them hovers Mrs. Pavinsky, the elderly organist, sporting a sweater like my grandmother used to wear, festooned with beaded mistletoe and holly.

"Time for singing," says Father Ryan.

"Let's get you to sit by the tree," Colleen tells him. I think Father Ryan means for her to start singing, but she cups his elbow with her right hand and propels him toward the seat intended for Santa. The high-back chair swallows him like a shrunken elf. The kids smile. I glance toward Mrs. Pavinsky, thinking she'll play the upright piano, but she sits on the bench with a baby in her arms. Colleen shrugs, then claps her hands and sings "Jingle Bells."

The kids clap, but no one sings along, making me wonder if they don't know the words. I wish I knew Spanish so I could translate. Colleen thrusts her left hip and changes the tune to "Jingle Bell Rock." Her voice gets gravelly like she's in a smoke-filled bar. She twists, swishing her skirt.

The children mimic her, wiggling and laughing. What will happen when they see there aren't enough gifts?

Their exuberance unnerves Father Ryan. He must realize the lack of gifts means disaster. His hands flap as he reaches for a bowl of candy canes under the Christmas tree. He signals for Colleen. "They'll have to share."

I am aghast. What kid shares a candy cane?

Colleen takes the bowl, grabs my arm, and pulls me to the middle of the room. The children swarm around us. My brain backpedals to age seven, and how I yearned for a Bridal Barbie, complete with satin gown, flowing veil, and silver high heels. When I found a box under the tree that was just the right size, I hugged it to my chest. My fingers trembled as I tore off the wrapping paper only to discover a knockoff doll in a blue dress and black flats. I'm sure my bottom lip quivered, but at least I got something. That these kids won't get to open their own presents makes me want to cry. I whisper to Colleen, "Not enough gifts. What can we do?"

She pauses, and I expect her to speak, but she hands me the candy bowl. Then she shimmies along, placing candy canes in outstretched hands.

And here's the amazing thing: Each kid who takes one, peels away the wrapper, breaks off a piece, and passes the remainder to the next kid. I don't hear whining or complaints. These children parcel out pieces of candy cane without being told, and all the while, they laugh.

Four boys with gangly arms elbow each other. When Colleen hands a candy cane to the tallest boy, his face becomes purposeful. He breaks it in pieces for his friends.

By the time we traverse to the open doorway, Colleen still has a fistful of candy canes. She distributes them to the kids at the top of the stairs. Like those inside, each breaks off a piece and passes it along to others on the sidewalk. None of them is at all upset. How can this be? I'm stunned. Surely the children realize there isn't enough for each of them.

"Señora Santa," chortles the girl in pink, clutching fast to Colleen's hand.

A boy waggles chubby fingers and reaches for the girl's other hand. Somehow the two of them set off a chain reaction, hands reaching for the hand that holds Señora Santa's. They thrill by simply holding hands.

"Ho, Ho," says Colleen. The children echo her. Their game of repeat ripples through the room and continues out the door.

Why aren't they angry at not having their own candy cane? I expect them to look around, eyes hungry for gifts. But there's no asking, "Where's mine?" I try to compute what their actions imply. They hold hands, pressing their palms together as if they yield an electric charge: the magic of the hands reaching for the next in the chain connecting them to the hand that holds Señora Santa's.

Without thinking, I pass a candy cane to a girl with red bows in her hair.

"Well, 'tis the season," snorts Colleen.

"Ho, Ho," cheer voices, mixing from all directions. Their words speed up, and they chant in silly rounds. Their playful harmony could rival a choir. How strange to discover such joy?

I step outside to the cement staircase. On the sidewalk, children lace hands, forming a link that stretches all the way to Big Blue under the street lamp. The kids laugh. They must be cold, yet they don't complain. The guy we'd seen upon our arrival stands guard at the rear of the line. He gives a thumbs-up approval I can't figure, but his gesture makes me warm to the spirit. "Ho, Ho," I say, laughing with the sound of my words.

A girl missing her two front teeth grins and tugs at my jacket. She points at the surrounding hills where colored lights twinkle.

My eyes widen. I know those houses need siding and new paint, yet the scene rivals a holiday image on the Hallmark cards Colleen sells.

The girl reaches for my hand.

She lisps, "*Feliz Navidad.*"

Puffs of breath rise with the night.

She and I watch as exhaled vapors crystallize into tiny specks of snow.

SIGNED SEALED
DELIVERED

IT WAS 1969. Mary Katherine watched her mother tap an airmail envelope against the kitchen counter. The tissue-thin paper, edged with red and blue parallelograms, a vocabulary word Mary Katherine recently learned in seventh grade, had arrived from Vietnam, the third letter in a week.

"Are you sure this soldier knows how old you are?" asked her mother.

"Course," said Mary Katherine. She reached for the envelope and tucked it in the pocket of her plaid school uniform. Hopefully her mother's interest in the other mail would prevent further questions.

"What does he have to say that he writes all the time?"

"Oh, you know, stuff about what's happening. Like the geography. What people eat, you know." Then, to avoid her mother's gray probing eyes, Mary Katherine slouched over to the refrigerator, "I take the letters to school and read parts to the class."

Swoosh, gurgle sounded from the bathroom. "Jimmy, stop flushing!" yelled her mother as she charged off. Mary Katherine smiled. Jimmy, her younger brother, occasionally came in handy.

Besides, part of what she told her mother was true. Mary Katherine did share the letters with some of the class: the other three girls in Group A.

Chair legs scraped against linoleum as Group A—the fastest readers—pushed desks into their customary circle at the rear of the room. They'd been assigned to the group when they were fifth graders, and with each new school year, the nuns continued the designation. Mary Katherine glanced toward the blackboard and, making sure Sister Immaculata wasn't watching, waved a letter. "Got another one yesterday. He signed it *Love Paul.*"

Four desk tops clunked together. "I get to read it first," demanded Colleen. She rolled back her shoulders, showing off a new pointy bra, and then crossed her calves. Colleen's mother let her shave her legs, and she made certain Group A noticed the smooth skin.

"I get it next," squeaked Beth. She tucked hairs behind a white plastic headband that she claimed highlighted her widow's peak. Mary Katherine thought the style made her look like a nun.

"I'll read it last, as usual," snorted Virginia. In first grade she had refused to play kickball. Instead she spent recess galloping around the playground, leaping over curbs, whinnying excitedly. And now, as Virginia scrutinized the letter, she spread her nostrils with each excited breath, "I think he's really in love."

The letters had started as part of a social studies project. With chaste Palmer Method script, Sister Immaculata listed on the blackboard the men from the diocese who'd been sent to Vietnam. She told each student to pick a name. "Write a cheerful letter," she commanded. "They're probably homesick."

Mary Katherine had chosen Paul McCarney because his name sounded a lot like the cuddly-looking singer with the Beatles. Having already sent five letters to Paul McCartney in England, with no reply, she needed to make this letter extra special. She pondered, trying to sound more adult than her twelve years, and remembered a joke from TV. It was just the sort of thing to write to a soldier. Her pen clicked with inspiration as she included a few one-liners from Johnny Carson, too. She sealed the envelope with satisfaction, glad she'd done *something* for her country.

"Hey McCarney! Here's a letter for ya."

"Bring it over. I can't move." Paul sat on his helmet, back pressed to the sandbag wall. "Die Fuckers!" He slapped his arm, then admired the pile of mosquitoes forming on his lap.

"What the hell?"

Paul nodded at the mass of dark bodies. "I've nailed a hundred of these, and if they're smart, they'll stay away from me."

Off The said nothing and dug his size fifteen combat boots into the mud. His name was really Anthony Insalaca, but during basic training, the guys named him Off-the-Wall after he strutted through the barracks wearing skivvies and boots while singing in a deep, smoldering tone to mimic Nancy Sinatra's "These Boots Are Made for Walking." Then, at a tattoo parlor in Tan Son Nhut, his nickname was shortened. He never said if booze made him slur his words, or if the other guys had played a joke, but the artist tattooed "OFF THE" directly below an eagle's talons.

From the opposite makeshift wall, Vinnie explained, "Paul's been at it for more than an hour. Real killer instinct." They laughed, for as far as Paul knew, none of the firing attacks had been successful, just making honeycombs out of the land.

Vinnie pushed his heavy-framed glasses higher on his face. He'd tightened them as much as possible, yet they continued to slide down his nose. Too much weight loss. The medics couldn't find anything wrong with him, but he'd been losing weight ever since the rumor—the hushed report about US troops firing mortars on a village full of kids and old people. Paul told Vinnie the report wasn't conclusive, but weight kept disappearing.

"It's postmarked Pennsylvania," said Off The. He dropped the envelope near Paul's hip, careful not to disturb the burial mound.

"Aren't you going to open it?" asked Vinnie.

"Probably from my mother. Last time she wrote, she asked if I could please go to Saigon and get her a good deal on a camera." He smacked a mosquito on his elbow. After manning this Howitzer in the I Corps, Saigon seemed as far away as home.

"Not my mother's writing," he mumbled. "Jesus, from some chick." Paul stood, scattering bodies. "This is wild. Did you hear about the salesman at the sorority house?"

The thrills of a soldier writing back! While the rest of the class recited rules about gerunds, Mary Katherine read his exchange to Group A. She moistened her lips and repeated the last line in a husky voice, "Write again soon and tell me what you like to do."

"You have to help me think of what to write him." When Group A failed to offer her assistance, she added, "Honest, he's adorable. I just know he has brown eyes like Paul McCartney. And he's really good with horses."

"We can't let him think we're—or rather you're anything like them," whispered Colleen. She snapped her wrist toward the class.

"Course, we'll only tell him good stuff."

Colleen sucked in her stomach and extended her chest. She pulled free a bobby pin that kept her red hair above the collar as stipulated by school rules. "Say you love driving around in Corvettes."

"And you drink sloe gin fizz," added Beth. "Whenever we visit my grandma, Uncle Charley sneaks me a drink."

Mary Katherine blinked. She'd always thought Beth was destined for the convent. Beth attended Mass each morning, sometimes praying the Stations of the Cross during recess. And now, the facts: drinking at Grandma's.

"Tell him you like to ride," offered Virginia. "Say it's best going bareback."

"At a beach, wearing nothing but a bathing suit," added Colleen.

The girls rocked their desks, unbridling energy. Within the hour, each member of Group A had written *him* a paragraph. Mary Katherine inscribed their sentences onto Colleen's pastel paper, for loose leaf was no longer worthy of Paul. At the closing, she hesitated. "Should I?"

Heads nodded emphatically: *Love, Mary Katherine.*

"Two more letters for you," said Vinnie. His pants flapped as he stumbled over rocks and handed Paul the mail. He glanced at Off The, "Nothing for us. I wonder why my sister hasn't written."

"It's from Mary Katherine," said Paul. His head still echoed from last night's firing.

Off The picked a tattoo scab, "She send anymore jokes?"

"Yeah, few of them. What did the elephant say to the naked man?"

"That's old," said Off The. "How do you breathe through that thing?"

Vinnie laughed. "How did Mary Katherine get your name?"

"Some list going around the diocese." Then Paul's voice cracked, "She says she likes horseback riding, especially that pounding rhythm."

"Between the legs is what she means," said Off The. "Catholic chicks can't wait—"

"Don't start," said Vinnie.

"I used to go with a Catholic!" Off The vibrated his hands in front of his chest as if holding large grapefruits. "I remember sitting at Kirby Park with her and her friends, each talking about how they'd *wait* till they were married. Then that very night, when her parents were gone—HOT DAMN. Rubbed my peter raw."

"Don't you ever think about anything else?"

"Hey, she's the one writing that stuff." Off The squatted on his heels, leaned against a sandbag, and lit a cigarette.

"She says she wants to hear from me. But I already wrote her one letter. What the hell am I going to say?"

"Ask if she has any friends and tell her about us."

"Like I'm supposed to tell her we spent three days riding in a truck through the jungle, hauling a 155 Howitzer. And my two safety-conscious buddies kept helmets over their dicks, because if we hit a mine, they didn't want their nuts blown off."

Off The shrugged while Vinnie stared blankly. Suddenly Paul laughed, that swirling eggbeater laughter that releases fear and preserves sanity. The others joined, but all the time watching, looking out from the artillery hill, quick to confront vegetation, the unknown lands.

Finally, Vinnie spoke softly, "Tell her about those kids we met at the last village. My sister always asks me to write that kind of stuff."

"Say things that'll make you sound important," bleated Off The.

"Yeah, I know. But what's impressive about loading powder?"

"I've got just the line."

As a shoe box filled with letters, Group A wrote on.

"I can't believe he wants to take you dancing," said Colleen.

"What's that I hear?" called Sister Immaculata, bustling toward them. Mary Katherine folded her hands and lowered her thick lashes, "We were laughing at the joke in the *Weekly Reader*." She paused, voice chiming like Bethlehem's angel. "They thought it might cheer up the soldier if I sent it to him."

Sister Immaculata said crisply, "How nice—a Corporal Work of Mercy." The starched wimple pinched her doughy cheeks. "May I see it?"

Mary Katherine shrank down and pressed her stomach against the desk top, frantically glancing toward Colleen, who provided no help. She merely stared at the dimes in her loafer's penny slots.

Then Colleen sat up straight. "Excuse me, Sister. Could you look at my SRA card? I might be ready for a new color." Colleen smiled and held out her card.

Sister Immaculata took the card and peered at the answers. "Good work dear," she said, and then waddled to the front of the room.

Yet Mary Katherine worried, "What if she remembers and asks to see the letter?"

"Never happen," said Beth. "She always forgets stuff."

Mary Katherine wasn't convinced. Something about the way Sister narrowed her eyes made Mary Katherine feel uneasy, almost sinful, like at First Friday confession.

"She'll never remember," added Colleen. "But just in case, I'll make a fake one. I'm great at disguising handwriting."

"Okay," said Mary Katherine. Lately, Sister had stressed the seriousness of dishonesty, warning about Purgatory. Yet the exchanges with Paul had never seemed sinful, even if she had mailed jokes she didn't quite understand. Mary Katherine pushed her tongue against her braces, then slackened her mouth, and breathed deeply. She, well Group A, made Paul happy. Mary Katherine was sure. After all, he said her cards and jokes were the best thing happening to him. It couldn't be a sin. They were helping a soldier—like Bob Hope and the USO.

Despite the heat, Paul wore his flak jacket. His body was molded against sand bags. He was so tired from last night's firing, he never unrolled his sleeping bag. The firing halted at dawn, but the noise, the echo, would it ever stop? Could he ever sleep, relax?

"Paul," called Vinnie, walking toward him. "I brought you some mail." Vinnie sat beside him, demanding Paul look at the letters.

"One from my mother—" Paul's voice rose. "And two from Mary Katherine."

"He's got mail from Mary Katherine," yelled Vinnie to Off The.

"Don't start. Gotta take a leak." During the last artillery move, Off The bragged about honking on a village woman. Within a week, he stopped mentioning his escapade, and instead, cussed about the burn, the gift that keeps on giving.

Paul rubbed powder traces from his brow and read from the letter. "What goes in hard and firm, coming out soft and sticky?"

"Ah, bubble gum," spat Off The. "That's a kid's joke."

"But it's funny," said Vinnie.

"There's something weird about that chick," said Off The. "I don't think she's a whore, definitely not a bitch, but she's probably ugly."

"Nu-uh," spat Paul, banishing images of female blimps his mother said had wonderful personalities.

"No, can't be," added Vinnie.

"Well if you think she's so hot, why hasn't she sent a picture?"

"He wants me to send a picture," moaned Mary Katherine for the tenth time. "Now what do we do?"

Virginia shrugged.

Colleen jiggled an ID bracelet, probably stolen from her cousin, but said nothing.

Beth crossed herself and remained silent.

"You have to think of a plan tonight."

"Four whole weeks, still no supply trucks."

"Even if we keep cutting back, there's not enough rations."

"Sergeant said this shouldn't happen. Nothing's getting through."

Off The loped up the hill. "See what I got?" He shook something feathery.

Paul stared more closely and realized it was a chicken. "How'd you get that? It looks run over."

"Bought it from an old woman."

"But there's no villagers left around here," said Vinnie.

"She was just passing through." Off The knelt, placed the chicken on the ground, and then clapped his hands. "Vinnie, you start the fuel while I pluck this baby."

Paul tucked in his shirt, ready for action. "What can I do?"

"Reread that letter. The funny one about Doing It."

As the class recited the Morning Offering, Mary Katherine watched Colleen loosen her bun and shake free her red hair. Then she pulled a photograph from her uniform pocket and held it behind her back. "I've got a picture."

Beth leaned over for a better view, gasped, and stared piously at the crucifix. "Thank you, our Lord."

Mary Katherine reached for the photo while Colleen explained, "I don't know who she is, but my dad took it when we were in Florida. Mom got mad. So, if Dad sees it's gone, he'll think Mom hid it."

Mary Katherine sucked the insides of her mouth to keep from cheering. The woman in the photo displayed everything Group A lacked: long blond hair, big smile, and a Barbie doll figure. But what intrigued Mary Katherine the most was the bathing suit. Sister Immaculata had warned all girls against the evils of baring their midriffs, and this woman wore a skimpy black bikini.

Colleen snorted, "It's so mature." Beth and Virginia nodded. Finally, Mary Katherine slid the photo into a scented envelope. She passed it around the circle, and each girl sealed it with a kiss.

Paul inhaled slowly, savoring the sweetness of gasoline. Supply trucks had rumbled in earlier. He held the envelope marked Photo Don't Bend, swooshing it like a fly swatter, shooing away Off The. "You don't deserve this."

Off The frowned and stared at his boots. That night, after feasting, the vomiting had started. For hours, they retched with machine gun repetition. Finally, their captain summoned a medic. Then Off The confessed. He'd found the chicken. "Honest, I didn't think it'd been dead long."

"We were lucky," said Paul. He slit open the envelope and enjoyed the look of tortured anticipation on Off The's face.

"Captain thinks we might get out early because of the supply screw up," said Vinnie. Suddenly his glasses slid down, "She's incredible."

"Talk about headlights."

Mary Katherine leaned over her desk top and gently rocked in her seat, "As soon as I get stateside, we should spend a weekend at the beach."

"Write that he should bring lots of wine."

"And tell him you love campfires in the sand."

"Rent some horses."

"Sure," whispered Mary Katherine. Sweet passion colored her ink. Group A floated through the afternoon as if they spent the lunch hour tilting champagne bottles instead of milk cartons.

When the truck grinded gears and slowed, Paul yelled over the engine, "What'll happen if Mary Katherine sees I can't swim?"

"You're not going to the beach to swim." Off The tapped the helmet protecting his crotch. "Just roll out a blanket behind a big dune."

"Read it again," begged Vinnie.

"'Dearest Paul, I can't wait to be alone with you.'"

"That chick is hot," said Off The.

Vinnie sighed, "Wish I could meet her."

"We'll have a reunion," boomed Off The. "Then we can all meet her. And maybe she can bring some friends."

Tonsillitis. Mary Katherine considered her illness a child's ailment, undoubtedly contracted from her wretched younger brother. When the doorbell rang, she didn't even get out of bed.

Her mother entered the bedroom, looking as pale as Mary Katherine. "That soldier you've been writing to—I thought he knew your age."

"Huh?"

Her mother glowered. "Get up."

Although Mary Katherine was dressed in a most undignified manner—pink robe, flowered pajamas, furry slippers—she marched ahead of her mother into the den.

He stood as she entered, bottle of wine in one hand.

Mary Katherine smiled weakly, and then puffed her lips like a fish, hiding her braces. She used to think her teeth gleamed with sophistication, but now her mouth seemed shackled, clumsy, and even worse, childlike. A sick feeling swelled in her stomach. If I run to the bathroom, will mom make me come out? She crept to the chair in the darkest corner: "I've kind of lost my voice."

Her mother gestured for the man to sit.

Mary Katherine peered at him. He looked nothing like Paul McCartney. His short hair, a soldier's buzz cut, was all wrong. Maybe if he grew it out for a Beatles mop-top, he could look more like the baby-face singer? The image made her smile.

He stared back at her with a Paul McCartney "I Want to Hold Your Hand" kind of smile. But Mary Katherine thought his eyes mirrored disappointment. How can I begin to explain? She watched him wrinkle his nose. His lips turned upward. No, no, she winced, don't laugh at me.

Paul sat beside her mother on the tan couch. His pants inched up his calf, white skin peeking out from dark socks. Mary Katherine looked at her own legs: ugh, the hair, the disgrace. She tucked her ankles under her robe.

"How was it there?" Her mother's voice shattered the stillness. "As bad as they say?"

"It wasn't good," he sighed. "But let me tell you, Mary Katherine's letters made life bearable. I shared them with my buddies. I promised them I'd come and see her as soon as I got home."

"You wrote those letters during class, right?" said her mother, turning toward Mary Katherine. "With Sister Immaculata?"

"I guess the nuns have changed how they teach since I went to school," he said. Then, as if Mary Katherine were the only person in the room, he dipped his chin, raised his eyebrows, and gazed in a way that made her stomach flutter. "You sure know how to write."

His husky voice both thrilled and worried her. What would he say next?

As Paul talked about the geography, the people, and what they ate, he sounded nothing like his letters. Mary Katherine was somewhat relieved. Yet she longed for his written words, the phrases that had quickened within her.

"I brought my new Polaroid camera with me," he said to her mother. "Mind if I take Mary Katherine's picture? I told my buddies I'd get more photos."

Her mother glared at the word more, but Mary Katherine avoided the accusatory eyes and looked down at her slippers.

"I know you're not feeling well, but it would mean a lot to me and the guys if I could take your picture. Could you stand up?"

Mary Katherine obliged.

"Please, can I have a smile?"

She nodded and puffed her lips like a blowfish.

He pressed the shutter button, pulled out the instant photo, fanned it dry, and then squinted at the image. "You know, I never realized until now, but you look a lot like my kid sister. You must be about the same age. She's in sixth grade."

Mary Katherine flared her nostrils. How could he compare her to a baby sixth grader? Rather than correct him, she prayed: Dear God, I know it was wrong to pretend I was someone else. I know it was a sin to keep writing the letters. But I never thought he'd come here. Please, I'll do anything if you just make him leave.

He walked toward Mary Katherine and held out his camera. "My sister has a blast taking pictures with this Polaroid. You want to take a picture? You can take one of me."

She shrugged and remained extra still as he leaned in close and showed her the button to push. He had a musky smell, nothing like the boys in her class.

Her mother suggested Paul pose by the fireplace. Propped on the mantle behind him was the framed 8×10 of Mary Katherine in her plaid school uniform, her hair braided, and beanie atop her head.

"Step a bit to the left, please," said Mary Katherine, determined not to include her ridiculous school photo in the Polaroid picture. She snapped the shutter, and after yanking out the photo, noted his brown eyes, the same color as Paul McCartney.

He told her mother, "I better get going." He shuffled across the room and bowed slightly in front of Mary Katherine. Next thing, he reached his hand toward her. She gulped and held her breath. She could practically hear Paul McCartney sing with Beatle John about wanting to hold her hand.

"I want you to keep the picture, but I need my camera back," he said.

She felt her cheeks warm and hoped he couldn't see them

turn red. As she handed over the camera, her fingers grazed his, creating a static shock, much like rubbing her feet across the rug and touching the door knob. She laughed nervously.

"I'll remember you," he whispered.

Mary Katherine wanted to say, "Same here." But she couldn't muster the words.

Off The kicked open Paul's door with his high-tops. He bolted into the apartment, his arms cradling a paper sack. Beer bottles clanked together as he gave Paul the bag of empties. "Hell of a long trip."

Vinnie entered close behind. "Don't ever drive with Off The." He shook Paul's hand. "Great to be home, huh?"

"I guess so," said Paul, walking to the kitchen, bell bottoms sweeping the floor. He dropped the empties beside the two other bags of trash. "I haven't found a job, plus my mother is making me nuts. She's always telephoning, reading me stuff from the newspaper about vets flipping out."

"Same with mine." Off The unzipped his sweatshirt and sat at the table.

"Yeah, but you were nuts before you went," said Vinnie. "My mother keeps trying to feed me. Can't understand why I won't eat chicken."

Paul laughed. He sat across from Off The.

"What's the story with Mary Katherine? When is she coming?"

"She's real sick. Can't make it."

"So, you've seen her?" asked Vinnie. New wire rim glasses rested on his face. "You spent time with her?"

Off The nudged him, "Did she put out?"

"Well I was really nervous."

"Oh hell," swore Off The. "Don't tell me you couldn't get it up."

"No," said Paul. Beer foam traced his upper lip. "See, while I was driving there, I wondered if maybe I should have phoned to let her know I was coming. Sometimes surprises aren't such a good idea."

Vinnie interrupted, "I know it. She has a boyfriend."

Paul shook his head. "Mary Katherine looks a little different now. Let me show you her picture." He stood and retrieved the photo from atop the refrigerator, and then teased, "She's only wearing her night things."

"Oh yeah," intoned Off The.

Vinnie snatched the photo. "Huh?"

"That's her."

Off The grabbed the photo. "What the hell? Who is this?"

"Seems Mary Katherine forgot to mention a few things."

Off The stood, knocking over his chair. "This is her. THIS IS HER!"

"Hey relax. She's really kind of funny looking," said Vinnie.

"Funny?" Off The staggered backward. "Bitches."

"Come on," said Paul. "She's only a kid." He held out his hand for the photo, fearful Off The might tear it.

Off The flicked the photo at him and snarled, "First it's my mother, then my aunts, even the lady next door. All of them watching me, like I'm a killer, going to murder someone."

"My mother wonders why I didn't get her a camera."

"She doesn't even have tits."

"The guy down the street asked if I fucked any of them," said Paul.

Off The circled the table, and then sank into a chair, "I don't believe it."

"Now my sister wants to know how many I think I killed."

"No tits."

"Does anyone understand what it was like for us?" murmured Vinnie. "How we could have got killed all the time?"

"That's just it. They don't know," said Paul, touching Vinnie's arm. "They have no idea."

Off The's voice quivered, "No one understands, and she's a kid. A fucking kid."

Paul stared at the photo. Strange thoughts whirled around him. Sure, she was a kid, but how would she look at twenty? Like that picture she sent? He smiled with visions of the bikini. Maybe their trip to the beach could happen someday? Then he caught himself. Who the hell knows where he'd be when she grows up? Would she even remember him?

Off The stood and lumbered toward them. "I got worked up over a kid." He embraced them with his enormous arms. His voice revved, an engine turning over. Suddenly he laughed, "A little girl."

Paul stepped away, rubbing his eyes with the back of his hand. He looked at Vinnie who was doing the same.

Vinnie snorted, "Yeah, a kid."

"You're right, she's just a kid," whispered Paul.

Suddenly they laughed, guffawing louder than they should. Tears mixed with gurgling noises. They snorted. Chortled. Words no longer served them. Perhaps now, they could begin the slow process of purging fears, horrors, and remembrances.

By the time Mary Katherine recuperated and returned to school, her mother had met with Sister Immaculata. Group A had been disbanded. Mary Katherine didn't say much to her cohort, mustn't strain the throat too soon.

Besides, Colleen asked, "Does he really look like Paul McCartney?"

"Can't talk yet," whispered Mary Katherine. How to explain the shame, the mortification?

At recess, she did her best to avoid them and sought sanctuary in the church. Liberally dousing herself with holy water, she genuflected at the Stations of the Cross and patted her hip pocket where she kept the Polaroid photo of Paul. No way could she show it to her friends. They'd never understand. And Mary Katherine? She'd keep his photo forever. She smiled with fantasies of her grown-up self and meeting him again. Then, she paused. Her bottom lip quivered. Would they recognize each other?

After returning to the classroom, Mary Katherine pressed her shoulder blades against the seatback as the students opened their *St. Joseph Baltimore Catechisms* and recited ways to atone for their sins. Her thoughts dive-bombed. Maybe she should write Paul a letter, saying she was sorry? But she knew she wouldn't. Somehow, maturity had become too complex.

Sister Immaculata didn't help to ease matters. She warned how those who died without making penance for their sins would be sentenced to Purgatory. Not only was it the dark realm between heaven and hell, but dead people couldn't talk. "Just lonely, suffering souls."

Each time Mary Katherine heard those words, her throat constricted. She slumped down in her desk and swallowed hard: Could she ever be forgiven?

SWEET THE SOUND

WHEN I turn off Anthracite Expressway and jockey Big Blue across River Street and into the parking lot of Our Lady of Perpetual Help Church, all the spaces are filled. Colleen sits in the passenger seat and taps her foot. "See, MK, I told you Craig's funeral would be packed." She crosses her arms over her chest, exhaling with such a huff, the pleats of her black dress unfurl like a billowing tent.

"I had to go slow around those bikers," I remind her. We got boxed in by geezers on motorcycles: gray ponytails hanging below do-rags, no helmets, just beer guts, green T-shirts, and denim vests. They passed us with their fists raised, oblivious to the double yellow lines, probably thinking I had Big Blue out for a joy ride. It's warm for November, yet I never expected them on our route along the Susquehanna River. We're way north of Lancaster, no draw of Amish farm roads or free tours at the nearby Harley-Davidson factory.

The hearse, parked by the church steps and flanked by men in military dress uniforms, blocks our way. National Guardsmen from Craig's unit, I suppose. I shift Big Blue to idle, and we open our windows. Big Blue hums a comfort purr. I came here many Sundays with my grandmother, but not since she died and left me the Buick in her will. Aren't places supposed to look smaller after you've been away? The church looms as large as ever, like an airport hangar topped by a steeple, but the façade of bluestone, mined from Slatington Quarry and sought by builders for its appearance and durability, has faded to chalky ash.

Colleen murmurs, "This will be a long service. Why didn't we eat more at lunch?"

We have the afternoon off from the mall, where Melanie, Craig's wife, now a widow, has a part-time job with Colleen at the Hallmark store. I work at Borders Books, but back when I started at the store, it was Waldenbooks. Most days, we take our breaks at the food court. Sometimes Colleen and Melanie swap stories from Vo Tech, even though Colleen graduated long before Melanie. Who'd have figured on a funeral, when a year ago, Melanie peered beneath dark bangs and said Craig was being deployed to Afghanistan?

"He gets a big increase in his monthly check," announced Melanie.

"That's good," I said as Colleen kicked my left shin under the table. I should have anticipated her reaction. Colleen gets enraged by many things, and her favorite rant is the Afghan War. She says Pennsylvania sends more National Guard troops than any other state in the US. "They signed up for extra cash while serving close to home. None of them imagined seeing combat."

Thankfully Colleen shut up as Melanie assured us of Craig's safety: "He'll do supply logistics, arranging who hauls garbage where. That kind of stuff." Melanie shredded her napkin, and bits of paper stuck to her fingertips. "The money will let us take over the farm when his parents retire."

Colleen nodded, jaws clamped tight. She was aching to foam about downturn economics, but I figured she'd wait and vent after work with a bottle of Merlot. That's when she gets going like she's on a soapbox, shaking red hair as she pounds her chest, spouting how her blood is spiked by Celtic warriors . . . until I beg her to cut the crap. Then she rants, "What will it take to get you involved and do something?"

Bob Jenkins, the director of Alderwood Funeral Services, walks toward Big Blue. He's put on weight, and his hair is butter-white. Leaning down to my window, he fills the car with Old Spice, the aftershave used by my grandfather: "Hello, girls."

I pray Colleen doesn't take him to task for calling us girls. We're women, well into midlife. Maybe he's thinking way back to when Colleen worked part-time at the funeral home. She'd taken cosmetology classes at Vo Tech and did the hair and makeup on dead bodies, no less. When Colleen had told me about the work, she said it was nice, the clients never complained.

Colleen smiles at Bob Jenkins. He has a calming influence, undoubtedly why he gets voted coroner even though he runs unopposed. "Best turn around and park on Mill Street," he says. His tone, flat and tired, makes me wonder if he's as sad as we feel. How could this happen when Craig's deployment was almost over?

No one speaks, and I hear the din of motorcycles coming from behind Big Blue. I check the rearview mirror but can't see much other than a green pickup angled at the curb, its tailgate down, the bed piled high with wooden poles sticking out the back.

Bob presses both hands against the car to push upright, "You'll want to avoid the crowd in the lower lot, so take the side alley."

Big Blue weaves past trash cans in the alley. Colleen sucks the back of her teeth, her prelude for home-baked history. How after Vo Tech, Craig said goodbye to farming and hello to the Army. *Be All You Can Be* meant an enlistment in Georgia, where he cultivated a hatred for chiggers, and long days at a computer, learning the ins and outs of trash management. Shortly before his tour ended, his parents sold forty acres to pay for barn repairs. The land was annexed to expand Rivendell, a gated development. Craig returned thinking everything he'd known was slipping away. *No more*, he vowed. But raising pigs and selling swine to kielbasa makers wasn't enough to get by.

Then a National Guard recruiter phoned, seeking a man with Army experience. He offered Craig a signing bonus, and the money was just what the family needed. Craig trained one weekend a month at Fort Indiantown Gap until Hurricane Katrina hit the South. He rode in a truck all the way to Baton Rouge, where in the ruins of Louisiana bayous, he sat at a computer under a tarp, pole in the middle like a circus tent filled with screeching noise and BO. After Katrina, what were the chances he'd also get sent to Afghanistan?

Months passed with Craig on deployment, and deep lines chiseled the skin around Melanie's eyes. Colleen started Ladies Stitch and Bitch Nights at her place. My job was to drive Melanie in Big Blue. She turned the radio on full blast and hummed along with Dido's "White Flag." The song was number one on the pop charts, and Melanie relaxed, even more so after we got to Colleen's apartment where Colleen poured wine and regaled us with her supposed novel-in-making.

"This is just what I needed," said Melanie. "I'm so busy, there's no time to read."

For Colleen, that was the perfect thing to hear, especially as I've yet to see a single typed word. She continues to write it in her head during her long shifts at the Hallmark store. "Lots of novelists start in the card business," she proclaimed, opening another bottle of wine.

"Writing cards, not selling them," I reminded.

Melanie laughed and held out her glass for a refill. She gushed about how she and the kids, Chelsea, six, and Dan, four, were planning Craig's welcome home Thanksgiving dinner. Having invited both sets of parents, brothers, sisters, and their kids, for a total of twenty around the table, Melanie was so excited she stayed up late and Googled recipes of sausage stuffing and snickerdoodle pie, special treats for Craig.

Then word came of a roadside bombing. Craig arrived two weeks ahead of schedule, his remains in a steel casket, flag draped over the top.

Colleen and I stand in the church under the stained-glass window of Jesus cradling a fuzzy, white lamb. Sandwiched between the other people who came too late to get a seat, we can't see the altar. The funeral dirge plays slowly, telling me Mrs. Pavinsky, who'd been friends with my grandmother, is at the organ. Halfway through the song, Mrs. Pavinsky loses her place and starts over. "When will they hire a new organist?" whispers Colleen.

I look out over mostly gray and white heads, a field of dandelions gone to seed. The music stops. Incense rolls over us, and I take shallow breaths through a tissue. Then Father Ryan ascends the pulpit. He looks shorter than I remember, and his collar swallows his neck. Raising his arms, he brings long-fingered hands together in prayer. The lucky people in the pews shift to cushioned kneelers. I look down at the cold tile floor and wonder what to do. *Suffer it up for Jesus* as my school nuns used to say?

Father Ryan rasps: "Dearly beloved, we gather here—" but a shrill distortion renders him silent.

"Same bad sound system," says Colleen. The man standing beside her smiles at us. He wears a tweed jacket and has dark, familiar eyes. Colleen nudges me with her elbow. Then I make the connection: Tad "Hottie" Hajduk. In high school, he worked weekends for Craig's father, but he moved to Colorado eons ago.

Did he come back for the funeral? On the other side of Hottie stands his dad, Jarek Hajduk, the sleeve of his suit jacked folded over his amputated forearm, the result of a battlefield injury. My grandmother said he often joked and named himself Stump, yet I wonder if the funeral ignites memories for him.

Father Ryan clears his throat and flutters his hands, so people will sit. There's a rustling as hips return to wooden seats, yet we remain standing. The National Guard, cordoned off in block formation by the right wall, gaze our way with blank expressions. I wish I could find Melanie. Colleen says she's been taking Valium ever since she got the news, and I figure that's good for her. I stand on tiptoe, hoping to see the front row where I'm sure she sits with the kids, her parents, and Craig's mom and dad. I stretch taller, sucking in my stomach, and then a sharp pain stabs at my bad knee. Too much standing can cause the flare-up of an injury from my jogging days, and this pain makes me stagger. Frantically, I grab for Colleen, but down I go.

Colleen kneels, fanning me with the hem of her dress. People turn to look, so I close my eyes, knowing that won't stop them from staring, but at least I can focus before trying to stand. Then I smell Old Spice cologne. "Need help? Maybe we should get you outside for some fresh air," says Bob Jenkins.

I nod, horribly embarrassed, and my knee hurts, too. With hands under my armpits, he and Colleen get me upright and guide me out of the church to the vestibule. A National Guardsman opens the heavy oak door, so we can go outside. I gulp air and sit on the top step.

Bob Jenkins says, "That incense could make anyone faint."

There's no reason to say I didn't pass out.

Colleen tells him, "You go back inside. I'll stay with her."

He gestures toward the door, "Call that Guard if you need him."

"Thank you," I say.

Colleen hunkers beside me and points to the lower parking lot. From this height, it looks like a big glove: the drive is the thumb; the sidewalk, open space, and the parking rows make four fingers. That's when I could swear I hear Sister Aquinas, my ninth-grade earth science teacher: *Behold the hand of God.*

"The bikers are here," says Colleen.

Am I dizzy? I didn't whack my head, but sure enough, I failed to notice the geezers. They straddle motorcycles and face the church. Propped against their handlebars are big American flags. Where did they get them? Then I remember seeing that green pickup with the bed full of wooden poles. The flags resemble the five-foot marching flag I carried in the Memorial Day parade when I was a Girl Scout. I wore a holster at my waist, fitted with the base to ease the weight, yet my arms ached.

A biker with a wide-brimmed camouflage hat sees us staring. He lifts his right hand, his fingers in the V-sign for peace.

"Veterans," says Colleen, her voice hushed.

They're way older than the National Guardsmen. Some have medals pinned to their vests. All wear dog tags with peace sign medallions. Could these guys have served in Vietnam? I wish I knew what was going on. That's when I spy another group of people in the far parking lot. About twenty men, women, and kids cluster behind a skinny, white-haired guy. He shakes his finger, and a woman in an oddly bright blue dress, standing smack in the middle, holds up a sign: *God Hates Fags.*

Colleen bolts down the stairs. Her dress swooshes out behind her as she stomps onto flat ground and raises her left arm, shaking her fist at them.

I think the group must be the fundamentalists that have been featured in the news. They picket at funerals of soldiers as retribution for the perceived sins of the nation—crazy stuff about God bringing war to punish our country for homosexuals. Last month, the group protested at a funeral in York, way down I-83. I never imagined them coming here.

I limp behind Colleen until I'm close enough to read more signs. A girl with pigtails and a pink skirt, looking the same age as Craig and Melanie's daughter, holds a poster board above her head: *God's Will*. Beside her, a tall man keeps his sign at chin level: *You're going to Hell*.

Colleen yells, "Get out of here!"

The old man cries, "God wants soldiers dead." His words incite fervor. The group cheers like a pep rally gone bad: "God kills soldiers for the sins of fags."

Colleen shudders: "Unbelievable."

The group yells with pinched, twisted faces. The bikers rev their engines. Throttles on full, the pitch accelerates over the chanting. The parking lot roars like warm-up at the Daytona 500. This is madness. Where are the cops? What about the National Guard? Then I remember: They're in church, same as Melanie and her family. The kids. We can't let them come out and see this.

"Celtic warrior!" screeches Colleen, loud as a banshee. Her foot paws the ground. Right arm raised high like she's holding a cudgel, she bulks up for the charge. I realize this could be the battle she was born to fight. Her head lulls back and forth, eyes bulge, and she wails. I yell too. Can we tackle them? We're not far, maybe forty yards. We ready our two-woman brigade.

Suddenly the biker with the camouflage hat zooms beside us like he's cavalry, mustering troops. "We'll handle this. That's why we came."

Colleen snorts, eyes wild.

The biker downshifts and uses the heel of his boot to lower the kickstand. He dismounts and moves in front of her. His surprisingly boyish face is a senior biker version of Beatle Paul.

I feel like I know him from somewhere. He stares like he knows me, too. Where could I have met this guy? A customer at the bookstore? Perpetual Help Outreach Center? Riverbed Tavern? My brain fails to make a connection, yet I can't shrug off the sense of familiarity. Maybe it will come to me later.

With trembling hands, he grabs hold of Colleen's wrists, "No violence."

I stiffen my spine: "We have to do something."

His voice is gentle, "Just bring your car. We can use it for the procession."

How can I run with a bad knee? Colleen vaults through the alley. I hop-along, leg-straight, trying to keep pace. Gasping, we careen onto Mill Street and reach Big Blue. The engine starts right up, a rarity, and I tear off toward the church driveway where the picketers have commandeered the blacktop. I want to topple them like bowling pins, but I motor over the sidewalk and lawn, rivaling any SUV as we approach the phalanx of bikers. Why don't they make room for us? I guess they're too intent on watching the congregation stream from the church. Big Blue hovers on the grass like a land yacht.

The mourners look out at the parking lot. They cluster on the stairs as if on risers for a photo shoot. No one smiles.

The old man yells, and his group chants, but they get drowned out as motorcycles rev their engines. Then the people on the stairs part in the middle like Moses at the Red Sea. The pallbearers, all National Guard, stride into the opening with the casket held on their shoulders. They move down the steps to the hearse. As they slide it through the rear door, I sense movement in my peripheral vision. The tall man charges from the lower lot. He looks like a running back making an unexpected dash for the end zone.

My breathing quickens as he gains yardage on the church. Why don't the bikers stop him? I swallow and realize there's no time to wait. I shift Big Blue into drive and gun it. We aim straight for him, getting so close, I see his jowls shake. That's when Colleen digs her nails into my shoulder. I pump the brakes, and the guy stops.

Biker Paul pulls up by my window. "Whoa now."

Colleen whispers, "What the hell?"

I'm panting too hard to speak, and then I see Melanie on the top step. Wearing a black hat with a veil over her face, she puts her hand to her brow and looks in our direction. The bikers swing their flags, creating a breeze that catches the Stars and Stripes to form a curtain against the hateful presence below. What So Proudly We Hail has never seemed so righteous. Then the veterans sing. They have gravel voices, but they chorus, and a few tenors project loudly: *Amazing Grace . . . How sweet the sound . . .*

I know Colleen thinks the song is schmaltzy, a term rarely used except by her, yet she joins in, same as do the people on the steps. They pivot, turning their backs to the man and his group. No one from the church looks their way.

The National Guard march in place. The singing intensifies and reverberates off the bluestone façade of the church. People press shoulder to shoulder, creating a human barrier for Melanie and her children. Heads bowed, they walk down the steps and get in the limousine that will follow the hearse to the cemetery.

The bikers brace flagpoles against their right shoulders and motor ahead. Engines thunder as they ride in formation alongside the vehicles. The funeral procession views waving flags and not those people with horrid signs.

Big Blue joins the line of cars, and I stifle a sob. Colleen gently raps her fingers against the dashboard. The small St. Christopher statue my grandmother had glued on wobbles a bit but stands strong.

Colleen takes a deep breath. Her voice quivers, *And Grace will lead us home . . .*

I stare through the windshield. It provides a kind of picture frame: late afternoon sun lowered to half-mast, the tree branches like dead limbs, leafless and forlorn. A shaft of light settles on St. Christopher. My eyes, awash, make me blink. I swear I see St. Christopher raise the arm holding his staff, and with the back of his hand, he rubs away tears.

YELLOW TAPE

ON A CRISP MORNING in 1990, Bob Jenkins wheeled the gurney into River Haven Hospital. His navy windbreaker flapped against his chino pants, making him look like a high school coach rather than a funeral director. Typically, he wore a suit for viewings and business matters at Alderwood Services, but these clothes were fine for a transport. It was rare for him to see anyone other than the supervising nurse.

The morgue was locked, so he hurried through the fluorescent hallway toward the critical care unit. The shift changed at 8:00 a.m., and nurses didn't want extra paperwork. Yet he paused when he saw bright yellow tape, the kind used at crime scenes, outlining the doorway of Room 112: CAUTION INFECTIOUS DISEASE.

"Your pick up is in there," said the nurse, Enid Walek, walking briskly toward him. She pulled latex gloves from the pocket of her green smock. "He's our first case."

Bob tilted his head. "Huh?"

"AIDS," she said.

"Matt Bryant?" Bob's voice rose tinny with disbelief.

"What? You never heard of AIDS?" rapped Enid.

"Sure. Who hasn't?"

"Then you better get used to it. We'll get plenty more." Enid put on a surgical mask, then handed gloves and a mask to Bob. Before opening the door, she paused and added softly, "When they've no place else to go, they come back here to the farms. Home to Mama."

Bob walked to the bed and lifted the sheet. Matt's arms and shoulders were all bone, fragile like a bird; his skin puckered with sores. "Sweet Jesus—"

"I'd just helped his mother give him a sponge bath," said Enid. "Mildred?"

Enid nodded. "I told her it would be best if she went home. I said you'd take care of everything."

"Good." Bob pursed his lips. He'd known Mildred and her family forever, not that they were close. They didn't go to the same church or socialize, but they used first names, and he handled her husband's arrangements two years ago. Bob sighed. Now this with Matt.

Shortly after Thanksgiving, he saw Mildred at Weis Markets. She wore a corduroy blazer with wool slacks, the sporty garb of bed and breakfast types, not a farm widow. Of course, Mildred had always dressed nicely, even when milk prices bottomed out. She waved to Bob as she placed cans of orange juice in her cart. "I'm buying for two again." She explained how Matt had left New York and moved back home. He'd been sick, so she hadn't been out much. "I don't care what the doctors say. What Matt needs is good homemade food. That will get him on his feet again."

"Always best," said Bob, patting his stomach. He was surprised Matt had returned and figured he wouldn't stay long. Northeast Pennsylvania lacked opportunity. It wasn't like the Lancaster area where farms gave way to commercial strips and housing developments. How could Matt do marketing? The boy, well, not anymore, had to be thirty. When did he leave for college? Fourteen years ago? Bob remembered because it was the bicentennial. The

Riverside Gazette had patriotic highlights, carrying the theme to the sports page: "Firecrack Matt" ran the headline after he placed in the mile at States. He was a top student, too.

Then like most talent to pass through Tunkhannock High School, Matt was gone, opting for a scholarship from Columbia over the Penn State Scholars program. Matt's father, Cletus, had told Bob he couldn't fathom his son's choice: "Off to the Seventh Circle of Hell," spat Cletus, eyelids drooping like a bulldog. And now, the two of them dead. The old man's aneurism was unfortunate, though not unusual, but who could imagine AIDS coming here? This was farm country. Yet if Nurse Enid was right, the hospital had better prepare. And not just them. Hadn't *Mortuary Management* featured an article about procedural changes? Something about the trocar and new bleaching chemicals to prevent the disease organisms from multiplying? Bob hadn't paid attention.

Gray sky replaced the dawn's purple stain, yet Mildred continued to lie on the couch. Her head swirled with questions: Why can't I accept he's gone? I know I'm supposed to think of his real home, but I can't. Mildred exhaled heavily as she recalled biblical phrases of The Saved going Home to Jesus. Yet Mildred also knew of the other place for sheep that had strayed. *If I could just have a sign*, she prayed.

When the phone rang, it so startled her, she sat bolt upright, shaking her hands anxiously until she remembered placing the portable on the coffee table. She put it there after calling her daughter. "Hello."

"I'm so sorry, Mildred. This is Bob Jenkins."

"I recognized your voice," Mildred's lips turned up briefly. Bob had a lilt to his words and could raise a person's spirit, no matter how low. That's why most people used his services. And he made a good coroner, too. Why he bothered to launch a campaign every four years Mildred couldn't imagine. No one ever voted for anybody other than Bob, especially since no one ran against him.

"You still there?"

"Yes, oh yes," said Mildred.

"This is tough for you. But I'm calling to make sure you haven't changed plans."

"Everything's the same. Like I told the nurses, I want what you did for Cletus." Mildred pulled at the green threads of the afghan covering her legs.

"You're sure now? I can come by and talk if you'd like."

"Actually, I was thinking about driving over and bringing you Matthew's suit."

"That's not necessary. I can pick it up."

But Mildred was insistent, "I want to come over before Debbie gets here." Mildred explained how her daughter in Johnstown would be driving on Highway 6 with her husband and three children. "The baby doesn't sleep through the night, so I want to give them a rest when they arrive. I'll feel better if I bring the suit, you understand how it is—" Her voice trailed off.

"Well, if that's what you want," said Bob. He didn't press the matter. Experience had shown him how small tasks often helped people cope with grief.

"I'll be there before noon," said Mildred. She hung up, and then closed her eyes. Her brain filled with pictures of Matt as a baby. When he was born, Dr. McFarland held him high and announced, "Mildred look at this boy! What hair!" Mildred laughed with amazement. Her son's head was plastered with white curls, and even though they were wet, the doctor teased them with his fingertips, shaping them into a kind of halo.

"My angel baby," said Mildred. Her baby seemed a miracle, the most wonderful accomplishment of her life. Maybe that's what made the present so difficult to accept. How could her greatest joy become her deepest sorrow?

If Cletus were alive, he'd tell her, "Now is the time for Scripture." She imagined him handing her the leather-covered Bible, but to consult it meant turning on the lamp and disrupting the comfort of the room's half-light. The harsh incandescence might make her eyes tear, causing her to cry, and Mildred feared she wouldn't have the strength to stop.

Bob put the phone on the charger and exhaled. Why shouldn't Mildred have sounded composed? After all, she was Baptist, and they kept hold of their emotions. He liked doing their arrangements the best. By the time they came in, they were done with the crying. They accepted death. It was part of their process for finding the Lord. Sure, it was hard if it was a young person or an accident. Then Baptists murmured about trusting the plan—even if they couldn't see it.

Bob walked across his office to the book case stacked with manuals and journals. Mildred didn't mention the AIDS, not that she needed to say anything. Still Bob felt uneasy, especially after he dialed Colleen Walsh, his part-time worker. She had completed the cosmetology program at Vo Tech, but never hired on with a beauty shop. He didn't ask why, pleased by the hair and cosmetics she did for the cadavers. Colleen crafted wonders from looking at photographs, and Bob often told her how families said the deceased looked better than they had in months. She smiled, "That's nice. They need that." Bob was never sure if Colleen meant the family or the deceased.

"I've got some work for you," said Bob when Colleen answered the phone.

"Anybody I know?"

"Maybe. Remember Matt Bryant?"

"Matt. What happened?"

Then Bob explained about the AIDS. He brought it up because of the lesions. Matt's face had a spray of sores the size of silver dollars, and Bob figured he better warn Colleen, but as soon as he told her, she said she couldn't come in.

"I'm working today at Hallmark." That was her other part-time job, the card store at the mall. Yet she often came in after she finished her shift. Not this time. "I wish I could help, but I can't risk catching something. I'm trying to get pregnant. It doesn't matter what they say about prevention, there's no cure. You better be careful yourself."

She had a point, thought Bob, as he scoured his bookcase for the missing journal. He rarely threw them away, only when a pile got too high. Besides, trade journals recycled the same articles every few years.

He opened the gray filing cabinet and found nothing. Then, he decided to call Grykowski, the coroner in Luzerne County. His first name was William, but Bob never heard him use it, simply identifying himself with a guttural blast: *Grykowski*. Sometimes they covered for each other or compared crime scene findings even though Bob disliked his crude manner. Grykowski was a blowhard, a weasel for getting his name into the newspaper. And he drank too much. At the annual association dinner, Grykowski was always the last to leave the bar.

"Good God. You poor son of a bitch," said Grykowski. "AIDS in Wyoming County."

"I know. I wasn't expecting it. Who'd think of it here?"

"Holy Jesus. You better be careful."

"That's why I'm calling." Bob explained how he'd read an article about procedure changes but couldn't find it. "I know I've got to use a high index spray and increase the bleach."

"Why embalm? Go direct cremation."

"That's out of the question here," said Bob.

For a moment, neither spoke. Then Grykowski wheezed, "I can hear what you're going to say next. Farm families want full burial. It's their ritual. But hell, they're going to have to change sometime."

Bob cleared his throat, "Arterial injection. I'll have to up the percent, right?"

"Hell, yeah. If you had more time, you could order venous tubes with double closures."

"I've got to do this now."

"In that case, best add extra bleach. Crank your injector way up. Use the whole damn bottle. Why risk it?"

Bob ground his heels into the wood floor. Their conversation was getting nowhere. "Thanks. I've got to go." If Bob completed procedures by midday, he could take a break prior to doing the face and hair.

Mildred pushed away the afghan comforter and walked barefoot to the window. She pressed her palm to the cold frame and stared at tufts of frozen grass, spindly tree limbs, and ever large, the yellow siding of an empty barn. Eventually a chill numbed her toes and settled into the small of her back. The view seemed so vacant from the days when Cletus kept forty cows, milked thirty, and maintained the cleanest stalls Mildred had ever seen. Cletus did well. Unlike many other farmers in the county, he didn't have to take on extra jobs: no driving a school bus, no snow plowing. He told Mildred, "We're blessed."

But Mildred knew their good fortune reflected his hard work. Naturally, Cletus couldn't do it alone. He hired help, and when Matt got old enough, he worked too. After particularly long days, when the family sat at the table, Cletus led grace, "We give thanks for all we're given—our food, our home, and my son by my side."

How Mildred treasured those moments. She never imagined they'd change, but after Matt entered tenth grade and his 4H friends began dating and making plans for homecoming, he resigned from the club. "I want to join cross country."

Cletus was troubled, "What about our prize heifer? You worked with her all year."

"I'll help some in the barn. But Debbie can start showing with 4H," he said, pointing at his sister across the table. She smiled eagerly as Matt told his father, "I can't miss practice. Coach gave orders. And the team travels on weekends for meets." Then after the cross country season ended, Matt joined photography club, spending hours in the darkroom, and in spring, he ran track. On the rare afternoon he was home during the day, he showed little interest in the new milking machines, even less for the planned addition to the barn. Instead Matt was thrilled about yearbook staff. "When I'm a senior, I might make editor."

Cletus told Mildred, "He doesn't notice our place. What happened?"

"Give him time."

And for a while, Mildred watched as Cletus listened to Matt's plans to study English. But Cletus grew agitated. "Can't you consider something useful?" he asked Matt. "If you're not going to farm, become a doctor or a vet. You're smart. All the teachers say so. We need educated people with training."

"I'm not coming back here after college." Matt covered his mouth with his hand as if surprised by his own words.

"I didn't realize—" Cletus clamped his jaw shut. He never mentioned it again, not after Matt's college graduation, or when he got an apartment with a bunch of young men in New York. Each time Matt switched jobs, Cletus shrugged and shook his head.

Mildred thought Cletus harbored a belief that Matt would experience an occupational conversion and return to work the farm with him. Yet when Matt visited for holidays, two or three times a year, he only stayed a weekend, and never brought a girl. Without asking straight out, Mildred fished for reasons. Her hints about starting a family like his sister failed to yield a response. So rather than dwell on the unknown, Mildred consoled herself with believing he'd always been a private person.

After milk prices took another dive, the farms on either side of them were sold at auction. Cletus tried to weather matters as best he could. He told Mildred, "Prices will pick up eventually." But they continued to drop, and Cletus filed paperwork to refinance. The bank turned down his request with a threat to put a lien on the property. Then, by chance, Matt arrived for a visit. Unusual, for it wasn't a holiday, and if it weren't for the difficulties with the bank, Cletus and Mildred would have been elated.

"What a lucky surprise," said Mildred, turning to smile at Cletus, who sat frowning at the kitchen table. She expected him to echo her welcome, but he said nothing. She hugged Matt, noticing how he'd grown thin, the skin beneath his eyes dark. "I can tell you're not eating right."

"Don't worry," he said, in his satiny voice.

How many times had Matt used that phrase? Mildred smiled at her son. "And work's good?"

"Work's work, but that's not why I'm home. I need to talk to both of you." He pressed his lips together, looked up at the ceiling, and then resumed talking. "Over the years, haven't you noticed I've changed?"

Mildred squinted. His hair did look different. No longer light, having turned dark by the time he was twelve, it was cut short, not a military cropped buzz, but rather like a skull cap.

"This isn't easy, but you're going to have to accept me as I am." Matt sat and held fast to the edge of the table. His words became puzzling—what Cletus termed bull crap—phrases about being accepted, his need for people to see him as he was, no matter how difficult. "You have to love me as *I am*."

"What now?" interrupted Cletus. "As soon as you turn around, you start something new."

"That's marketing," said Matt. "There's lots of quick changes."

"You did the same thing at college."

"I was trying to find what to do with my life. I got good grades." Matt coughed, and his voice sounded heavy, "It's not like I ever asked you for anything."

"Mr. Scholarship. Like we needed reminders," snapped Cletus. "Don't kid yourself. Your mother and I still paid—we paid with our hearts."

"Dad, please."

"And look what we got." Cletus pursed his lips.

That's when Mildred spoke, "Iced tea. I think we could all use an iced tea. Let's go out to the porch. There's a nice breeze."

"I can't. I've got to get back." No, Matt wouldn't stay for supper. He hadn't planned to spend the night. The rental company needed the car.

Mildred knew he lied.

After twenty-six years in the business, Bob Jenkins was certain of one thing: he got the final look at the best and worst of Wyoming County. And while that aspect of his job held merit, he couldn't deny how some cadavers were harder to deal with than others. Bob shifted into motions that gave little cause for thought. He held the trocar, the long thin needle with the flexible tube for draining the body and hoped he wouldn't have a problem. There'd been no autopsy, no removal of organs, so it wasn't as if he needed to add padding to restore shape.

Then, for the first time since he'd brought in Matt, Bob took a closer look. From head to toe, bones poked against nearly transparent skin. Bob realized Matt had been sick for a long time. The disease had ravaged any semblance of muscle, and his face prompted Bob to mutter, "Sweet Jesus!"

Matt had been handsome, not in a movie star way, but healthy and athletic. He had brown hair and a strong jaw with wide cheek bones. Now his chin, covered by dark stubble and a spray of lesions, had sunk toward the cavity of his mouth. His lips, cracked and swollen, held cankers. Bob rarely let physical decay bother him, but he cleared his throat, "You poor man."

When it came time to mix the bleaching solution, Bob paused. How should he figure the ratio? Grykowski had been little help, simply warning: *Can't be too safe*. Bob knew Grykowski was right about precautionary measures. *If I were you, I'd add the whole damn bottle*. And with that thought, Bob poured in sixteen ounces.

Alderwood Services was only five miles away, but Mildred felt so overwhelmed, she wondered if she could drive there before Bob Jenkins left for lunch. Where had the morning gone? A rising tide of inertia had engulfed her, making her legs heavy, as if she walked through mud. Not that she'd much to do—just enter Matt's room, open the closet, find the gray suit, white shirt, and tie and put them in the car.

Her thoughts bogged her down. She asked questions she knew she couldn't answer. Still they took shape. Maybe if Matt had stayed in the area like Cletus wanted, this wouldn't have happened. Yet she knew he had the right to choose his own path. But what if Matt had chosen the wrong one?

When Matt came home for Cletus's funeral, he brought a gym bag of vitamins and special pills. The alarm on his watch sounded each time he needed to take them. Why hadn't she realized the obvious? How could Mildred be so ignorant?

Not until four months ago, when Matt, who had stood a foot

taller than she, started to shrink beside her, did she begin to comprehend. "Mama, this is it." He coughed so violently, blood mixed with spit.

Mildred helped Matt to the couch, coaxing him along by whispering, "You'll be okay."

"I've told you, it's AIDS. You know what that means."

Mildred called Dr. McFarland. He no longer made house calls, having joined the county's HMO, but Mildred was firm, "You must come here."

Dr. McFarland arrived with cloudy eyes, the same eyes she'd seen when the vet came to put down a cow. As he gave Matt an injection, he told Mildred, "This will help his cough and ease the pain, too." His shoulders drooped. "Call me when he's ready for the hospital."

Before Mildred could fully register the extent of the disease, Matt lay on a hospital bed. The nurses put up that awful yellow tape, and insisted Mildred wear gloves, gown, and mask. Matt gasped and wheezed, thankfully oblivious, yet each breath rattled the inevitable. Her son was dying.

Mildred sang to him—lullabies, hymns. She patted his forehead and clutched his hand. How she prayed to ease the suffering. But what could she do but hold him? His entire body tightened each time he labored for breath; then grew calm, only to struggle again. Did the morphine patch really block pain? How long would the pattern continue?

Then, without warning, the nurse turned off the monitor: "He's gone."

In the seconds that followed, a curious relief washed over Mildred, but with it lingered one thought: where had Matt gone?

She turned her Dodge into the Alderwood parking lot, and the same question persisted. For a fleeting moment, she considered driving to see Pastor Richter. No, best to wait and phone him after she delivered the suit. She worried what Pastor might say, especially after that odd Sunday, shortly after Matt moved back home, when Mildred failed to understand he was so sick. She arrived early at church, thrilled to tell Pastor Richter, "Matt's home."

"Really?" rasped Pastor Richter.

Mildred chattered about the changes she wanted for the house and how Matt would need a car, "How I wish Cletus were alive."

"He had faith Matt would find his way back. His own Prodigal Son."

"Hardly that," bristled Mildred. "Matt would be here today, but he's sick."

"Maybe next Sunday." Pastor clicked his tongue against the top of his mouth and walked toward the pulpit.

Mildred thought he was uncharacteristically abrupt. Perhaps he was thinking about his sermon? She sat in the second pew, eager for a spirited talk, what she called his golden nuggets, but Pastor Richter skipped over prayers for the sick and shut-ins and cautioned about sin. His voice railed as he preached how God condemns the sin but loves the sinner. Clearing his throat, he looked right at Mildred: "Beware of enabling the sinner." Unbelievable. Mildred folded her hands, cheeks hot. At the end of service, she rushed off.

Bob Jenkins opened Alderwood's oak door. "Why Mildred, come in." He held her elbow and guided her to the foyer, where Mildred glanced at the pedestal with a vase of white and yellow chrysanthemums.

Bob followed her gaze. "They're nice, aren't they? Especially for this time of year."

Mildred nodded. "I've brought Matt's suit." Her arms cradled his dress clothes.

Bob reached for the hanger's metal hook and held the suit

upright. With his free hand, he touched the sleeve, "Beautiful material."

"It's one of the few things Matt brought home. I don't know what happened to his stuff. I guess I never really thought to ask."

"Why don't you have a seat while I put this downstairs," said Bob. He guided her to a wing chair in the receiving room. "I'll be right back."

Mildred inhaled slowly. The light blue carpet calmed her, same with the walls, and she remembered how peaceful Cletus had looked when he was laid out. Everyone said so. Mildred knew her husband was at rest, even if he did go suddenly. With Matt, it was so different. How he suffered, and yet last night, as Mildred patted his head and placed ice chips on his lips, soothing him as best she could, she never actually thought he'd die. Mildred pressed her tongue to her lower teeth. What had she expected? A miracle?

Bob returned and placed his hands together.

"I'd like to see him," said Mildred.

"Of course. You'll have private time before the viewing."

"I mean now."

Bob opened his hands. "This isn't a good time, you should wait. He's not dressed. And I haven't done his hair."

"It's okay, I don't need special treatment. I took care of him before he went to the hospital. And even there, I helped to bathe him."

"Trust me, this is different."

Mildred stood and raised her chin. "I want to see him while I'm here."

"I really think you should come back later," said Bob, his voice slow and sure. "Maybe your daughter could bring you over?"

Mildred shook her head. Her tone was firm. "I'm his mother. I need to see him. NOW."

"Okay then," sighed Bob. "Let me take you downstairs." He

walked a few steps ahead of her, trying to shake his sense of resignation. He feared the sight of Matt could have a lasting impact, the image she'd call up for years.

Mildred followed close to Bob. Her loafers made a squeaky noise against the carpet, so she lifted her feet higher than usual. What Mildred didn't tell him, and perhaps failed to realize, was that more than seeing Matt, she wanted something to show her he was at peace.

As soon as Bob entered the procedure room, he paused. Vapors of bleach and phenol swept over him, stinging his eyes, but more disorienting was Matt's skin tone. Uncovered from the chest up, the body lacked pigment; no color remained. Even his hair was bleached porcelain white. Why had he listened to Grykowski? *Use the whole damn bottle.*

"Look at him," gasped Mildred. She dug her fingernails into Bob's arm.

Bob stiffened. What must Mildred think? He searched for words.

Mildred released her grip and walked from Bob to her son. With the back of her hand, she grazed Matt's cheekbone, then rested her palm on his head.

"I'll fix everything," said Bob. "Sometimes chemicals have an odd effect on skin. That's why we use makeup." Yet he'd never seen a chemical reaction happen this way, much less so quickly.

Mildred looked up from her son. Her eyelids flickered as she made a rounded *O* with her lips, but no sound came forth.

Bob hesitated. What next? Would Mildred scream? Perhaps faint? Maybe a lawsuit? Mildred had every right to sue, for her case was legit—the court would impose fines, perhaps suspend his license. His shoulders sagged, "Let me try to explain."

"Sshh," whispered Mildred. What she needed had come. More than she'd prayed for: "The Lord does provide."

Bob punched a fist into his palm.

Mildred bent and kissed Matthew's head. She laced her fingers through his white hair, caressing it with circles. His hair was as downy as the day he was born. It was the sign she needed. She raised her eyes to heaven and smiled, "My angel baby."

"Forgive me," pleaded Bob.

"My angel baby's home," said Mildred. Her glance penetrated Bob with a strange mixture of sadness and relief, "Can't you see?"

LESS SAID

BLOOD in women's armpits. As a fifth grader, I thought that's what happened each month. And that's why when Jenna started middle school, I couldn't tell her my notion of female biology. She'd have thought I was an idiot. Yet I'd been a top student. I could recite fifty state capitals and spell them perfectly. I was nothing like eleven-year old Jenna—quick to define the purpose of fallopian tubes, not to mention safe sex.

At my school, Our Lady of Perpetual Help, the Sisters created an atmosphere as chaste as the Palmer Method penmanship they scripted on the board. The word *sex* was never spoken. I had gym, not Physical Education for Preteen Health and Body where young Jenna tackled a project on menstruation: "We're searching websites. I get a free starter kit if I do the extra credit report. That's why you have to tell about getting yours."

I had wanted to claim that my skewed ideas reflected the times, but I knew Jenna would laugh the way she did when I turned on the radio, begging me to switch channels if she heard the jingle: *Grooving with Gold from the Seventies and Eighties!* Those were the days before Stayfree Thong Maxis with Wings, no female athletes promoting panty liners for lighter days. And TV commercials for tampons?! Unimaginable. Mine was the culture of inference: the less said the better.

The misinformation began in the Off Limits. I never entered my mother's bedroom unless summoned, and on that distant day, I stood as my mother sat on the white stool by her vanity table. She talked while I gazed above her bed at the crucifix where the wallpaper's dizzying blue flowers collided with the crown of thorns and blood.

My mother hushed *uter* and *menstra*. I nodded knowingly, lest she think I didn't understand. Her habit of whispering body parts, other than head, hands, and feet made them seem disagreeable or, worse, forbidden. So, despite my curiosity—after all, I was something of a word aficionado having spent hours with my friends looking up swears in the dictionary—I didn't ask.

She dipped her chin. Her nose seemed even longer. "You've heard this?"

"Sure."

She clucked, "I suppose with Colleen in your class. She's a big girl."

I crossed my arms over my chest.

My mother continued, "When it starts, let me know, so I can—."

The door banged open, rattling the Virgin Mary on her maple dresser. "What's going on?" demanded my little brother Jimmy.

"Ever try knocking?" I asked.

He bounced on his heels. Jimmy never closed doors, not even the bathroom. He pointed to the box on the bed. "What's that?"

"Not for you," I said.

"M-O-D-E-S-S," spelled Jimmy, showing off his letter skills. "MOM!"

My mother shooed Jimmy out of the room, and then turned to me. "Put the napkins in your room."

"Fine," I snapped. There was no good reason to be angry, but I stomped down the hall, locked my door, and sat cross-legged on the pink fluffy carpet. With the box in my lap, I ripped open the top. Inside were stacks of what looked like ice cream sandwiches. I pulled one out and squeezed the soft, padded block. Napkin? I looked in the box for explanation, but finding none, I invoked Nancy Drew's *Quest of the Missing*, and shredded the thing in less than two seconds: tissue wrapping, layered cotton, and thin blue plastic. I grabbed another, recalling the crescent shapes my mother pinned in armpits of her fancy dresses.

"Shields," my mother had said.

I held a surfboard napkin at eye level, appraising the end tabs, and sniffed baby powder instead of the camphor I'd expected. My mother had a thing about Vicks Vapor Rub, advocating its use as an all-around cure all. In fact, her bedroom had the perpetual odor of camphor. Whenever I sneezed or coughed, she attacked, rubbing the salve onto my chest, dabbing at the base of my nostrils if she could get away with it.

One time, my older brother Robert pointed out, "Says external use only."

She dismissed him with THE LOOK, the same look she'd used when I asked why she needed shields: "To protect the material," she said. "You'll use them when you're older."

I hadn't thought to ask: protect from what? But now I knew. Bleeding pits.

The following day at school, I couldn't wait to report to the other three girls in Group A—the fastest readers. Soon as Sister Paracleta sent us to our circle of desks in the back of the room, I whispered, "You won't believe what my mom told me." I twisted my finger around my braid, then caught myself at fidgeting, the behavior of little kids.

"Mine said so, too," cut in Beth. She smoothed back her white plastic headband so her long dark hair looked like a nun's veil.

"Same here," snorted Virginia. She no longer galloped around the playground during recess, but she still made horse sounds for effect.

"School sent home The Letter about seeing The Movie," said Colleen. She reached inside her blouse and tugged at her bra strap, making us feel inadequate about our lowly cotton undershirts.

I wanted to ask what movie but remained cautiously mute so I didn't sound stupid. Colleen was in the know from Susan, her older sister at St. Rose Prep. My mother said Susan was flashy, having been sent home from the high school for wearing eye shadow and rolling up her uniform skirt.

"Fifth grade girls watch the movie at the end of the year," explained Colleen. "No boys are allowed."

That was fine with me. I was glad to get rid of them. The boys were immature plus.

Virginia kicked my chair leg. "What'd your mother say?"

My lips brimmed with sophistication: "Certain adult words."

"Mary Katherine! Do I hear talking?" roared Sister Paracleta.

I leaned over my paper and pretended to list vocabulary words as I jotted phonetic spellings of my mother's terms. When Sister turned back to the board, I passed the list to Group A.

Heads bent studiously. Virginia shook her ponytail. Colleen traced her finger over my script, "My sisters tell me a lot, but I never—"

Beth took the note, and spell-burped: U-T-A-R-U-S. In first grade, she was an accomplished alphabet belcher and had recently revived the art.

"Now I remember," gushed Colleen, chest extended. "My sister told me how—"

"Five more minutes." Sister Paracleta rapped her knuckles against the board.

I hurried with the assignment, but my fountain pen kept making inkblots.

"Stains?" said Beth.

"Too much flow?" laughed Virginia.

Colleen smirked, "Need a napkin?"

I wasn't finished when Sister collected the papers and told us to line up for Mass.

"What about the movie?" I whispered.

Colleen rolled her eyes. "They show it after Mass, right before we go home, so they don't have to answer a bunch of questions."

With boys on one side, and girls on the other, we marched silently down the tan cement block hallway, past the green doors that opened with a push bar, and into the bright parking lot. We squinted as we walked single-file across the pavement, up the twelve stairs, to the hot, stuffy confines of the church.

Beth, Virginia, and I knelt in one pew. Colleen was behind us, making it hard to communicate, but not impossible. Beth, her shoulder pressed to mine, placed her hands over her face, ever prayerful, then whispered out from the side of her palm: "You have to read Colleen's note."

"Whoa," neighed Virginia.

"Huh?"

"Our Friend," said Beth. "Big Red."

How could I get the note? I pretended to read my missal in case Sister was watching, but she was all prayer, kneading her black rosary beads. Then I turned toward Colleen and sounded a half-sneeze, Group A's secret signal: "Give me the note."

Colleen pointed to Beth, who said, "I don't have it." Colleen mouthed something else, and then Beth nodded and whispered to me, "You need to pass her my Kleenex packet. She'll put the note inside."

To initiate the pass, I had to sit part way on the bench and send the packet over my shoulder. The action was simple, unless Sister noticed. Then I'd have to think fast. I figured I could say I was giving Colleen a tissue for her allergies. I glanced at Sister Paracleta: All clear.

No sooner had my rump graced the wooden bench than Virginia neighed and drew back her lips—hardly the moment for horse antics.

Sister Paracleta snapped her fingers at me: "Who gave you permission to sit?"

"My stomach hurts." Why did I say that? It wasn't the plan. But suddenly my stomach did hurt.

"Suffer it up for Jesus."

I slid my hips from the bench and knelt. I knew what Sister would say next: "He died for your sins." She pointed to the stained-glass window of Jesus on the Cross, staring down at me, skin pale except for the wounds at his side, bright with *blood*.

Then Father Mullen ascended the pulpit for his homily, a little pep talk. His voice rasped extra loud. "Vacation starts soon, and while you may have the best of intentions, many will be tempted." I expected him to launch a tirade against missing Sunday Mass; instead he hissed, "Implore the Holy Spirit lest you succumb to the flesh." I knelt straighter. We'd been warned repeatedly against the evil of exposed midriffs—two-piece bathing suits and, banish the thought, bikinis. Father puffed his lips, "Some boys will try and take girls in the woods to lift up their petticoats."

Students gasped. Not me. I closed my eyes and held my stomach. For once I was safe. I never wore petticoats. The crinkly stuff made me itch. "Sensitive skin, just like your grandmother," said my mom.

"Stop daydreaming!" ordered Sister Paracleta.

I blinked, realizing how Father Mullen had ended his talk as quickly as he began it. All the girls stood: Time for The Movie.

We marched out and onto gummy black top. Sun blazed against my skin, creating moisture everywhere. I stuck my finger into my armpit and checked: wet but clean.

"Same old stuff from Father Mullen," hissed Colleen.

"I didn't get it."

"He figures he has to say something because we're seeing the movie, you know."

Upon entering the stifling school, I longed to stop at the water fountain, but Sister Paracleta allowed no diversions and led us directly to the Multi-Purpose Room, used for gym, cafeteria, weekend bingo, and movies. The shades were pulled down, making it even hotter. As the lighting dimmed, chair legs scraped against linoleum, and I sniffed dirty socks and cheese. Sister started the projector: "No talking."

The title, *Personally Yours*, flashed on the screen. I wished I hadn't made up the story about my stomach because I really and truly felt bad. I took a deep breath. Sweat dribbled from my lip.

"Smells like a stable. We need a fan," whispered Virginia.

My nostrils quivered. It was the first time I'd ever noticed my own body odor. Next thing, I focused on an animated cartoon of girls. They looked more like cats than people, and the stench of the room ripened.

"This is dumb," complained Beth.

The characters talked in high kit-kat voices, and I envisioned litter boxes. Even worse, I seemed to taste cat turds. My stomach loop-de-looped.

"Boring," whispered Colleen.

"Exclamation point or PERIOD," croaked Virginia.

And then, I blew chow.

When I returned to school for the final two days of fifth grade, Group A laughed and mimicked upchucking.

Virginia said, "You barfed like a horse."

Beth burped, "P-U-K-E."

Colleen said, "We named you Mt. Vesuvius."

Menstruation got swept away like sawdust on vomit. Too embarrassed to speak, I welcomed a summer vacation away from them.

June brought endless games of backyard baseball with my brothers. Robert, wielding a bat and power as eldest, assigned me to the outfield. "Where's your glove?" he yelled. "You can't catch a fly ball with your hand in your armpit."

How to explain, much less ease the worry? Did napkins attach to tank tops? Would my brothers notice? What about bathing suits?

Finally, Robert left for camp. No more baseball. Even better, I could ride his new, red, twenty-six-inch English racer bicycle. Of course, if he'd been home, he'd never allow it. But he was gone, so who could stop me?

My mother. "The bar is not safe for girls," she said, pointing to the frame's crosspiece. No further explanation.

So, I had to remain content with my fat tire clunker. That is— until my mother watched her soaps and Jimmy had rest time. Then I hopped onto the Forbidden. It was too big for me, so I stood while pedaling up hills, panting for the joy-of-joys: Downhill. With my bottom planted firmly on the seat, I kept my legs up and out. How I soared!

At the end of the week, I awoke tired and achy. I felt like I'd swallowed marbles. After breakfast, I went to the bathroom. My pajama pants had brown and red streaks. Not skid marks, but blood swirls. They smelled bad, too. Suddenly I remembered my mother's warning: The bike bar. But I had never banged against it or used it for a seat. Just to be safe, I chose not to ride for the day.

"Aren't you going outside?" asked my mother.

"I want to finish *Mystery of the Ivory Charm*." I lounged on my bed until chapter twelve. Then I took a bathroom break.

More Blood. I tossed my underpants in the hamper on top of my PJ bottoms. Returning to my room, I had a hard time focusing on the book.

After lunch, I found blood again, and it had leaked through to my shorts. I took them off and dumped them in the hamper. Luckily my mother and Jimmy failed to notice my different clothes.

Twice more I changed my underwear. What if my mother found out I was riding Robert's bicycle? I'd have to think up a good story. But all I did was put on clean undies. Four? Five?

My mother called from the laundry room, "Are you okay?"

"Course."

She started to say something, and then paused, "Well you know I respect your privacy, but if you need me—"

"Could we go to the library?"

"Not today. Did you forget? Elizabeth is coming."

"Right," I said. My cousin was two years older and very bossy, so I wasn't thrilled about her sleep-over visit.

"She's bringing her bike. You can ride together."

My mother had a point. Maybe we could go to Pinky's Sweet Shop. If I rode Robert's bike, I'd zip right past my cousin. I liked that idea. But when I used the bathroom by my parent's bedroom— the other one had been cleaned for guests—I reconsidered.

Skulking out of the bathroom, I passed by my mother's bed and spied the crucifix on the wall. Suddenly I remembered Sister Paracleta's parting words: "In times of need, seek Jesus." Relief surged as I quickly changed and announced, "I'm going for a walk."

I marched the half-mile to my school's playground, now ghost-like and empty, and then hurried across the steaming parking lot and up the stairs to the church. The inside walls were dark and foreboding, so I double-splashed with holy water, then knelt in the front pew, and stared penitently at the stained-glass window of Jesus surrounded by little children. Etched into the glass were the words, *Come unto Me.* I clasped my hands and prayed: I know I should listen to my mother. I know it was wrong to use Robert's bicycle. I promise not to ride it again. So please, dear Jesus, stop the blood. I glanced up and saw Jesus smiling.

All the way home I skipped, for I believed in Divine Intervention. I couldn't wait to check my underwear. I felt better all over. Then I saw Jimmy dancing back and forth, gesturing at my mother, who stood, arms crossed over her chest, tapping her foot on the front porch. "YOU'RE IN FOR IT NOW!" sang Jimmy. He pointed to a lawn chair holding my cousin. A bra strap hung limply from her sleeveless-shirt. I walked closer and realized she shaved her legs, too.

"Hey Libby," I said.

"Elizabeth," corrected my cousin. "No one calls me that kid name."

"Right." I took note of the Band-Aid on her ankle, another on her shin bone.

"Mary Katherine," said my mother sternly. "Help her carry in her things. Then open the cot and put on the sheets. After she unpacks, you can peel the potatoes, and then set the table."

"Yes, Mom." My contrite tone was convincing, for she disappeared into the house.

Elizabeth rummaged through her shoulder purse and took out a piece of gum. She removed the foil. "Your mother is really ticked. Where were you?"

"Church."

"Yeah, like I'm supposed to believe that."

I grabbed the handle of her blue Samsonite suitcase, and then with my other hand, reached for the small bag that looked like a bread box.

My cousin pushed away my hand. "I'll take my makeup case."

I knew she was trying to impress me, and as much as I wanted to ask about mascara and shadow, I trudged up the stairs, banging her bag against each step, and then kicked it through my doorway. "Be right back. I have to go to the bathroom."

When I returned, she asked, "Have you been crying?"

I shrugged.

"It's a guy, right? He wants to break up."

"No."

"I have a boyfriend too." She produced an ID bracelet from the pocket of her pedal pushers and jangled it in front of me.

Under other circumstances, I would have examined the bracelet's authenticity, but so absorbed by my own dilemma, I blurted, "This is worse." Then, longing for the comfort of Confession, I grabbed her hands. "I'm dying." I sniffled and pictured my own funeral: white coffin, my mother weeping, the assembly of children at Mass.

"What are you talking about?"

"I'm bleeding to death." I described the rides on Robert's bicycle. My words, pumped by details of sleek tires zooming down hills, then shifted to low, same as when I hit the flats: "The bar—I don't remember bumping into it."

"A boy's bike can't do that." She hopped onto my bed, sitting queenly on the pink flowered pillow, and then filled in the blanks. "You thought what? Armpits?!"

"I missed the movie."

She demanded I produce the box of napkins stashed beneath my bed. As I inch-wormed below, she bounced on the mattress hard enough to squeak the springs. What followed was an explanation of pads. She used a nasal tone, emphasizing her importance now that I needed her. "Your belt? Where is it?"

From the top drawer of my white dresser, I produced the yellow and blue beaded belt I had made in Scouts.

Elizabeth shook her head: "Ask your mother for the right one."

My mother told me to follow her into her room. From the closet, she brought out another box of napkins, as well as two small packages. "I forgot to give you the belts. Do you know how to use them?"

"Sure."

"Know what this means?" Her voice fluttered all happy sounding. "It's a miracle. Your body's preparing to have babies. But not until you're older. And married."

In that instant, I pledged my life to the convent. A missionary nun might be nice. They wore beautiful white habits with long flowing veils. They traveled all over the world. No continent was too far. No task too daunting. I hugged myself, sensing my destiny. I would save the pagan babies of Africa.

"Does your stomach hurt? Need a St. Joseph's aspirin?"

I shook my head, fearful a dose of Vicks Vapor Rub would follow the aspirin.

Jimmy banged on her bedroom door. "Use my bathroom. I'll deal with him," said my mother.

After I finished, I walked toward my bedroom with great purpose, for I'd seen the *Nun's Story*. Who wouldn't be infatuated with her calm air, her small and dainty steps?

"Why are you walking funny?" demanded Jimmy.

"Don't ask what you don't need to know," answered Elizabeth. She tried to push him out of my room and looked to me for assistance. I puckered my lips in a half-arc. Missionary nuns smiled that way.

Jimmy screwed up his face and made a fist. "Don't look at me like that."

His stance reminded me how Sister Paracleta said that missionaries were sometimes martyred. She described grizzly tortures involving whips, spikes, and lots of blood. Gingerly I sat on the edge of the cot and pivoted to accommodate the strange bulk in my underwear. From missionary to martyr wasn't necessarily a bad thing. After all, to be called Sister had charm, but Saint sounded better. Maybe they'd put my picture on holy cards, and school children all over the world would pray to me.

My brother stamped his foot and growled.

I closed my eyes and mustered strength, my capacity for suffering. Folding hands over my heart, I lay back and conjured visions of myself as missionary, martyr, saint: *To think . . . A miracle . . . For me.*

LOVE, MASQUE, AND FOLLY

TIM pumped the lettuce spinner like he was performing CPR. He pressed his hips to the kitchen sink and stared out the window. Leaves zigzagged across the yard. Should he have a Yuengling? A shot of Stoli? Best wait until Susan got home. She'd know how to take the edge off.

He tossed the lettuce in a teak bowl and heard Susan's heels clack on the porch. The door banged open: "Colleen and I went shopping. Look what I got you for our Halloween party." Her short hair, spiked by the wind, made her eyes wild. Tim wondered if she and her sister, Colleen, had stopped at the Riverbed Tavern for happy hour.

Susan held out a garment bag and grabbed for his hand, placing the hanger's crook in the soft dip between his thumb and index finger. "I need to get the head from the car." Off she rushed with more energy than Tim had seen in months.

Tim sniffed moth balls and debated whether to peek inside. No way did he want to upset Susan. He was uncertain if what she termed *menu-pause* made her prickly, or if it was the stress of having Zack in college, Brandon with special needs, and Heather, ever ready to argue. Last night, they had another go around with her.

"So, what if I'm a good student?" Heather was seventeen and slouched in the den, wearing a satin top that looked like lingerie. Her hip bones jutted above low-ride jeans. "Why waste a Saturday taking those stupid SATs? If I go anywhere after graduation, it'll be to Empire."

"The Beauty School?" asked Susan.

Heather rolled her eyes and huffed, "I knew you wouldn't understand."

"You're right."

Heather's veins stood out on her neck. Then she pivoted and stomped up the stairs toward her room.

"Well, that's a new one, even for her," said Tim. He moved closer, arms wide, ready to ease the pain in Susan's face.

Susan backed away. "Some mammals eat their young."

Tim hadn't responded, figuring she joked. But now, as he walked to the breakfast nook and hung the garment bag on a Windsor chair, he realized they needed to talk. Where to begin? Especially as Susan claimed he'd gotten set in his ways. Tim exhaled slowly. How could Susan think like that? Had she forgotten how he changed his work schedule, getting home first each night to cook meals he saw on *Food Network*?

"Check this out," said Susan. She waltzed into the room, waving an enormous pig head, twice the size of a beach ball, and fuzzy too. "The Salvation Army thrift store is having an amazing clearance. Colleen knows that place inside and out. She helped me to find this for you, and I got a shirt that Brandon can wear for his reenactments."

Tim thought Civil War nuts were weird and hygiene challenged, but he felt relieved to have Brandon, their youngest, involved with something. Brandon showed little interest in junior

high school, finding it difficult to make friends until he joined
Frosty Sons of Thunder. He chose them because they held their
reenactor meetings at the VFW that had a wheelchair ramp.
Every few months the group traveled to Gettysburg and shot
canons during campaigns. The man in charge let Brandon light
the fuse.

But why did Susan buy Tim this pig head? Fat cheeks stuck out
as far as the snout.

Susan pointed at the garment bag, "You haven't even looked at
your costume."

Tim tugged away the white plastic and discovered pink bristles.
"You got this for me?"

"It's an original," said Susan. She set the head on the counter.

Tim scratched his thumb against his chin. Susan wasn't passive
aggressive, and despite having some differences, they were like
most couples transitioning to midlife. But a pig costume?

"Try it on. I'll help."

Tim swallowed, as Susan, saucy and pert, slid the costume off
the hanger and unzipped the rear seam. She held open the sides
until he obliged her by lifting his right foot and stepping into it.

"Isn't this better than that old cow costume of yours?" trumpeted Susan. "Here's the head."

"I thought you loved my cow suit."

"You wear it every year."

Tim crossed pink arms over his chest and briefly envisioned
the white flannel with black Holstein print, its hood of horns
and round ears, and jangling from waist to thigh, his favorite: the
plastic udders. "That costume's in great shape. People expect me to
wear it. They like it."

"You like it. I swear, you strut around like the udders are a
bunch of penises shaking out in front of you."

"I do not."

"You get off on the idea of having them yanked and sucked." Susan laughed as if she had said the funniest thing ever.

Tim was so stunned, he lowered his arms. His shoulders drooped. He barely noticed as Susan plopped the bulbous pig head over his skull, tightening the chin straps to keep it from moving. "You should see yourself."

"It's too heavy," said Tim, disliking what was more mascot than regular costume.

"You can just wear shorts underneath. Use lots of talc." And then, without bothering to ask if he wanted to wear it, Susan added, "Colleen gave me a local history book. Did you know the Pennsylvania Dutch rubbed piglet bellies for good luck?"

For their first party, Tim had purchased the cow suit as a joke, some humor for Susan after his deployment in Germany ended. She couldn't wait for them to leave the drab Army housing and return to Northeast Pennsylvania. Tim got hired as a machinist at Charmin, the paper plant, using skills he learned in the service. He did maintenance on machines that made giant-size rolls of toilet paper. Plus, he got time off for long weekends at the Tobyhanna Army Depot, where he trained once a month after signing on with the National Guard.

While he and Susan had looked to buy a house, they lived with Colleen in Wilkes-Barre. Each time a realtor took them to see listings in Luzerne or Wyoming counties, Susan frowned: "I'd forgotten how you can smell manure around here. Why did I want to come back?"

Tim tried to make her think positive. "The farms mean the food and milk are really cheap. We're saving a lot of money."

Indeed, the low cost of living allowed them to snag a brick Victorian in Tunkhannock, prompting Susan to envision parties on the wrap-around porch: "It will be perfect for Halloween."

"Right," said Tim.

And so began a tradition that included a pumpkin quest to Oak Grove Nursery. The pick-your-own place was autumn cutesy, but Tim feigned enthusiasm for Susan. He clenched his teeth as they boarded a hayride. Susan leaned in close, smelling musky, her breath warm against his neck. "Thanks honey—the kids are happy. Me too." She smiled and rubbed his thigh with wide circular motions, edging in and upward.

They gathered so many pumpkins, Tim couldn't shut the hatchback. Zack and Heather, both toddlers, clapped as he tied down the hatch. "What if we get rear-ended?" said Tim.

Susan stood on tiptoe and kissed him: "I love you."

"Mom, I have to pee," said Heather.

"Me too," echoed Zack.

Tim waited for them in the gift shop. Barn stars and hex signs hung on the walls. Two display tables were crammed with jars of apple jelly, pumpkin butter, pickled beets, and chow-chow. In the far corner, next to a shelf of whoopie pies and kettle corn, Tim spied the cow costume. Stuffed with paper and tacked upright on the wall, its head inclined as if conversing. "Moo," said Tim. His fingertips graced the soft nape of the material, flirting across the belly to udders, pliant and full.

"Half-price. One size fits all," called the clerk.

Tim lowered his hand and turned toward a large, shapeless woman in a blue calico dress with a lace-covered bun. She smirked when Susan entered and pointed at the cow.

"Too funny. That's great," said Susan. She smoothed the sides of her sweater, accentuating curves long gone from the clerk.

"I'll take it," said Tim.

For their first party, Susan dressed as a milkmaid. She wore a scoop-neck smock and swayed abundant and free. "MOO," bellowed Tim after a few beers. Susan grinned, same as each year when he donned his cow suit. Initially, she coordinated with him, but always something new: farmer, scarecrow, milk carton, and then, after Brandon was born, and the kids got older, she shifted into their horror themes of ghoul, mummy, chainsaw-wielding maniac. Regardless of what she wore, Tim kept to the tried and true.

How could he switch his cow costume to a pink porker?

"You're thinking of that old cow suit, aren't you?" Susan stood behind him and rubbed his ham-hock. "I suppose you'll feel lost without udders, but I like this corkscrew tail." She pulled him close, and he rump-bumped against her. Susan laughed and held tight. All play, they shifted back and forth. Tim snorted as Susan tottered and teased. "Oink," he grunted, but the plaster snout muffled the sound and reduced it to a mere squeal. He tried again. He breathed deeply to cleanse his lungs and airway. Then, opening his mouth and nostrils wide, he gulped air from within the pig head. His chest expanded. His shoulders heaved: "OINK!"

At that moment, Heather entered the room. She looked her father up and down. Tim waited for a sarcastic remark.

"Do you like it?" asked Susan.

Heather blinked, and rendered mute, exited down the hallway.

"This costume is so good," whispered Susan.

The days leading up to Halloween were stark and gray. Cool air rustled through the trees, shaking off what few leaves remained. Heather made no more mention of beauty school, but as Susan had predicted, she refused to go with them to gather pumpkins. Brandon begged off, too. On a whim, Tim called Zack in State College to see if he could come home for the weekend, but the voicemail flustered him: "Just wondered how you're doing, son."

"What college kid comes to his parents' neighborhood party?"

said Susan. She steadied the ladder as Tim hung pumpkin lights along the porch posts.

"Zack always seemed to like it." Tim's voice rose over the CD player, blaring near Brandon, who wheeled beside a coffin, swishing a paintbrush across the plywood.

"Mom look!" Brandon raised his chin, seeking approval.

"We can put food in there," said Susan, obviously delighted.

Tim treasured her upbeat tone, but when he saw Heather walk onto the porch, he figured the mood wouldn't last. Heather held out the phone, "Guess who?"

Susan said hello, and then yelled to Tim, "Zack's on the phone." She spoke quickly and attempted a three-way exchange by repeating bits of conversation. Tim had difficulty following until Susan laughed, "Yup, Aunt Colleen helped me find him a new costume. He looks great."

Tim almost fell off the ladder. NO. Not that pig suit. He leapt from the top rung, landing hard on the porch, and faced Susan.

"This is going to be the best party ever."

From upstairs, Tim heard shrieks of the first-to-arrive guests. Earlier, he had watched Zack and Brandon rig a fog machine by the entrance. The green box, no bigger than a tool kit, had a nozzle at one end. Zack poured in glycol and water before turning on the heat exchanger. The fluid vaporized into clouds. "See what I learned in Chem-E?"

Brandon grinned and adjusted the nozzle to rotate at different angles.

Zack patted his shoulder. "Did your reenactors tell you how the firing at Gettysburg caused billows of fog?

"Seen it," laughed Brandon. "The fog covers everything."

Zack slapped Brandon's palm with a high five.

How Tim longed to wallow in that fog. The pig suit waited on his side of the bed. Tim's stomach churned. Surely Susan had to understand why he couldn't wear it. Not only would people look at him, they'd listen. Could an oink, paltry and sniveling, ever hold up to his resounding moo? He blasted the rafters: MOO! But the mighty cry failed to embolden him, much less erase Susan's image. Her face had been jubilant when he tried on the pig costume, and it made her frisky, too. How could she claim he'd gotten set in his ways? He wasn't becoming a geezer. Tim tugged at the waist of his boxers, and a strange resolve took seed, gathering strength as he strode toward the walk-in closet. With a firm hand, he reached for his ever-familiar cow costume.

He straddled the corner-edge of the bed, yanked on leggings, and then stood, pulling the suit up over his hips and rib cage. He push-punched his arms through the black and white print sleeves, finally adding the hood. All the while, he had the uneasy feeling someone watched him.

"Hey Dad, Mom wants to know what's taking you so long." Zack, dressed as a gladiator, filled the room with his body, that self-assured bearing of males at twenty.

"Let me explain," started Tim. He glanced down where Zack stared. The cow suit had lost much of its elasticity, causing it to sag at the knees with udders limp and flaccid.

"I thought mom bought you a new—"

"She did. I'm wearing this underneath the pig suit," interrupted Tim. He arched his back and paused. Why had he said that? He squinted at Zack, expecting to find an expression that said: Hey man, you're whipped.

But Zack, eyebrows rising, did a wrist-snap with his fingers. "I get it. You come in one costume and then what? Strip to the other?"

Tim replayed Zack's words: Had his son offered redemption?

"Bump and grind music," said Zack. "I can download from Rhapsody. Just don't let Mrs. Adams get in the act."

Tim shuddered. Sonia Adams, a neighbor who dressed once too often as a tavern wench, ended parties by clambering atop the picnic table.

"You better hurry," said Zack. "You know how mom gets."

Tim tapped his index finger against his lips and thought of Susan. He'd do anything for her. She knew that. Why worry about stripping from pig to cow? It was a joke. His act would show the kind of spontaneity she said he needed. Tim grasped the pig suit, surprised at how easily bristles slid over the cow layer. Before adding the head, he glanced in the pedestal mirror. A pink doughboy stared back: Set in my ways? Ha.

Tim walked past the fog machine. It spit clouds that drifted around the porch with the stop-and-go of parking garage exhaust. Bob Jenkins, the county coroner, had dressed as King Kong. He aped his hands in his armpits, "Hey Timbo. Makin' bacon?"

People huddled by the coffin, balanced on sawhorses, including a big woman with flaming red hair, who was dressed like a Viking, with a plastic chest plate, black gauntlets, thigh high boots and a brown skirt. It took him a minute to recognize her—Colleen, his sister-in-law. Beside her was that other woman who worked with her at the mall, MK, wearing a costume of a retro rock star—spiky green wig, pink tutu, and combat boots. The women laughed, plucking up monster eye meatballs and mummy wrapped sausages.

Colleen smiled at Tim and thrust out her chest plate. "I like your new costume. Susan told me you looked good in it. Change keeps you young."

"No more cow suit?" said MK.

"Where's your cow costume?" asked others. "I can't believe it."

Tim waved his piggy hoof. If only he could tell them his plan. You'll see. I still have what it takes.

Then Susan appeared, rising beside him. Tim tried to grasp

what she wore, and as comprehension registered, he cringed. Susan had on a white cap and shirt, dark pants, butcher apron, and hanging from her belt, a meat cleaver. Susan hadn't said anything to him about her costume, not that he had asked, as mired as he was in his own dilemma. "To market. To market," cheered Susan as Colleen and MK shouted with her.

Tim cleared his throat and walked to the keg. Stationed by the tap, he gave the appearance of being involved. It was easy to avoid conversation in the blare of Warren Zevon's "Werewolves of London." He watched the coffin transform to a trough. Guests rooted for chips, leaving crumbly pieces on the rim, along with broccoli florets and little carrots. Spinach dip oozed down the sides, and when the wind shifted, the air smelled flat with beer.

Heather, wearing a black gown and long, black wig, walked toward him. He knew better than to ask if she was a Goth diva, for she'd frown and say something to make him feel like an idiot. He wondered if she imitated a video game, her character obvious to teenagers, but not him. Heather whispered, "Zack let me in on the plan."

"What do you think?"

Heather shrugged. Her lack of comment proved unsettling. She moved toward her brothers near the CD player. Bonded by conspiracy, they smiled.

Were they smiling with him or at him? Tim had seen his children laugh during sitcoms where parents played the fool. Those shows were ridiculous, yet maybe not so different from his plan. While stripping had seemed a good idea, he wasn't so sure anymore. Yet Tim couldn't forgo his cow suit. He had to make a stand.

"Everyone's milling around, even you," said Susan. She tackled Tim's side and hugged him across the stomach. "What have you got under that?"

"Hmm?" said Tim absently.

"Time to get people dancing. I'll ask Zack to start playing "Monster Mash," said Susan.

Her feet hadn't moved when a deep drum roll began—Da, da, da, DAAA—followed by heavy bass. The riff pulsed with a thumping, primitive beat, accompanied by sultry, brass horns. Sounds blended and throbbed, creating a sleazy melodic rhythm. The pitch grew edgy. Tim stepped away, shy of reckoning, and fixated on the night sky. Mottled by rising fog, it had a strange similarity to cow print.

"Is this stripper music?" asked Susan.

"Dad," crowed his children. Next, he heard clapping, and soon others joined, pounding their feet on the wooden planks. The snaky tones increased. Tim felt small and hemmed in. He considered vaulting the porch rail to disappear in the dark.

"Look at the kids. They're laughing like when they were little," said Susan. Her voice trembled. "Do they know how happy this makes me?"

Tim inhaled and tried to focus on the grinding beat. Would it be better to romp forth or start slowly? The pitch grew fevered, making his brain whirl with goofy lines from old movies: *A man's got to do what a man's got to do.*

Susan must have sensed what he couldn't say, for she laughed, that same impetuous lilt he remembered from when he met her. But it was her face, so bright and reassuring that encouraged him to trot across the porch. He shimmied, dipped a shoulder, then shook and wangled his tail. He looked back at Susan and rolled his hips with hula-hoops of promise.

"Go Dad!"

Tim reached an arm behind his neck and pulled down on the zipper. Off came the right sleeve, and then the left. He raised his chin, pig head shaking, and struggled with the clasp. The deck vibrated, all stomps and bangs. Sounds roared to a crescendo as he broke free. He tossed the head toward Brandon, but his pass came up short. The snout smacked against the wheelchair, and then rolled across the deck. Everyone gasped. Not Tim. He wriggled off the pig suit, stepping away from the ankle-deep bristles and bowed. With his right hand, he scooped up the pig togs from the floor, flourishing the suit like a toreador's cape. A circle formed around him. Tim rapped his heels and twirled.

More yelps and shrieks erupted. Amidst the cacophony, Tim heard a faint moo. From Susan? He glanced about until he found her, hovering in the shadows, lips rounded and eyes wide.

"Moo?" called Tim. It didn't sound right. Best try again. He hoisted low-hung udders and sucked in air until his lungs ballooned. He looked straight at Susan. Why did she stand so still?

The music ended. Hands stopped clapping. Quiet ensued. Tim pressed cow arms close to his sides. If he hadn't watched the others cluster behind Susan, he'd swear they had left the party.

Susan puffed her cheeks and furrowed her brow. For a moment Tim thought she might cry. What have I done? He wanted to tell her the act was meant as a joke, a lift that had fallen flat. He stared imploringly, but she snorted, a savage gleam in her eye. Tim blinked. Susan had never shown aggression, not even in play, yet she clenched her fists and charged toward him.

"Let me explain—" Tim closed his eyes, awaiting the punch. He widened his stance and peeked through heavy lids.

Susan let loose with a deep, sonorous moo, lusty and unrestrained. She grabbed his shoulders and hugged him so forcefully Tim staggered backward. Susan laughed, "Too funny. I love you. You're such a geezer."

Caught by the porch rail, they pressed together and stared up at stars that peeked through the vanishing fog.

COMPLICADO

COLLEEN charges into Borders Books an hour before my shift ends. She wears a black tunic, leggings, and pointy-toe ankle boots, resembling a medieval knight on crusade rather than a cashier from the Hallmark store. Her red hair, pulled atop her head like marching band plumage, flags a warning: "MK, we need you."

"Why are you still here?" Usually I give her a ride home from the mall where we work, but Colleen rearranged her schedule so she could get off early to take photos of the English as a Second Language class taught by our friend, Rachel Wojtowitz. Tonight, is her class's graduation at Our Lady of Perpetual Help Outreach Center, and Colleen, championing yet another social cause, has volunteered to photograph the event.

Colleen's voice quivers, "Rachel was supposed to pick me up half an hour ago, but her car won't start. We don't have much time. Can you take us?" Rachel lives too far into Wyoming County for Triple A, and I shudder at what a tow will cost. She teaches the evening class for extra money. Rachel's a single mom with two boys, and "Mr. Oxycodone," as Colleen calls the former impregnator, is long gone, packed off with officially stamped divorce papers. That he works on an oil rig in the Gulf of Mexico is Colleen-speak for the fact he's an inmate at the Frackville State Prison. Colleen claims she invented the oil rig code phrase to avoid bringing shame to his children.

How can I refuse to offer up the charitable service of Big Blue? Amazingly, the forty-year-old Buick still chugs over Northeast Pennsylvania roads like a newbie. Sure, the engine makes funny noses, but the rattles are its Proclamation of Survival. No way will I consult with some mechanic. Next thing I know, Big Blue will be laid out with the junk cars rusting beside coal mine slag heaps.

"Turn!" shouts Colleen from the passenger seat.

"Yelling won't get us there faster." I swing left and try not to look off the side of the road at the Susquehanna River, far below. All too often, cars zoom through poorly banked curves and plummet down to its depths.

Colleen fiddles with the radio, ushering in Froggy 101: "News from Tunk-a-han-knock." The announcer mocks the pronunciation of Tunkhannock. Obviously, he didn't go to school around here, for in sixth grade social studies, students learn how the Susquehannock Indian name has spiritual meaning, but just what that meaning entails remains unknown. My guess is the name has something to do with the river where far below, rock mounds are splayed out in the middle unlike any place else between its banks. I glance at the water, which is higher than usual owing to excessive rain. Mud rushes with the flow to create water the color of instant iced tea.

"I'm not listening to that crap on the radio," I tell Colleen.

"It's the only station we get," she says, but turns it off. She takes a deep breath, and in my peripheral vision, I see her lift her arms high as if trying to channel her Celtic ancestors. Colleen embraces her heritage in ways that give me pause, but I try to keep my opinions to myself. She heightens her audible rasp—*inhale*—*exhale*—and then asks, "Can anything rival the smell of river mud? Real bowels of the earth kind of stuff, huh?"

I'm not sure if her question means she wants me to shut my window, or if she's revving up to begin another yarn from her novel-in-the-making. Who is she kidding? At first, I indulged her, playing the role of the ideal editor, listening to her yap and repeat lines for a supposed book jacket. But such charades tax even the best of friends, so now I try to silence Colleen lest I become a writing enabler. No easy task.

We skid through the last sharp curve, spitting gravel, and find Rachel Wojtowitz standing by a row of rural route mailboxes. She waves, and Colleen leans over me to honk the horn hello.

I elbow Colleen back to her side of the car and ease off the gas. I'm glad Rachel has walked out to the flat, open area of the road because pulling a K-turn by her house gets tricky. The road hasn't been graded since the Department of Transportation scaled back funds for county maintenance. Ruts have transformed the surface into a washboard of fluted ridges that cascade down to the water.

Colleen sees me smile, and she probably thinks it's for Rachel and not the inviting turn-around spot. "Rachel looks good, considering all she's been through," whispers Colleen. "I'm amazed she kept teaching after the bicycle crash."

"Right," I say, shifting to neutral. Rachel approaches Big Blue, and the windshield creates a frame: she's younger than we are, mid-thirties, and thin, with spiked brown hair. She wears tan slacks and a pale, blue sweater. From this angle, there's no hint of her broken jaw, wired shut ever since she wiped out while trying to show her son, Joey, how to ride a bicycle without training wheels. What happened remains unclear other than Rachel's impact with the paved parking lot behind Our Lady of Perpetual Help Church. They were there practicing bicycling since it was a Wednesday, when there isn't a Mass or any other service, so no cars were in the parking spaces. Thankfully Rachel wore a helmet, proving to Joey the importance of always wearing a brain bucket.

Colleen opens the passenger door and scoots out, holding it wide for Rachel. "You sit up front. I'll get in the back."

Rachel mumbles and steps into Big Blue, jostling her hips onto the seat. I smell patchouli oil as she puts her woven bag—more shoulder purse than a teacher's briefcase—on the rubber mat beside the floor hump. She forces words from the clenched teeth of her wired jaw: "Thanks-for-coming-to-get-me."

Before I say no problem, Colleen, speaking extra-loud, enunciating slowly like I'm hearing impaired: "SHE-THANKS-YOU-FOR-DRIVING."

"I understand her," I say.

"I-called-Father-Muzwongo-to-say-we'd-be-late," adds Rachel.

Colleen rests her chin on the vinyl ridge-top of the front seat: "RACHEL-TOLD-PRIEST-WE-ARE-LATE."

"I know." Father Muzwongo is the replacement for Father Ryan who retired several months ago and moved to Riverview Assisted Living. Then, inexplicably, I smile at Rachel and pat her arm like she's one of those special employees who pack grocery bags at Weis Markets.

Rachel parts her lips. Thin silver wires hold her teeth and jaw in place, reflecting rays of the setting sun. I am reminded of junior high school and the kids who wore elaborate head gear for their orthodontia. Shaped like the rims of a Frisbee, the apparatuses stretched out with arcs in front of the kids' faces as if they could commune with distant planets. I decide not to mention this to Rachel, for she might feel self-conscious, and then Colleen will call me insensitive.

Rachel looks at her watch and curls her lips, trumpeting words: "Graduation-starts-in-fifteen-minutes."

"Don't worry, I'm speeding up," I say.

"Oh yeah—that's you, putting pedal to the metal," laughs Colleen.

I hadn't considered Rachel's adult learners until we parked at the Our Lady of Perpetual Help Outreach Center. The squat, prefab building has a stripe of windows along gray siding and looks like a train car without wheels. When I was a kid, catechism class met inside, but now Father Muzwongo sponsors all sorts of programs—Bingo, Food Pantry, Alcoholics Anonymous, Parenting Class, Veteran's Motorcycle Association, and Senior Citizen's Line Dancing. Colleen says that's what churches should provide, and I guess Father Muzwongo reaches out, for I'm told his pews are packed on Sunday despite sparse money collections. Colleen says the parishioners come to gawk and listen to his French accent. The priest is from the Democratic Republic of the Congo, what my grandmother called Belgian Congo, yet I learned in school as Zaire. He looks nothing like the congregation, and Colleen jokes about his placement. "Ironic, huh? Africa sends us missionaries." Colleen has a point. I can remember back to the days when Pennsylvania exported nuns and priests. I used to sit at Mass with my grandmother, fantasizing about becoming a missionary as I placed a quarter in the Maryknoll collection basket. Who wouldn't dream of wearing a flowing white habit to save pagan babies? Now I rarely get closer to the church than the outreach center.

I wonder if Father Muzwongo understands what happened in the surrounding hills to bring Rachel's students here for English lessons. Their relocation has a shroud of mystery, one we don't mention, for *less said* is the prevailing dictum. Sometimes I think the lack of talk is an attempt to deny hateful incidents. Yet when Colleen Googles the terms—*Hazleton Area, Latino, Anti-immigrant*—she brings up enough harrowing information to plot another supposed novel. Just where did those poor people go when they got forced out of Hazleton?

"They're here! Welcome!" cries Father Muzwongo as he waves us into the room. He stands in dark contrast to the white crepe that streams from the ceiling lights. A trellis of fake lilies, used at Easter and weddings, is arranged at the front of the room.

Colleen grins, "Father Muzwongo has been decorating."

Then I notice about a dozen women standing off to the side dressed in jeans, high heels, and tank tops. Soon as they see Rachel, they smile and wave. They speak through clenched teeth: "Hello-good-to-see-you."

Rachel claps: "Nice-job."

"THANK-YOU!" they chorus without moving their jaws.

Colleen nudges me, "Hold my camera case. I've got to get a picture." She snaps photos with the frenzy of a paparazzo and acts as if there's nothing askew with their pronunciation.

"Did you notice they all talk the same way, just like Rachel?" I ask.

"I think they're paying her a compliment. ESL students always mimic the teacher. You wait, after they get jobs, put their kids in school, and start going to the bars, they'll figure it out."

School? Bars? Has Colleen forgotten why these women packed up their families and left no forwarding address?

A few months ago, some high school boys kicked a Mexican man to death. What happened *back there*—pronounced like a distant country rather than Shenandoah, thirty miles away—was an explosion of violence that had started brewing when Hazleton officials tried to pass an ordinance aimed at penalizing landlords for renting to illegal immigrants. Even though the ordinance failed, it provoked animosity, especially as people lost jobs and moved out of the deteriorating neighborhood. That the arriving Spanish speakers found work picking cherries and pruning Christmas trees heightened anger against them. Three families grew to several hundred people, but they kept to themselves. They didn't need to know English to recognize the slurs painted on sidewalks and road signs.

But the real problem, according to Colleen, is downturn economics. She loves bringing up the issue when we're on break at the food court. Most days, we get coffee from the Java Bean. Tiffany, a senior in high school, works there in the afternoons. Recently she got a nose ring and dyed her hair purple. Colleen, older than Tiffany's mom, talks all chummy with her and acts like they're BFFs.

Tiffany became our font of insider info about what happened: "You have to realize Mexican kids caused problems unlike the others," she told us. By *others* she meant the few black students who mostly live in Mennonite foster homes, and the two students of Asian descent whose parents are doctors at the hospital. According to Tiffany, those *other* kids participated during class and attempted to fit in. Of course, they knew English, but Tiffany doesn't consider that. "The new kids didn't even try to speak English. Instead, they laughed."

"Maybe they were embarrassed?" Colleen patted her chest like she had heartburn. "Teenagers laugh when they're insecure about saying the wrong thing."

Tiffany shrugged, "Why do people judge what they can't understand?"

Colleen flared her nostrils. I could tell she restrained herself. She had liked Tiffany since the first time she served us coffee and chatted about her twelfth-grade creative writing class. Colleen, ever quick to promote her purported book, forged an instant connection. No matter that Tiffany was a teenage slam poet and hardly an avenue for publication.

"Tiffany, remind me again. Why is it you drive all the way over here every day?"

"Duh, for my job."

"Might that reflect a lack of jobs near your home? Hayna or no?" Colleen used the phrase employed by old timers. They swallow word endings with a dialect passed from Polish and Slovak relatives who came here to forge a scant opportunity by farming or coal mining. Most of those farms have been sold—land for developments—and the mines closed long ago.

"Like I don't know there's hardly any jobs," snapped Tiffany.

"That's been the case for decades, but the decline has gotten worse," said Colleen, voice hollow. "Latinos became the scapegoats because they are least able to defend themselves. When you consider other factors, like how drug arrests have risen within the white community, but not for immigrants, you realize—"

"What? Drugs had nothing to do with that guy getting killed."

Colleen drummed her fingertips on the table, "He was a newcomer, and they pose a threat to existing jobs. Limited work makes easy avenues for drugs, particularly when they mask a blighted future. Next thing, amid all of the at-risk warning signs, four high school boys jump a Latino guy in a park with his girlfriend."

"She grew up in our town—and was pregnant by him. And most people don't know he was drunk."

I blurted out, "Channel 28 reported that the boys were drunk. They'd been drinking at the Corner Pocket even though they're underage." Tiffany sneered at me, so I never asked who started the punching that led to the man getting beaten. Did the guy fall to the ground right away? The reporter said his girlfriend kept screaming while the boys kicked him in the head. No one rushed to his aid. Maybe he yelled *Ayudeme*, and people didn't understand his cry for help? When the cops finally came and called an ambulance, he was comatose.

Not until two days later, with the boys back in school, did the Geisinger Medical Center in Danville announce his death. The cops never said why the boys didn't get charged for another two weeks, but on the night that they actually got charged, rocks got thrown at the houses where Latino families lived. Then pouf: The newcomers disappeared. No one asked where they relocated. No requests were made for moving the trial to a different county to avoid conflicts of interest.

I look at the women behind the trellis, awaiting their certificates. They should be laughing and joking, eager to celebrate their accomplishment, yet their faces are pinched. They stare at the door.

A woman with an orange headband is the first to walk below the lily-framed arch. "Congratulations," says Father Muzwongo. His white collar looks most official as he presents a scroll, tied with a gold ribbon, and shakes her hand.

"Thank-you," she says, her teeth clenched, strong and deliberate.

Each woman follows her, and I clap double-time to compensate for the lack of an audience, wary that the empty metal folding chairs are a portent.

"Very good," says Father Muzwongo, clapping for the final graduate.

A thunder of clapping echoes behind me, and I smell fried chicken. By the steel door, set open with a rubber wedge, several men cluster with Mrs. Pavinsky, the small and wizened church organist. She seemed old in my grandmother's day, yet in she totters, wearing red-check oven mitts and carrying a crockpot, "I hope we aren't late. Carlos gave me a ride."

"Let me take that," I say, rushing for her ceramic slow cooker. She no longer has a blue coif. Her hair is close-cut, dyed almost flesh color, and matches her pants suit. She blinks, accentuating wrinkles on her round face, and I flashback to the movie *ET*. I try to banish images of the tiny extraterrestrial, hardly complimentary, for she and my grandmother spent scads of money on Avon beauty products back in the day. Her voice is scratchy, "Carlos and his family moved in next door to me, but they don't have a phone, so I let them use mine. Carlos called the church to say we might be late. But no one answered."

"Phone Home" rattles my brain as she adds, "The kids started calling me *Abuela*. No, I told them—say *Babcia*. I'm *Babcia*. Now they call me *Abuela Babcia*." Her chin bobs up and down.

Standing close to her is a dark-haired man, and I figure he must be Carlos. He grasps the handle of a brown valise. The worn leather, strangely familiar, looks heavy, the size of two stacked cases of Yuengling. Carlos nods hello. Eight men follow, holding trays of food. Their boots and pants are caked with gray dust, probably from Riverside Quarry where I hear they hire day workers and pay cash to eliminate the expense of providing insurance and W-2 forms. The men march toward the cafeteria tables positioned in an L-shape along the side wall. They arrange their items as children surge in, wearing green T-shirts. Have they run from the baseball fields? No teenagers appear.

Mrs. Pavinsky taps Father Muzwongo's arm, "Thanks for waiting for us. I better get started. We can't have a graduation without music."

"Oh dear," says Father Muzwongo, turning to Rachel. "I thought the families weren't coming. I felt so badly for your students. Was it my Spanish?"

Rachel stares blankly. Then Colleen holds out her camera as if a toy steering wheel and drives it back and forth. "There's plenty of film. Let's do it again."

"Good-idea," says Rachel. She walks to the women, and they

huddle around her. Laughter erupts, and then the women line up by the trellis.

The priest raises his arms and brings his hands together. "Welcome."

A man with huge biceps makes the sign of the cross. I expect to hear tinny chimes from the center's upright piano, so I am startled by the forced air bleats of an accordion. Sure enough, Mrs. Pavinsky, sits on the piano bench and faces us, holding the instrument against her chest. As she stretches the bellows, her arthritic fingers slip on buttons and keys, meshing chords in a strange hodgepodge of "The Wedding March" and "Pomp and Circumstance."

Colleen looks toward me and rolls her eyes.

I recall how Mrs. Pavinsky's husband used to play this very accordion at Christmas and Easter. How I thrilled at the ivory keyboard, the casing inlaid with mother-of-pearl, its gold trim aglitter from rhinestones. When the bellows expanded, the folds with silver diamond shapes enhanced the magical sound. His performance was a rare treat, and so after he died, Mrs. Pavinsky took over for him, but my grandmother urged her to stick with the organ.

"*Mira*," call children as the women file below the arch. Colleen clicks the shutter for the re-graduation. At the finish, Father Muzwongo hails, "All Good." The room echoes with so much clapping, the walls vibrate.

The graduates join their families. Colleen and I make our way toward the buffet. "My kind of men, they bring food," says Colleen. "Glad we went easy at lunch, huh? Let's enjoy."

Discipline is the variable of our never-ending diet, but today we'll splurge. Yet as I grab my paper plate, I hesitate and say to Colleen, "Maybe Rachel should lead the buffet line?" After all, Rachel is the teacher, but it might seem odd for her to start the food line since she can't eat solids and must use a special straw for protein shakes. Then I add, "The graduates could go first. We've come to recognize them. Or Father Muzwongo could have the honor?"

"You're blocking the food," scolds Mrs. Pavinsky, moving ahead of us. "Have you been to that new grocery aisle by the kielbasa? Goya, that's the brand I bought." She removes foil from a pan and reaches in for the folded dough. "I helped make these empanadas. They're not so different from pierogis," she laughs.

We're about to sample them when a boy tugs the hem of Colleen's tunic. His eyebrows squeeze together in a dark-V: "Lady, why you take pictures?"

"You want me to take one of you?" asks Colleen. She smiles at me, for we know how kids, shamelessly narcissistic, love having their photos taken.

"No." He puts his hands on his hips and stands taller, almost to Colleen's shoulder. "We don't want no pictures. Nothing in the paper. No trouble here."

Colleen tilts her head. "No worries. The pictures are graduation gifts." She turns and looks across the room at the men who watch her. Arms crossed over their chests, they could pose for a sports club photo, but no one smiles. They eyeball Colleen. Under other circumstances, Colleen would thrill to garner such male attention, but she says, "Must be a misunderstanding." She lumbers toward them.

A little girl taps my leg, "We eat?" She holds hands with another girl. Both are missing front teeth. "You like tostado? Plantain? Yum."

"Let's get your moms," I say. The women stand beside the men and finger the gold crosses on their necklaces. Most frown as they squint at Colleen. What is it about her photos? She holds out the camera, a chunky Nikon that uses film unlike slim, digital models. Colleen says it gets better definition, but regardless, she can't afford something new. Her head wobbles, so I know she's talking, probably venting about photo journalists and how they've sunk to an all-time low.

Rachel stands beside her. She places her hand on Colleen's elbow to make her shut up. Then Rachel speaks. I watch the group listen to her. The man with thick biceps sucks in his breath, puffing out his cheeks. The woman beside him pats her heart and blinks at Colleen. Then Carlos grins. That's when I realize they must think Colleen is a nut case, and not a reporter, or worse, a rep from Immigration Services.

Rachel turns and walks to me: "To-think-a-picture-could-be-bad."

"Who'd have figured?" I say, wondering about the Spanish word for complicated. How could a Kodak moment go so wrong? It's unsettling to consider what problems the photos might cause for families trying to make a new home.

Colleen opens the back of her camera and pulls up the knob to unwind the film. Her cheeks are pink, and she breathes heavily with each circling motion. As she removes the spool, now ruined by its exposure to the light, she says, "No worries."

The woman with the orange headband reaches for it. Her teeth are clenched, and I can't determine if her stiff jaw reflects tension or pronunciation: "Thank-you."

"*De nada*," says Colleen. She turns and moves with a labored gait. I guess she's headed for the food, but she stops by Rachel and me, and pivots toward the group.

The woman smiles and calls, "Maybe-husbands-take-English."

The men stare at us, and we nod, shifting weight from foot to foot. We mirror the sway of the graduates across the room as our hips list in slow motion. There must be some sort of cultural exchange taking place, but just what seems blurred and unfocused.

"Eat," says Father Muzwongo.

"Carlos, it's your turn to play," calls Mrs. Pavinsky. She cradles the accordion in her arms. "If Aloysius were here, he'd insist you play."

Carlos walks toward her and slides his hands along the vertical pleats of his Mexican-style, guayabera shirt. The white cotton fabric is finely crafted, and he tugs the patch pockets at his hips. Then, projecting ceremony, he reaches for the instrument. Mrs. Pavinsky beams. He hugs the accordion close to his chest, placing the straps over his shoulders, and then leans his chin into the keyboard. Carlos presses his left fingers on the ivory keys. With his right hand, he inflates the bellows as silver diamonds peek from the folds. Instead of oompah-pah, we hear spicy riffs. The Latin sounds create fusion in a room steeped with polka fests.

"It's like our own Cinco de Mayo right here at Perpetual Help," says Colleen. She laughs a belly snort that I interpret as both a nervous reaction and a way of trying to understand what she can't explain. But then again, Colleen may just want to eat.

Children squawk, adding to the laughter, followed by the high tones of women, and guffaws from men. I feel a change in the room as if the air has levitated us to a new place. Maybe this is the language we're meant to share?

The tune accelerates, generating promise. Women fill their plates, and children grab cookies. I glance out the narrow windows on the far wall. Street lights illuminate the parking lot where Big Blue bears silent witness. Carlos follows my gaze. He smiles and briefly lifts his hand, pointing toward the food, a signal for me to join the others.

HAND AGAINST THE HORN

MRS. PAVINSKY stared at her white slacks and pictured them with black, horizontal stripes. It was easy to envision prison garb, sitting with the other senior citizens in route to Keystone Mall. The mini bus, painted cobalt, resembled a transporter from the Pennsylvania Department of Corrections. No matter that the side panels are marked Luzerne-Wyoming Counties Agency for Aging, more like Jailbirds on Wheels.

She placed her hands together to stabilize her thoughts. Mrs. Pavinsky needed to buy books for the youngsters who had moved in next door. By reading to Carlita and Ibbie, she could help them to learn more English.

"I've never seen you take this bus," called the man across the aisle. He wore a beige sweater unlike the passengers up front who sported red, athletic jackets. Were they a team? At their age? She shook her head and figured they shopped at the same sale.

"You don't remember me, do you?"

Mrs. Pavinsky pivoted her hips and angled toward him. A gray mustache, neatly trimmed, offset eyes, bright and familiar. Had he attended Our Lady of Perpetual Help Church? She had watched parishioners come and go, having played the church organ since her twenties.

He raised his right shoulder, elbow wagging where the sleeve was folded over his missing forearm: "It's me, Stump."

Mrs. Pavinsky grinned. She couldn't forget Jarek Hajduk. He'd fought in Vietnam, long before the peace marches or fiery press. Back then, infantry received little training to detect landmines, and his platoon never saw what hit them. That he survived and returned to Factoryville, hell bent on taking over the family's dairy farm, made folks wrinkle their brows with wonder. "I'll get me a hired hand," he joked, and he insisted they call him Stump. For decades, he thrived—he got married, had a son—but after milk prices bottomed out, he got done-in like other farmers forced to sell their land. Somehow, he kept the house.

"Our stop is by the food court," he said. "I like a late lunch before going home. You should eat then, too."

She lifted her chin. He still had good posture, and his smile showed nice teeth. When had his wife passed? Maybe around the same time as Aloysius.

"I have coupons for Subway."

Mrs. Pavinsky liked a man who came prepared. "I might be hungry after I shop. I'm looking for children's books."

"Grandkids?"

"Sort of," she laughed. "They call me *Abuela Babcia*."

"Nana seems easier."

"Not for them." She bypassed how the children spoke Spanish. Ever since the violence broke out in Shenandoah, where high school boys beat a Mexican man to death, she safeguarded the arrival of the new family. So much had changed from her girlhood when each spring, right about this time of year, Sal's Grocery hosted fundraiser tables near the entrance. The Perpetual Help Rosary Society sold peanut butter eggs, alongside Temple Hillel's chocolate dipped Matzo, and St. Mark's Methodist Welsh cookies. She grew accustomed to English mixed with Polish, German, and

Welsh. Sure, they had differences, but they tried to accept each other. These days, Mrs. Pavinsky wondered if getting along had been lost with the past. *The Riverside Gazette* ran editorials that clamored for tolerance, making it seem a totally new concept.

"You know the bookstore is closing," he said. "Borders filed for bankruptcy."

She nodded. "I read it in the paper."

"They've marked down everything, even the fixtures. Not much left."

"I need books about bunnies and lambs. To put with candy and eggs in the Easter baskets."

"Anything on the shelf, you can get dirt cheap."

Gears downshifted, and the bus wheezed to the curb. Like a flock of cardinals, the red jackets rose, displaying the word PUMPERS on their backs.

Mrs. Pavinsky blinked.

"Mall walkers," said Stump. "This is their heart surgery rehab. Commonwealth Hospital gives them jackets if they keep at it for six months."

"Are you getting one?"

He pounded his chest: "Ticker's just fine. But I come every Wednesday. You can't beat the price of the trip."

She laughed. He was as corny as ever.

The pumpers hustled toward the catacomb of stores while Stump ambled beside her. She hoped he didn't expect her to walk laps, for she got a full workout from the organ. Her legs stretched for foot pedals as arms reached across the keyboard. Sometimes the coordination proved a bit much, and she confused the notes, having to start songs all over again. Father Muzwongo failed to notice unlike that red-haired volunteer, Colleen, who offered to turn pages, so she wouldn't lose her place. "Not necessary," snapped

Mrs. Pavinsky. She knew Colleen worked here in the mall's Hall-mark store, a guarantee Mrs. Pavinsky wouldn't shop there.

Stump gave her shoulder a squeeze, "What's the matter? You're frowning."

"Am I?" Mrs. Pavinsky sniffed Old Spice cologne, the same scent her husband had worn. Stump stared at her closely. She fluffed her hair, glad she'd kept her appointment at Golden Touch Beauty Shop. When the newly hired stylist, Consuela, applied a lemon rinse, she whispered: "I add a splash of tequila. Make you intoxicating."

Mrs. Pavinsky thought she was kidding, but maybe not. Eyes shiny, she told Stump: "I'll need a snack after I buy books."

"So, you'll come to the food court?" His voice had a rich timbre.

"I think I will."

"Good, see you there." He loped after the pumpers.

Three teenage girls shuffled past her. They wore black leggings and suede boots, walking as if they had shoe boxes on their feet. Maybe they dressed alike so no one could tell them apart and report them for cutting school. Did adults report such things anymore?

Then three boys practically bumped into her. Were they following the girls? Their jeans hung so low their underwear showed. Mrs. Pavinsky thought saggy pants had gone out of style, owing to something that was said on a talk show she'd watched last week. Just what, she couldn't place. All too often, her brain operated like slot machines at the Mohegan Sun. The harder she pulled the crank, the likelier she got at a mismatch: cherry, grape, banana. Rarely did her thoughts line up on the first try.

The boys slowed, forming a huddle. She could see the label on the doughy one's skivvies, inside-out, no less. Two more steps and she'd plow into him. Mrs. Pavinsky veered to the left, and the boys did too. Then the kid with a green, sideways baseball cap shimmied in her direction. Why did he sneer?

She held fast to her pocketbook. The plastic wicker pinched her fingers.

The boy burped, a low, snaky emission. It made the others laugh.

Her nostrils twitched from the sour smell, like bread with too much yeast. She knew she should step away, but her feet felt leaden.

He scuffed closer, eyes vacant, lips like worms.

Mrs. Pavinsky had to show him she wasn't afraid. Her breathing quickened. Then she spied the neon sign of Aeropostale. Could she make it inside?

A woman's voice chortled lyrics from "Pants on the Ground," mimicking the ridiculous tune that played on Froggy 101.

Mrs. Pavinsky clamped her jaw tight. Would the boys think the song came from her? Again, she side-stepped. Same for them. The boys bulked up so large, she felt caged. Next thing, someone even bigger came up on her right, blocking her escape. The woman continued to chant words from the song.

The boys merged into a dark mass. Mrs. Pavinsky swallowed hard.

"You, clowns, what're you doing?" called the loud voice.

Mrs. Pavinsky stopped. Beside her stood red-haired Colleen, clad in a khaki jumpsuit, the garb of a mechanic rather than a middle-aged sales clerk. She carried a carton filled with French fries.

The boys snorted, but within seconds, they scattered.

Colleen sighed, "They ditch school, only to come here, begging for attention."

Mrs. Pavinsky made a chirping noise.

"You okay?"

How Mrs. Pavinsky wanted to sit, but she said, "I'm buying books for the children that I watch. You've seen them with me at Perpetual Help." She pointed ahead. "I have to go to Borders."

"Me too," said Colleen.

"They're closing, you know."

"Could be all the stores," sputtered Colleen. They walked past the blue sign for Old Navy, and next, the green letters of American Eagle. "The owners defaulted on their loan. Now Chinese investors made a bid and want to gut the retail space for a fracking truck depot."

"Being close to I-81 must be a draw," said Mrs. Pavinsky.

Colleen shuddered. "What does it matter if we lose our jobs?"

Mrs. Pavinsky bit the inside of her mouth. Is that why Colleen wore the jumpsuit? Surely a trucking depot would need to hire mechanics. But Colleen had no such skills. She sold greeting cards and assisted at the Perpetual Help Outreach Center.

"You must be upset to see me with fries—what with my diet— and how I joined The Program."

Mrs. Pavinsky knew the outreach center sponsored a weekly Big Losers competition, modeled after a reality show. "Your secret's safe with me."

Colleen smiled. "I'm bringing comfort snacks to MK and her coworkers. Borders got so busy, they can't take breaks." Her eyebrows pulsed conspiratorially. "And in case you're wondering, I've never said a word about *you know what.*"

Mrs. Pavinsky's knees grew weak. If she spotted a bench, she'd plant herself. That she no longer drove and took the senior bus to the mall proved a sad reminder of how her husband had chauffeured her everywhere, even though she had a license. After Aloysius died, she motored downtown, but switching from passenger seat to behind-the-wheel gave her a troubling perspective. Each time she got on the road, the car seemed wider, especially in December, when she drove to an afternoon Christmas gala at the church. Although it wasn't dark enough for headlights, the sky had shifted to the same gray as the trash cans propped in front of the curbs. The cans crowded the streets, and try as she might to avoid them, if she merely glanced at one, the right fender made contact, knocking it down like a bowling pin. How she prayed to St. Christopher, pleading for safe travel. Finally, she rumbled into a parking space at the church hall where Colleen, dressed as Santa Lady, stood on the sidewalk and welcomed guests. She offered to carry Mrs. Pavinsky's bag: "You seem upset."

Her hands trembled, and in a halting voice, she told Colleen what happened. "I can't drive. How will I get home?"

"Not to worry," said Colleen, putting her arm around Mrs. Pavinsky's shoulders. "I can drive you in your car, and MK can follow us in Big Blue. Then she'll take me to my place."

Mrs. Pavinsky fought back tears. "Please don't tell anyone what happened."

"Me?" Colleen spoke extra slowly. "I know nothing."

Since that day, the Chrysler had slumbered in the carport. Mrs. Pavinsky thought about selling it, but she couldn't place an ad in the *Penny Saver*. Strangers would come to the house. Plus, she had no idea of pricing. If she asked her son in Scranton, he'd take it as a sign to move her into Riverview Assisted Living.

Then, like an Act of Divine Providence, Carlos and his family moved in next door. He and Rosalina helped with chores previously done by Aloysius and drove her to church with them. In exchange, Mrs. Pavinsky watched the children after school until they got home from work.

The bookstore swarmed with shoppers. "How can this place go out of business when it's so crowded?" asked Mrs. Pavinsky.

"Ironic, huh?" said Colleen. "You poke around while I take these fries to MK."

Near the front, five bins held pen sets, coffee mugs, boxed cards, puzzles, DVDs, night lights, and in the middle, red signs wobbled on metal stands: *80% OFF*. Shoppers tossed about items, never grabbing to buy, and Mrs. Pavinsky didn't blame them. The stuff was so picked over, it looked used.

She squeezed past bodies toward the bookshelves. Banners dangled from the ceiling: *Final Sale*. Rather than exult at low prices, she studied the placards on the wall indicating various sections: History, Literature, Women's Studies, Travel, Self-Help, Gay and Lesbian.

Why not use alphabetical order? The shelves, a complete hodge-podge, caused her to move slowly, wary not to bump into anyone. Where were the children's books? Surely, they hadn't sold out.

Low snickers caught her attention. She peered into the section marked Sex and Relationships. THEM. There stood the Devil Boys.

Mrs. Pavinsky tip-toed to the next row. She hunched down and reached for a yellow paperback on the bottom shelf: *Poetry for Dummies*. Why had the boys come here? They were hardly the type to buy books.

Inch by inch, she skulked along the row and smelled cigarette smoke, undoubtedly from their clothing. She peeked through the open space. Chubby fingers grasped a hardback book. The boys snickered at the cover. A figure-drawing depicted a naked man holding the breast of a woman doing a backbend: *KAMA SUTRA*. Mrs. Pavinsky stifled a laugh. The Ladies Auxiliary gift-wrapped that book each holiday season, causing hilarity at their white elephant exchange. She crept out to the aisle and ignored the sensation that someone followed her.

Thud, thud. Footsteps struck the linoleum floor. Mrs. Pavinsky smelled cigarettes. More thuds. The dull sound had to be them. No way would she let them think they bothered her. She hurried toward purple and pink blossoms highlighting a mural on the back wall: *Children's Garden of Books*. A short, circular display rack, the height Carlita and Ibbie could reach, stood beside two green beanbag chairs and a rocking chair.

"Hey!"

Mrs. Pavinsky pivoted and squared-off with Sideways-cap, his worm lips curled as he wielded the *Kama Sutra*, advancing so close, she raised her arm, palm out and fingers up like a traffic cop. The movement sent her backward, and she whacked against the hard edge of the rocker. It dug into her ankle bone, making her lose balance. She winced, yet kept hold of her pocketbook, reaching aimlessly with her left hand for support. Her wrist hit the slats of the rocking chair, and she dropped full-force into a bean bag chair. Too startled to yelp, she opened and closed her mouth.

The boy's eyes widened, "Shit, she's hurt. Let's get out of here."

Mrs. Pavinsky felt no relief. She had plunked down like a frog. Knees above her ears, she pushed with her hands but couldn't get up. The bean bag swallowed her. Briefly, she closed her eyes and slowed her breathing. Again, she struggled to rise. No go. Could she call for help? Her lungs were so compacted, she emitted a mere croak. Stay calm, she whispered. Do not panic. Surely someone would notice her.

With each second of imprisonment, tears threatened. She recited multiplication tables to banish thoughts of getting buried alive. The AARP claimed math exercises promoted mental acuity. Yet at 9×9, she paused. Why such indignity? She blinked. Inhale. Exhale. The laborious task exhausted her, yet determined, she moved on with 9×11, 9×12. She snorted over the 10s, tacking zeroes onto the digits, and the 11s proved easy, too. But with the 12s, she sucked the back of her teeth. She never liked those multiples and figured a short rest would help.

"What happened?" A man's voice swirled from above. "Are you okay?"

Mrs. Pavinsky's eyes fluttered open. Stump knelt beside her, and behind him, forming a tableau, hovered Colleen with MK.

"Give me a hand," gasped Mrs. Pavinsky.

Stump extended his good arm, and she latched on, but couldn't rise. "My legs are pins and needles."

"Should I call an ambulance?" MK held her cell phone.

"They're just asleep," said Mrs. Pavinsky.

"Not a stroke? You're sure?"

"Yes." Her stern tone prompted Colleen and MK to step forward. They reached under her armpits and lifted her upright.

Stump rose, too. "I sat and waited at a table in the food court. I wouldn't order until you got there. I kept waiting. Then the bus came, and you didn't show. I couldn't leave. I had to look for you."

"We couldn't find you either. I thought you had left," said Colleen. "I told MK you wanted books for those new kids whose parents drive you to Perpetual Help."

"We went to the Travel Section," said MK. "For dual language picture books."

Colleen spoke quickly, "There's no *Peter Rabbit*, but I found some kid favorites." She held up a chunky book, ideal for little fingers. *Go, Dog. Go!* The words loomed above a brown mutt driving an orange putt-putt car, and beneath the wheels: *¡Corre, perro, corre!*

"*Go, Dog. Go!*" roared Stump. "Kids love that book."

Mrs. Pavinsky smiled. "I better pay for these, or we'll miss the bus."

"It's gone," he reminded her.

"But how will we get home?" She opened her purse as if searching for the answer.

"We'll take you," offered Colleen.

"Are you sure?" said Stump. "I live out past the collier on Ridge Road."

"Our shifts ended an hour ago. This is good timing," said Colleen.

"I could call us a cab." He placed his arm around Mrs. Pavinsky's shoulders.

"I'm happy to drive," said MK.

Stump held open the passenger door of the front seat as Mrs. Pavinsky stepped into Big Blue. Then he opened the driver's door for MK, followed by the back doors for Colleen and himself. Mrs. Pavinsky fastened her seat belt and said, "Your grandmother used to give me rides to Canasta in this car."

"I know," said MK. "You were friends."

"You've kept it as clean as when she bought it," continued Mrs. Pavinsky. "When was that? Thirty years? Forty years? Maybe more?"

"Funny how time gets away from us," said Colleen.

Stump leaned forward and placed his hand on the seat-top by Mrs. Pavinsky's shoulder.

"Time has become my most precious commodity," she said and kneaded her thumbs against the handle of her pocketbook. "Someday you'll realize the same thing."

"See how I still have my grandmother's St. Christopher statue?" MK tapped the figure on the dash. "But I had to glue him back on a couple of times."

Colleen added, "I can't believe the Church dropped his feast day from the calendar."

"Just awful," said Mrs. Pavinsky.

MK tightened her grip on the steering wheel. "Good thing my grandmother didn't know. She believed St. Christopher saved her many times, especially during the Agnes Flood."

"Same for all those folks living by the Susquehanna River," added Stump.

Afternoon sunlight filtered through the windshield, anointing the statue in its glow. Both St. Christopher and the child Jesus on his shoulder seemed to smile. "Some days I feel like my grandmother is near," said MK.

"I know what you mean. I can feel Aloysius, too. There are days I feel I can talk with the two of them," said Mrs. Pavinsky. "That's what happens when we get close to the check-out."

"It means you need to get out of the house more," said Stump. "The VFW has bingo on Friday night. We should go."

"We can give you a ride," said Colleen.

"They have a fish fry, what with Lent, and we can—" Stump paused in mid-sentence. "Look at those Canada geese. They're so early this year." The birds rose from the river, flapping wings and forming a V-shape.

"Global weirding," spat Colleen.

The flock ascended, and Mrs. Pavinsky fixed her gaze skyward. The geese flew higher and shrank to the size of bats in a coal mine. She elected not to tell the others what she'd come to understand: loved ones welcomed her to the other side. They awaited her arrival, and she looked forward to joining them.

But not quite yet.

Mrs. Pavinsky needed to paint Easter eggs and put books with candy in the baskets. Carlita and Ibbie liked when she read to them. She didn't know if they grasped all the words, but as she pointed to pictures, they sat with rapt attention and smiled at the right places.

"So, you'll go with me to bingo?" asked Stump.

The birds swooped down, growing large as they soared over tree limbs. Mrs. Pavinsky felt bold. She relished the here and now. It wasn't her time to depart. Not for a while, at any rate. How best to announce her realization?

The geese honked.

Mrs. Pavinsky reached across the seat toward the steering wheel, much like she stretched when playing the organ, and pressed her hand against the horn. Big Blue honked. "That's for Aloysius and your grandmother. They need to hear I'm staying put."

MK grinned and pumped the horn, too. Colleen and Stump laughed. Then like a choir heavy with altos, the Canada geese gathered force and trumpeted their refrain: Honk. Honk.

Mrs. Pavinsky clapped, pleased to herald the sound

PIXELATED

THE MAIN reason I'm driving Colleen in Big Blue to the Luzerne-Wyoming Counties Arts Center is to help Hottie Hajduk. I'd prefer sleeping late, what with tombstone-gray skies lurking overhead, but Colleen had activated her sunshine voice: "Come on, MK, we can do a good thing. He needs us for his internship." Along with Colleen's many social concerns, she has taken to championing the arts, or more specifically, Hottie's photography workshop. Colleen says creative outlets can ease our woe. She's full of it, all right, being as our jobs are near goners. For now, I work at Books-a-Million, the store that took over the space left by Borders, but it's not doing well, same for the rest of the mall, including the Hallmark store, Colleen's employer, yet she says, "We must look on the bright side."

Hottie's good looks is more like it.

Colleen sighs, "There's a purpose when nice guys find their way home again."

I nod, lest she babble about the way-back days when Hottie set off for the Denver School of Design, saying Pennsylvania was a good state to be *from*. Next thing, he landed in Vail, taking pictures of skiers on vacation. Who wouldn't smile and give him big tips?

For decades, all went well. Then came the urgent phone call. His dad, who'd been spending time with Mrs. Pavinsky and planning to take a cruise arranged by Boscov's Travel, had suffered a stroke. It happened so unexpectedly, Colleen and I were shocked, same as everyone at Perpetual Help Outreach. Hottie packed up his jeep, drove nonstop, and became the caregiver for Jared Hajduk's final months.

Colleen and I attended the viewing at Alderwood Funeral Services. As I raised my arms to give Hottie a hug, Colleen swooped in, latching on with such force, he lost his balance and sat in a straight-back chair. "Thanks, I needed the break," he whispered.

"I'm available whenever," gushed Colleen.

Only Colleen makes a proposition under the guise of condolences. She harbors the belief that men crave big women during times of duress.

Hottie hasn't taken her up on the offer, but he has stayed put, renovating his dad's farmette. Hottie claims that when he left the area, he was too young to appreciate how we live in a ground-zero kind of place. Now he's back for the long haul and wants the graduate degree he never finished. That's why he enrolled in a low-residency photography MFA. His internship requires him to teach a photography workshop. Problem is, no one signed up, even though it's free, and his supervisor is traveling from Wilkes-Barre to observe him. Colleen offered our assistance, which is typical of her, and so we'll be his students for this session. She would have taken his class, but she must work three Saturdays a month, and although each day with a paycheck is a good thing, Colleen is lucky to have today off.

"I don't like the idea of pretending to be his student," I say, drumming my fingers against the steering wheel. "I don't even own a camera."

"Not a problem," says Colleen. "His supervisor wants to see him. He won't notice much about us."

Let's hope so, I think, glancing at Colleen. Over her standard black tunic and leggings, she sports a tan vest with lots of little pockets, the kind worn by fishing guides. Undoubtedly, she got it on sale from Salvo. Colleen could be the poster woman for the Salvation Army thrift store. She pats the vest. "Makes me look like a *National Geographic* photojournalist, don't you think? Maybe Hottie and I can collaborate on a coffee-table book. He can do the photos, and I'll write the story."

Please no, I pray, fearful she'll yammer about another book-in-waiting. I used to believe she'd actually write something, but she never puts a word to paper, always rushing to some volunteer effort of the month with the notion that good deeds provide the core for her stories. Dream on. And worse, she thinks my driving her to events will keep me here. Yet again, I made the mistake of telling her that I was thinking about moving to Point Pleasant, an ocean town where I vacationed as a kid. Who wouldn't want to leave? This area is going rock bottom. But living paycheck to paycheck without a lead for a new job or friends to stay with forces me to stay put. In a weird way, I know I'm lucky to have Colleen. Sure, she's a mess, but her intentions are good, most of the time.

Thankfully she stays quiet as we turn onto Mill Street. The rambling houses, originally built by coal barons, are divided into two- and three-family dwellings. Most have plastic on the windows with siding the color of steel wool. Front porches hold couches, not patio furniture, overstuffed pieces moved out from living rooms, deposited by people too tired to haul them any further or weird enough to think they're decorative.

We stop for a red light. No other vehicles pass through the intersection, unlike when I was a kid and the road swelled with Saturday shoppers. The light turns green, and Big Blue charges ahead, seemingly on autopilot, having motored here regularly with my grandmother. Are any of the current residents from those days? How my grandmother loved taking me to Jennowitcz Clothing & Fine Apparel, the sprawling stone building at the corner of Mill and River, and across the street, Donovan's Shoes, where I got my first loafers and put dimes in the penny slots. Those stores closed about the time my grandmother died and Hottie went west. The mall was built then, too. My brain goes haywire from all the connections, and I'm relieved my grandmother can't see the plywood nailed across windows, spray-painted with black hieroglyphics. Although it's hard to imagine gang activity, I wager the graffiti hints at trouble.

"Pull over at the next block," says Colleen. We pass the VFW, a skinny, stucco building with blue trim, and then, a rectangular shop with yellow neon lights: Hornet's Nest Tattoos & Piercings. At the cross street towers a brick building, Luzerne-Wyoming Counties Department of Aging, with a wheelchair ramp parallel to the stairs. We're as low as we can get without running into the railroad tracks and after that, the Susquehanna River. Brown dust tinges every surface. Remnants from the Agnes Flood, I figure. A tin marker nailed to the wall shows the twenty-foot high water mark.

"How could anyone pick this area for an arts center?" I ask. "It's so depressing."

"That's the point," says Colleen. "This is where the arts are needed more than ever."

"What they need are jobs." I swing into the parking space. The rear end of Big Blue shakes, and we settle to a stop. I peer past the St. Christopher statue on the dash at what used to be Marko's Office Mart. Sometimes my grandmother took me inside. They sold typewriters, ribbons, carbon paper, and best of all, adding machines that resembled a toaster with raised number keys. I'd tap-tap, pulling the handle as paper unfurled with curly loops. The business has long since closed, and for a while, the building housed Social Services. When that left, a sign was taped in the window, telling people to contact them via the internet. Do people in need of public assistance have web access, and if so, are they savvy enough to manage online forms?

I stare hard at the arts center and try to recall its original use. Grange Bank? The two-story box has an oyster-stone facade, mined from Riverside Quarry. Not even a power wash could freshen the exterior but, shocker, the picture window in the middle is wiped clean.

Colleen gets out of Big Blue, and I join her on the sidewalk. Each concrete section heaves up at a seam and makes the surface uneven. Colleen grinds her heel against a crack. "Not once has Hottie mentioned a woman. Do you think some mountain skank burned him? Most guys his age talk about relationships. Unless, of course, it's too painful to discuss."

"Maybe there was a boyfriend?"

Colleen vibrates her head, red hair swishing, and I know she's checking her Gaydar. When we attended the reunion for Our Lady of Perpetual Help Elementary School—a huge event for any student who'd ever gone there during its existence—she pulled me aside: "Remember those guys we thought were gay? They've come out." Now she thinks she's an expert at detecting gay, straight, or whatever.

She yanks open the door, and I follow her inside, taking shallow breaths against the musty air. The ground level is closed off, and the light filters from yellow transom glass above the entrance. We march up wooden steps to the second floor. Hottie stands by a tripod near the *clean* window, and off to the side is a metal table with folding chairs where I guess we'll have the workshop. He smiles, his face surprisingly healthy. All that time in the Colorado sun should have baked his skin like a brown potato.

He walks toward us, having swapped his cowboy boots, jeans, and denim shirt for sneakers, khaki pants, and a green cardigan that resemble cast-offs from *Mister Rogers' Neighborhood*. Has Colleen taken him shopping at Salvo?

"Mary Katherine, thanks for coming," says Hottie, reaching for my hand. I'm glad he avoids the cliché of me not having changed a bit, for we're long past our days of sitting in the same classroom.

"MK. Everyone calls me MK."

"But you *are* Mary Katherine," he insists. "That's how I think of you."

Wary of time warps, I extricate my hand from his.

Colleen says, "Remember how most girls had Mary tacked to their names?"

"Mary Katherine," he repeats. His voice has a molasses-thick texture. "I can picture the time you came to school wearing moccasins and a buckskin dress."

"Some memory, Thaddeus," I say, using his baptismal name, just like the nuns who refused to call him Tad.

He and Colleen laugh.

"Actually, the outfit was brown felt, sewn by my grandmother."

Again, they laugh, a reminder of how our school celebrated on the day after Halloween, November 1, known as All Saints Day. Forgoing uniforms for the garb of patron saints, most girls chose blue gowns with white veils to resemble the Virgin Mary, but I wore the get-up of Katherine Tekawitha, *The Lily of the Mohawks*. It did not matter that my name honored my grandmother as well as an Irish virgin-saint martyred under an oak tree. I figured my real patron saint had to be Katherine Tekawitha. Our nuns extolled the orphan girl's chastity and her refusal to marry an Algonquin. We prayed for her canonization, and I could imagine myself in buckskin, hiding by the river rather than being forced into marriage. Rarely did I think about the Jesuit who found Katherine Tekawitha, taking her to a Mission where she prayed until poor health caused her to die young. I preferred thoughts of her miracles, especially her appearance to Polish prisoners during World War II. They had no idea who she was, but the buckskin-clad female explained she was their patron and promised their release. Not until the men were freed and told Jesuits in Warsaw about the Mohawk girl they'd seen did they learn her identity. It was my kind of story.

"Mary Katherine no more," murmurs Hottie, his brown eyes velvet soft.

Colleen butts in: "Today's her first time here. I couldn't get her to come to any of the showings."

"Quite a place," I mumble, being as I don't go for artsy-chat, much less the surroundings. Why did I agree to this?

"I've told her about your amazing photos," spouts Colleen. "I can't wait for the workshop."

"My supervisor texted he got lost, so we're starting a little late. Seems he drove up before dawn to go fly fishing, but he got confused by the river. Had I known, I would have taken him."

Colleen hooks her thumbs in her vest pockets; the other fingers dangle like bait. "A perfect morning for fishing."

What? I squint at her. She never goes fishing.

"Morning's the best," agrees Hottie. "When the fog shroud lifts, and light plays on the Susquehanna, you discover a charm that can keep you here forever."

I tighten my jaw. Is he for real?

Colleen pats her heart, "Such words belong in a book."

Yet I notice she doesn't write them down, and no way will she remember what Hottie just said.

"Your novel?" He smiles.

Colleen beams. That's why she hasn't said much to me lately. I thought by refusing to listen, I'd get her on task, but instead, she blabs to him.

Avoiding her pleased expression, I glance around the room at shelves displaying local art. A sign, etched with calligraphy, hangs from a support post: For Sale. From the highest tier droop Afghans, woven like American flags, and squeezed beside them are round saw blades painted with farm scenes. On the middle shelf, I spy toilet paper doll-covers with red and white crochet skirts, and a framed needlepoint: Bless Our Home.

"Don't you love this stuff?" says Colleen.

I cross my arms over my chest. Crafts and folk art appealed to my grandmother. What grabs my attention is the set of six margarita glasses. Each glass is filled with color-specific knitted balls, the size of jumbo marbles. I step closer and note how each glassful displays its own specific knitting pattern. My grandmother, who tried her best to get me to learn to knit, realized I was a lost cause, but she succeeded in teaching me to recognize patterns. The glass with yellow balls displays a four-point stitch, red is double moss, pink a bouquet lace, green a basic basket weave, but the purple and blue balls feature stitches I've never seen. Propped at the base of each glass is a recipe card for the drink that inspired the knitted balls.

Hottie notices my interest. "What do you think?"

"Kind of fun, I guess. But who takes the time to make stuff like this?"

"My sister, Susan. How could you forget?" says Colleen. "Remember how I told you Susan took up knitting when Tim got deployed to Afghanistan?"

"Oh, right. And I can see your influence, too," I say. My glance shifts to the next shelf where a ceramic cow sculpture reminds me of Susan and Tim's annual costume bash. For years, Tim had dressed as a cow until Susan bought him a pig costume. Colleen and I always make it a point to go, but with Tim gone, I'm not sure if Susan will have the party this year.

"Check how Susan titled her collection," laughs Colleen.

I reach for the business card leaning against a glass: *Yarn Over Not Hang Over.* That's never been the case after their Halloween party.

Hottie steps close to me, so he can read it, too. I sniff spearmint and fir trees, a he-man kind of smell.

"What's with the tripod?" calls Colleen. "Is that for us?"

He turns and points to the window. "Yeah. It's a good prop since you're supposed to be working with mirrors and windows."

I walk from the shelves and look through the glass at the shop across the street. The "*T*" in *Touch* has burned out of the pink lights: *Golden ouch Beauty Shop.*

"Before and after photos are the best," says Hottie.

My abs tighten. Is he mocking the customers? My grandmother used to get her hair done there. She said it was worth the long drive into town where Tressa, the beautician, never tried to sway her from a blue rinse. "You better not be making fun of those ladies."

"No, you don't understand." From the table, he picks up a Contac sheet of twenty or so matchbook size photos and offers it for our inspection.

"Another prop?" asks Colleen as she grabs it.

I move beside her and squint at a series of double exposures. They merge into one full picture. Did he intentionally blend images together?

"I shoot from behind and side views, never their faces."

Colleen, lips turned up like a know-it-all, hands me the Contac sheet. I scan the arc of superimposed shots and figure the collage offers a significance that eludes me.

"The technique is all about angles and impressions," continues Hottie. "From afar, you have a bird's eye view. But get closer, and you see more than a new hairdo. You appreciate the change in posture, how they carry themselves."

"So true," interrupts Colleen. "They arrive stooped and retiring, but afterward, they look taller, their faces raised.

"Beauty wells up from within," says Hottie.

From the corner of my eye, I perceive movement on the sidewalk. Mrs. Pavinsky, the church organist who seemed old in my grandmother's day, leans on the arm of her neighbor, Rosalina. They walk slowly toward the beauty shop. Mrs. Pavinsky wears a paisley scarf on her head, what my grandmother called a *babushka*. Mrs. Pavinsky stops, and after a moment's rest, resumes her measured gait. Colleen says Mrs. Pavinsky's son, who lives in Scranton, wanted to put her in Riverside Assisted Living, but he's eased off since Rosalina and Carlos have moved next door. They're happy to do the driving and yard work, and in return, she watches their kids after school.

Rosalina holds open the door for Mrs. Pavinsky, so hunched over, I chide my sagging posture and straighten my spine.

The click-click of a camera registers from behind me. I pivot and see Hottie with his head at tripod level. He snaps photos in quick repetition.

"What are you doing?" I shake the Contac sheet. "How do you think she'd feel?"

He steps away and rubs his forehead with the back of his hand.

"She'd love it," says Colleen. "You've seen her ham it up on the organ. Mrs. Pavinsky thrives on being the center of attention."

Spoken like one who knows, I think.

"You're missing my intent," says Hottie.

I should ask him to explain, but he distracts me by staring deep into my eyes. He breathes slowly, sure and deliberate. Briefly, I think he's flirting. What made me tease Colleen about him being gay?

BAM bangs the lower door, followed by the drum of lug soles on the staircase. A tall guy enters, looking like he stepped from a Cabela's fishing catalog: Gore-Tex boots, green zip-off pants, and over his wind shirt, a vest that's almost identical to Colleen's, except his pockets have fly-tie feathers stuck to them.

Hottie rushes through the introductions. I had expected a much older man with a gray beard, but Ben, as Hottie calls him, not Professor or Mister, is about our age. Hottie shifts from foot to foot, and I gather he wants to start the workshop before Ben gets wise to us. I'm wary, too. Should I keep standing if I'm a student?

"Sorry I'm late." Ben smiles apologetically. "My GPS got no reception, and the dirt roads aren't marked."

"Reception is terrible because of the coal mines up in the hills," says Colleen. "I keep a gazetteer in the car."

What? Colleen hasn't had a car for ages, and without me driving her in Big Blue, she wouldn't go anywhere. Her claim about using maps is a joke. If I ask her to check the atlas, she pooh-poohs, opting to look for landmarks that, in most cases, no longer exist.

"The gazetteer is so hard to read," he says. Then he reaches into the waist pocket of his vest and pulls out a silver charm, the size of a half-dollar. "This got me here."

"A St. Christopher medal?" blurts Colleen.

"My grandmother gave it to me when I was a teenager," he explains. "It used to be on a chain, but that broke, so I keep the medal in my fishing vest."

Colleen rasps, "You and MK could be related."

He cocks his head, failing to understand. "I don't meet many female anglers—unless they're fishing with their husbands."

Colleen presses her left palm against her chest, luring attention to her ring finger that lacks a wedding band. Rarely does Colleen surprise me, but I'm unprepared for her whopper: "Morning is the best. When the fog shroud lifts, and light plays on the Susquehanna, you discover a charm that can keep you here forever."

"How poetic," he says.

Hottie coughs: "Let's get started."

We move to the chairs, and Ben pulls his seat in close to Colleen. Hottie continues, "Today, we'll find ways to capture undiffused light to form the image."

I glance frantically at Colleen. What the hell is Hottie talking about?

Colleen provides a little assistance, smiling at Ben as he reaches for the Contac sheet I'd placed on the table. He holds it at eye level and scrutinizes the details. His voice goes nasal: "Good effort for a beginner. A series, no less. How did you determine your level of pixels?"

Pixels? I start to explain the photos aren't mine, but Colleen nudges me with her foot, a reminder to play along, so I answer without lying: "Hard to say."

Ben persists, "Did you consider heightening the resolution?"

I kick Colleen under the table, begging for help, being as she got me into this. What a mistake. "If MK hadn't missed so many classes, she'd tell you."

Ben's jaw protrudes, and his tongue flicks out like a frog. "Hmmm, well, the VGA display will improve with more pixels."

That word: pixels. No wonder Hottie clears his throat. He balances his upper teeth against his lower lip and radiates tension. Clearly, he's worried about our charade, but then I wonder if he's been slighted. Does Ben fault Hottie's technique?

Out stretches Ben's tongue, long enough to snag a fly. He catches me staring: "What you have is adequate, but it could be better pixelated."

"Come again?" says Hottie.

"Better pixelated." His pronunciation sprays saliva, bathing me in memories of watching a black and white movie with my grandmother, and how she joked about the film's old lady stereotypes. Each time the main characters, two biddies, helped a drunk man to cross the street, they tittered: "He's pixalated." My grandmother thought they were hilarious and chimed in with them. I can practically hear her. "Pixalated," I snort.

The room gets very still. Colleen looks at me strangely. I try to make them understand: "The golden oldies movie, you must have seen it—the one where Jimmy Stewart, or maybe it's Cary Grant—gets drunk, and the two old ladies who help him across the street keep saying 'pixalated.' "

Colleen and Hottie shake their heads no, but Ben nods enthusiastically: "A classic film. I never expected someone here could joke about pixelated with pixalated."

The way he says *someone here* causes me to clench my fists, thumbs tucked in, and press my arms to my sides.

Colleen's voice is clipped, "What's that supposed to mean?"

Hottie scowls. I am certain that pretending to be students was a bad idea.

Ben's eyes bulge until he blinks, settling them back into the sockets. "I like your play on language, same with the pixels. If you connect each rendering for a broader picture, the structure inherent in the window will admit light while serving the function of the subject."

Huh? Is this his way of saying he sees through our pretense?

"That's the focus for our workshop," says Hottie. He explains how we'll find ways for capturing light and image.

I stare across the room, searching for balance against their photo-speak. One large canvas, about 18×20, occupies a shelf. There's space for other works, but the portrait sits alone, directing my attention to an elderly woman. The artist used pale gray brush-strokes for a background and switched to bright green for the dress. The subject, looking straight at me, has white hair shaped to her head like a turban, and sympathetic eyes revealed behind glasses. Her expression, elusive and mysterious, offers no visual clue as to what she is thinking, and I speculate that the straightforward depiction suggests the artist's respect for her. An older woman, no less. Pleased by that notion, I smile, for I hadn't expected to be moved by anything here. Quickly I put my hand to my mouth lest the others see me and ask for an explanation. I can just imagine Colleen spewing on with more fervor for the downtown arts.

"Me! I'll shoot first," says Colleen. She jumps up and struts to the tripod.

She fiddles with the camera, and I stand, thinking I missed the directions. Hottie hovers off to the side and glances out the window. I follow his gaze, where below, the beauty shop door opens. Out wobbles Mrs. Pavinsky, minus the head scarf. Light plays on her newly coifed hair. She pauses, less stooped than earlier, and then straightens, seemingly transformed. Maybe it's the effect of her fresh, cottony pouf? Rosalina walks out, too. She smooths her dark hair, cut like big *Cs* around her face, and smiles broadly at Mrs. Pavinsky. They link arms and walk up the sidewalk, passing close to Big Blue. The headlights wink as sunlight ricochets off the glass.

Colleen snaps the shutter. Click. Click.

Ben raises his index finger in a gesture of approval.

Hottie looks at me, his eyes gentle and kind. "If there's enough pixels, we'll print it with the series."

Amazingly I sense his purpose. He's not making fun; rather, he documents small measures of respect. How do I tell him I understand? "The photos can go on the shelf with the painting of that woman," I say.

Mrs. Pavinsky stops. She turns, face held high as if looking up at our window. Her arthritic hands, cupped like nests, pat chicken fluff at the back of her head. Is she laughing? Then I realize the sun in her eyes makes her squint. How happy she seems. Quite lovely. Perhaps this is the moment I needed to see. So much depends on the frame of perception.

RAMP

ORDINARILY Brandon spent summer mornings with his wheelchair pressed to the computer desk, playing *Medal of Honor*, but today, he sat on the back porch and avoided his mother. Yet again, she had phoned the Tunkhannock township supervisor, having called his office every few days since the 4th of July. Her voice, extra loud, carried out through the open windows. "School opens next week. If the ramps aren't done, I'll sue. Do you know what you'll pay for violating the Americans with Disabilities Act?"

Moisture glazed Brandon's forehead. In the past, he'd attended Camp Spifida, an adaptive day program for kids like him. This year he begged off: "It's for dweebs. I'm fourteen, starting high school." No way would he ride the short bus with the window lickers. Bad enough during the school year. That's why he looked forward to high school. The school was four blocks away, and the access ramps would let him use the sidewalk like everyone else.

His mother rushed from the house, wearing her Weis Markets cashier's smock. "Why are you sitting in this heat?"

Brandon shrugged.

"Guess what the supervisor told me? *We'll get right on it,*" she mimicked.

Brandon nodded, glad she sounded in a better mood.

She leaned down and kissed the top of his head. "Got to hurry or I'll be late. Aunt Colleen will bring you lunch."

Brandon smiled. Aunt Colleen, totally different from his mom, played cards, and when she brought wine, his mom laughed a lot. But his aunt didn't drink and drive. That lady, MK, who worked with her at the mall gave her rides in her old Buick. Brandon thought it was funny that Aunt Colleen called the car Big Blue and talked about it like it was a person. No matter. He liked going in Big Blue to the food court for soft pretzels or ice cream. Aunt Colleen said the mall was in a bad way, and any business could help the place survive.

Thoughts of food propelled him to the kitchen. Fruit flies hovered over the bananas, so he made do with a Pop-Tart. He considered eating another one when gears ground in the street, so loud his wheelchair vibrated. What the heck? Brandon wheeled out to the porch, down the wooden ramp and along the path to his secret vantage point: the forsythia bush. Its yellow flowers had fallen off weeks ago, and leafy branches stretched akimbo like an octopus gone mad. He peered through the greenery and spied a tan pickup truck, parked midway between his house and the corner. The door, stamped with the township's spruce tree logo, swung open, and a huge man stepped to the curb. His arms bulged from a gray T-shirt, and his legs, sturdy as tree trunks, squeezed against jeans that draped over his work boots. He wasn't blubbery, but so big Brandon figured he used to play football, probably defensive tackle.

"Too damn hot," spat the guy, rubbing his hand across his neck.

Brandon considered telling him that when his mother phoned weeks ago, it was ten degrees cooler.

A short man with an orange safety vest walked from the passenger side to the truck bed.

"Why the hell are we doing this today?" said the big guy.

"Crap with handicap laws, you know," said Orange Vest. He released the tailgate and reached in for a sledge hammer.

"Handicap my ass. Some shithead complains, and we got extra work."

"Quit bitching, Klooch."

Brandon tried to register that name. Klooch sounded weird, but it suited him.

"How many damn ramps have we put in? Who the hell uses them?"

"Shut up and get working. We can knock off soon as it's cleared and formed." Orange Vest strode across Bridge Street to the opposite curb. With feet set wide, he raised the sledge and smashed at the cement. Bam. Bam. His rapid action made chunks of the pavement.

"Too damn hot. We need jackhammers," called Klooch. He yanked his shirt over his head, revealing a tattoo of red lips sprawled across his back—a kiss planted between his wing bones. As he swung his sledge, the lips puckered up and spit sweat.

Did the humidity make Brandon see things? The air felt weighted, and despite his mesh athletic pants, his legs stuck to the chair. Brandon knew he should go inside to the air-conditioned family room. He could almost taste the cold, but he liked spying on these weirdos. Maybe he was getting bored like his mother had predicted would happen if he didn't go to camp. Whatever. Briefly he wished she were home to bring him his water bottle filled with ice. Perhaps he'd go get it from the kitchen, hook the bottle to his chair, and return to watch the men.

With that plan, he backed away, but a branch caught in the spoke of his wheel. Lacking the ability to reach down and work it free, he tried rotating back and forth.

"You know what I'd tell those bastards about their access ramps?" said Klooch.

Again, Brandon attempted to move the wheels. The branch jammed in deeper. He exhaled as sweat rimmed his brow, stinging his eyes.

"Handicap's the worst," continued Klooch. "They all got a sense of entitlement."

"Quit bitching. I'm almost done here."

Brandon stared at the branch, bent like a wishbone, and realized its angle meant he'd have to roll forward. But how could he move ahead with the bush so thick? He jerked his chair a half-spin and almost tipped over. Panting, he backed up, but more branches grabbed at the wheels. The forsythia trapped him like he was in a jungle.

"What's with that bush behind you?" said Orange Vest. "No wind, but it's shaking."

Brandon held his breath.

The sledge hammers stopped. "Damn squirrels," said Klooch. "Gray rats with furry tails."

"Too big."

Eyes shut tight, Brandon recalled a book where the main character used psychic powers so that people couldn't see him. Could he focus his energy and become imperceptible? Brandon sat extra still, and with shallow breaths, willed himself incognito.

"What the hell?" called Klooch.

The voice sounded close. Brandon tried to banish the approaching smell of cheese and onions. He scrunched up his face and mustered all his powers of concentration. The smell got stronger. Then he heard a snort, followed by another. Unable to ignore the sound's proximity, he opened his eyes.

The guy's face loomed large: "I'll be damned."

Sometimes Brandon had difficulty speaking; that's why Miss Kaminski, his speech therapist, had taught him to make an *O* with his mouth. He formed the rounded shape as Klooch crouched down beside him. "Damn, kid, you got yourself a mess." He poked at the wheel, "What the hell happened?"

"Stuck," forced out Brandon.

"No shit." Klooch called to Orange Vest. "Hey, High Power, bring me the loppers out of the truck."

For some reason, Brandon laughed.

Klooch grinned. "That High Power may be short, but the dude eats Energizer Bunnies for breakfast."

High Power handed Klooch the tool, and then spoke as if Brandon weren't there. "Do you think the kid heard what we were saying?"

"So, what if he did?" said Klooch. "Ain't no crime to bitch about people."

Snip, cut, Klooch pruned away the vegetation. "You're lucky, kid. The wheel spokes seem okay." Klooch stood, grabbed the handles of the chair, and yanked it onto the walkway. He pushed Brandon to the shade of the window awning attached to the brick house. Then Klooch secured the brake and stepped across the cement walkway. He stood beside High Power.

That's when Brandon noticed how Klooch had another tattoo: a pair of female legs with each foot set in a red high heel. One leg extended down the side of his chest, and the other leg stretched along his inner arm.

"He likes your tattoo," said High Power.

Klooch raised his arm, flapping it to spread the legs and expose a hairy pit.

"See why they named him Klooch?"

Brandon squinted, "Huh?"

High Power laughed, "From the Eskimos, when he was stationed in Alaska. Klooch means asshole."

Klooch grunted, "Twenty years in the military, and I come home to Pennsylvania, having to work with this asshole."

Brandon wanted to tell them his dad was with the National Guard in Afghanistan, but this didn't seem the right time.

"Hey Kid, no more talking my ear off. High Power wants back on the job."

Brandon watched the men pummel the sidewalk into cookie bits, and around noon, Big Blue rumbled onto the driveway. Aunt Colleen eased out of the passenger side. His mom often said she gave new meaning to plus sizes, and Brandon agreed. Aunt Colleen wore a long, Hawaiian print skirt, ablaze with red, yellow, and orange flowers. Grasping handfuls of material, she lifted it halfway up her thighs to fan her legs. "Air conditioning's broke," she called. "Too damn hot."

Klooch pivoted in her direction. He placed the sledge upright like a pedestal and rested his hands. That's when Brandon realized Klooch was checking out Aunt Colleen. Even worse, she rocked her hips, walking slowly with her skirt bunched up.

The horn tooted as MK backed Big Blue out of the driveway and motored away. Aunt Colleen smiled and asked Brandon, "Ready for lunch?"

Brandon shrugged.

"Aloha," said Klooch. He put on his shirt and sashayed toward them.

Aunt Colleen steadied her gaze on Klooch, and slowly, inch-by-inch, lowered her skirt.

Oh, brother, thought Brandon, both grossed out and fascinated.

Klooch puffed out his chest, "Thought you should know, I fixed your son's wheel."

"Thanks, but Brandon's my nephew." She rolled back her shoulders, and her voice got husky, "I'm not married."

Klooch gave Brandon a conspiratorial nod.

Ugh, weird. Brandon released the brake and wheeled toward the porch.

"Be there in a minute," called his aunt.

Brandon spun toward the house as Klooch bragged, "Let me tell you, it takes real skill to build these ramps. We're about to do the forms, so tomorrow we can pour the concrete." Then he spoke softly, and Brandon strained to hear, having learned how adults whisper the good stuff.

"Kid's got some problems, huh?"

"Depends how you look at it," said Aunt Colleen. "There's the spinal cord damage, what with his leg paralysis and speech difficulties, but he manages okay."

Brandon clenched his teeth. Why did she keep blabbing?

"He wants more independence. The ramps will let him wheel to the high school."

"He goes to regular school?"

"Yeah, he's smart, gets good grades, a computer whiz," chimed Aunt Colleen. "He won prizes at the science fair."

Can't she shut up? Brandon turned and wheeled toward them.

"Hey kid, I've been telling your aunt how building these ramps is the best part of my job. I love building them."

"Yeah, right."

By late afternoon, Aunt Colleen cheered at the sight of gaping holes in the sidewalk. Brandon thought they resembled empty sandboxes. The men had removed the entire corner sections, not just curb pieces, and formed them out with two-by-fours. Klooch claimed a full replacement would last longer, especially if water seeped into the cracks and expanded during the winter freeze: "It's a matter of physics. We can't just redo the curb."

"You're full of it," said High Power. "That's not how we did the others."

"Completely different terrain," said Klooch. He crossed his arms over his chest and detailed how a load of gravel would ensure proper drainage. He had ordered the gravel to arrive first thing in the morning. "We'll set the grade, get the cement mixer, and finish it up fine."

"Glad I'll be here to watch this," said Aunt Colleen.

Klooch leaned toward Brandon: "Know what it's like to pour concrete?"

Brandon shook his head.

"Massaging a woman," intoned Klooch. "We work it back and forth, mixing nice and easy, and as the aggregate comes to the surface, we start vibrating."

Aunt Colleen laughed.

Klooch cocked his left eyebrow: "Pretty soon the whole surface heaves up. Man, it's intense, and then, *whoosh*, everything relaxes and goes smooth."

Brandon pursed his lips. He didn't know why this guy bothered him, but he did.

"I'm about to make sangria," said Aunt Colleen. "Can you stay for some?"

Klooch nodded, but High Power said no. They had to get the truck back in the maintenance lot before their supervisor knocked off for the day. As they walked away, Brandon heard High Power scold Klooch: "See what you missed? I told you to get working, but oh no, not you."

Rain. The forecasters hadn't predicted it, but showers poured in at midnight, smacking the earth with a vengeance that continued into the morning.

"Why so glum?" asked his mother. She grabbed her umbrella and headed for the door. "The rain should cool things off."

Brandon worried rain would delay the ramp. What if it wasn't ready for the first day of school? He turned on the radio to Froggy 101. The DJ said the storm had unexpectedly dipped down from Canada and warned how another front had formed in the Atlantic. If the ocean storm shifted west, the two forces might collide, producing gale force wind and rain.

No way would the men show up for work. Brandon wheeled across the room to the computer. Then he heard a truck backfire. He swiveled his chair toward the window. The pickup pulled to the curb, followed by a dump truck filled with gravel.

Klooch got out and waved his right arm, directing the dump truck to a perpendicular position at the sidewalk. The truck blocked the street, so High Power stood by the corner to signal drivers even though few traveled there other than residents of the rambling houses.

Slowly the dump truck raised its bed, and with a hydraulic blast, the tailgate opened. Gravel spilled into the open space. A mound formed, and Klooch yelled, shaking his hands. After the gravel stopped, Klooch walked to the driver's window, and the men conversed. Next thing, the dump truck backed-up, jockeyed around, and repositioned to the space on the other side of the street. The truck dumped the load and rumbled off.

Klooch and High Power wore orange slickers, but their jeans, thoroughly drenched, clung to their legs like second skin. Each man worked on an opposite corner, wielding metal rakes to smooth the gravel. Klooch swore with each pull of his rake while High Power revved his arms and dug the sharp teeth into stone. The rain persisted. Mud oozed over the wooden forms. Watching their exertion made Brandon hungry, and he wheeled to the kitchen.

He found a granola bar and returned to the window, munching the chocolate chips and granola as High Power slowed his motion. He dropped his rake, lifted his arms above his head and clapped. Klooch yelled something, and High Power pointed at his smooth bed of stone. Klooch shook his head and pointed down to his uneven space. High Power raised a fist, but he picked up his rake and sprinted across the street to work beside Klooch. Like wind-up machines, they leveled the surface. Klooch smacked High Power in the shoulder, and the men laughed. Then they stared directly at the window and gave Brandon a thumbs-up.

Brandon sat motionless. How did they know he was there?

The men grinned and stood as if waiting. Finally, Brandon raised his thumb in approval. With high-five gestures, they slapped palms and got back in their truck. But they didn't pull away. Did they listen to the same alert that Brandon heard on the radio? Storm tracker predicted floods in the low-lying areas.

As he watched the men eat sandwiches, he had the odd feeling they stayed for Aunt Colleen.

After a while, their heads turned toward the driveway. Big Blue motored onto the macadam. Aunt Colleen emerged, cloaked in a long yellow slicker, the kind worn by cops, and on her feet, she sported purple rain boots, bright with pink and yellow polka dots, looking like she puddle-jumped from the game board of *Candyland*. She carried a Subway bag, and Brandon hoped she brought his favorite, a teriyaki chicken wrap.

Klooch ambled out of the truck, holding an umbrella, no less. He marched toward Aunt Colleen, and when they converged, he held it over the two of them. Wind rattled the umbrella, and Brandon thought his aunt stood unnecessarily close to Klooch. Hopefully she'd keep the Subway bag from getting wet. Klooch escorted her toward the back porch, and Brandon wished he could hear them talking. He wheeled to the kitchen door, grasped the handle, and opened slowly. "Be sure to tell his mother about the gravel. We'll pour the concrete soon as it dries a bit."

"Might take days," said Aunt Colleen. "Whenever it rains this hard, I think of Hurricane Agnes. I was just a girl, yet I remember that rain."

"I'll never forget it. But if something like that happens, they'll postpone the opening of school." Klooch added, "That might buy us time to finish the job."

Aunt Colleen squeezed his arm: "Such a positive sign to find the good in a situation."

Ugh, groaned Brandon from the doorway.

"Hey kid, you should have told me about this aunt of yours," boomed Klooch. "Not to worry about the ramp. Gravel makes it drain fast. We'll finish soon as the rain stops."

The next morning, his mother told him to quit frowning. "This rain is not the end of the world."

Brandon glanced out the window. Gravel spilled like soup from the wood forms. Even if the rain stopped, he didn't think the spaces would dry enough to have the ramps ready by the first day of school.

"I know what you're thinking, but I can drive you to school for a few days."

Brandon didn't respond.

Long after she left, he sat, staring at nothing. He didn't feel like turning on the computer. No TV either. He considered sending his dad an email. But what to say? *If mom drives me to school, I'll look like a loser.* Besides, it could be weeks until his dad had access to any communication.

He wheeled to the keyboard, but his game strategies for fighting enemy supply routes provided little satisfaction. Midway through the game, he felt a warm sensation on the back of his neck. He turned away from the screen. Sunlight filtered through the window. His eyes smarted. Never had the sky looked so blue. He wheeled across the room and stared out at the ramp-in-making. The water had receded. "Oh, yeah!" he cheered, amazed that the gravel created a drain. Maybe Klooch knew what he was doing?

Brandon wheeled outside. The heat spell had broken. Birds sang loudly. Then he heard the putt-putt rumble of the township truck.

He spun along the walkway to the front yard. "You're here," he called to Klooch.

"Good conditions for a pour. No rain expected for days."

High Power joined him, "If we work fast, we'll finish by tonight."

"Is your aunt coming over?" asked Klooch.

"Yeah, but later," said Brandon.

Klooch gave him a thumbs-up, and then walked to the truck bed with High Power. They retrieved rakes and smoothed their gravel plots. When the cement mixer roared onto the street, they grabbed shovels.

Klooch signaled the enormous cement mixer into position and then spoke to the driver. Brandon wondered what Klooch said, for the man extended his arm out of the open window and gave a thumbs-up.

High Power positioned the mixer's curved metal spout over his sidewalk space. Wet cement cascaded down as he shoveled the slop across the stone and into the corners.

"Keep it coming," chanted Klooch. He stood beside High Power, matching his frenzy, pushing and smoothing with the flat blade of his shovel until the cement solidified. Flecks splattered their jeans and boots. They carried their shovels to the pickup, rested them against the tailgate, and guzzled from gallon-sized jugs of water. Then the driver blasted his horn, and High Power sprang to action. He repositioned the slide in the space on Brandon's side of the street. The cement flowed with a loud, slurping noise while the men used their shovels to slap it into place. Brandon watched them so intently, he failed to notice the arrival of Aunt Colleen.

"The truck's blocking the street, so I got off at the corner," she told him. Her outfit, purple leggings with a matching tunic, seemed familiar. Then he remembered his mother saying that's what Aunt Colleen wore for wine tasting night.

Brandon smiled. He was glad she was here and could see them finish the ramp.

The cement mixer left shortly after the pour. The guy honked his horn repeatedly, and Brandon waved with Aunt Colleen.

Klooch didn't stop to talk. He and High Power grasped trowels and flat rectangular blades with handles. Each man knelt at his slab, smoothing and edging.

"It's an art," said Aunt Colleen. She had dragged a folding chair from the porch and sat next to Brandon. He nodded, amazed that Klooch worked so meticulously.

"Looks like you're icing a cake," called Aunt Colleen.

The men nodded, never wavering from their task.

Just as Brandon considered going inside for a snack, Klooch shifted back on his heels. "Time for the final buff," he announced. He held out the trowel and brandished it with exaggeration.

"He likes hamming it up, huh?" said Aunt Colleen.

Klooch took a deep breath and held his arms wide. Brandon laughed, for he knew the tattoo moved under his shirt, but he didn't mention it to Aunt Colleen. Klooch patted the cement one last time and stood. Aunt Colleen jumped up and hurried to him, standing close enough to whisper. High Power shot over from his side of the street, and the three talked, but Brandon couldn't catch a word. Then, flanked shoulder to shoulder, they advanced toward him.

"Ready to leave your mark?" asked Klooch.

Brandon stared quizzically.

"You have to put your name in the cement," said Aunt Colleen. He smiled and wheeled to the slab.

"High Power and me will tilt the chair forward, keeping it steady," said Klooch. "Your aunt will make sure you don't slide out. Soon as you're close, go for it."

The chair lowered to the wet, gray surface, and Brandon sniffed a muddy odor. He extended his hand, stretched his index finger, and wrote *Wheel Man*.

"Just like Hollywood Boulevard," said Aunt Colleen.

On Monday, Brandon was up and dressed, his backpack hooked on his wheelchair by 7:00 a.m. "Did you eat breakfast?" asked his mother.

"Yeah." Brandon pointed at the cereal bowl on the table.

"Let me get my sandals, and I'll walk with you. I've arranged to go in late for work since it's your first day."

Brandon shook his head no: "Going on my own."

His mother rubbed her hands together.

Brandon sat as straight as possible and stiffened his jaw.

For a moment, his mother's eyes seemed to glaze with water. She whispered: "I wish your dad could be here to see you."

Neither spoke as Brandon wheeled to the door. Then his mother called, "Have a good day."

Brandon coasted from the porch to the path, keeping wide of the forsythia bush. He heard a deep voice: "Too damn hot."

The township truck had parked on the street, two houses from the access ramp. What were they doing here?

Brandon wheeled along quickly, making sure not to look at them. He stared hard at the cement, but the sight of *Wheel Man* made him grin. He eased down the ramp, crossed the street, and rolled onto the new incline. When kids yelled, he looked ahead to see two boys he didn't know. They waited on the sidewalk. "Come on," they called.

Brandon wheeled faster, but then his shoulders stiffened. They weren't calling to him. A kid wearing a Steelers shirt ran out from a side yard, and the boys jogged toward the school. Brandon paused. The truck's horn tooted. He rotated his chair and looked back across the street.

Klooch watched from the driver's seat, and High Power leaned against the passenger door.

Brandon took a deep breath and exhaled. Maybe, after a few days, those boys would walk with him? His shoulders relaxed.

Klooch and High Power waved from their open windows.

A gum wrapper, probably dropped by one of the boys, skittered across the pavement. Brandon nodded to the township truck, and then turned his chair in the direction of the high school.

AFTER ALL
DANGER OF FROST

SATURDAY, 5:30 a.m. I'm driving Big Blue to the mall with Colleen, hours before the stores open and we start work. I glance across the seat at her, clad in a green tunic and pants, probably chosen to resemble a Girl Scout uniform, but in the briny dawn, she looks like a stuffed pickle. Last night, Colleen volunteered us for a sunrise hike with the Luzerne-Wyoming Girl Scout Troop. We had just clocked out of work when a dozen girls roared into the food court. They carried sleeping bags and were followed by a tall woman, her hair pulled atop her head like duck feathers. "We know her," said Colleen.

Leader Deb, a single mom, lives at Colleen's apartment complex, and the connection prompted the invite for a hike. Colleen never asked me, yet I couldn't refuse after she made the offer. And Leader Deb gave me pause. What sane person takes kids on a trail in the dark with the likes of Colleen?

My thumbs press against the steering wheel. "What possessed you to go hiking? You don't even walk much."

"Girl Scouts camping *inside* at the mall? They should explore like we did."

"We made S'mores."

Colleen grunts, same as when Leader Deb told us the girls lacked funds for cabin rentals, having had their cookie money ripped off. That's why they couldn't stay at the Grand Canyon of Pennsylvania like the other scouts for Earth Day. "We won't build a campfire," chirped Leader Deb as the girls positioned their sleeping bags on the floor of the atrium. "But our lock-in allows them to earn their Journey Badge."

Colleen didn't question the term lock-in or why the sleepover merited a badge. She was too eager to brag how we had been Girl Scouts, and how back then, Troop 193 did a sunrise hike up the hill beyond the parking lot. "Of course, the mall wasn't here when we were scouts, and we started down by the Susquehanna River."

Leader Deb raised her eyebrows, shaped like lopsided parentheses. "Must have been a long time ago."

I expected Colleen to huff at the age inference, but the troop clustered around us, and she pounded her fist to her palm: "Girl power, that's what we had, and you can, too."

The scouts blinked. Several rubbed their cheeks, pudgy and full.

Then Colleen went random, spewing like a social studies teacher: "In colonial times, fur traders and Susquehannock Indians traveled the very same path behind the mall. It has significance all the way to the top."

Dubious of her claim, I pursed my lips. The dirtway leads to slag heaps from abandoned coal mines. Shoppers who bring dogs in their cars take them to crap out there. Yet Colleen was on a roll: "You can hike the trail of history and find meaning by watching the sun come up."

Leader Deb clapped her hands. "Hey girls, we can do a hike tomorrow."

Chins dipped. Eyes studied the floor.

Colleen sputtered on, "Ms. MK and I will guide you."

Ms. MK? Guide? I feather the gas pedal. Big Blue grumbles, telling me to ease off. The muffler agrees. Big Blue is overdue for inspection, and the Jiffy Lube mechanic says it won't pass without replacing the turn signals, discontinued parts that need to be salvaged from junkyards. I'm taking Anthracite Expressway rather than Highway 29, the more direct route, frequented by cops. They'd notice Big Blue's long hood with a smiling front grill. Big Blue attracts as much attention now as when my grandmother bought the preowned Buick in the eighties. She willed Big Blue to me, certain I'd keep on driving, a cause for appreciation rather than scrutiny from cops looking to score ticket quotas, or worse, impoundment.

"We only have an hour 'til sunrise." Colleen chomps her gum. "Floor it, Mary Katherine."

She knows my childhood name annoys me and probably thinks I'll speed up. I consider slowing down, just to hear her groan, but I feel sorry for the girls, especially as I was working the day their cash box got stolen. The mall gave them permission to sell cookies at a table by the atrium. There's too much risk going door-to-door through neighborhoods. Scouts used to get space at Sal's Grocery, but the Thin Mints and Shortbreads ate into his profits. That's how bad his business has gotten. I guess the economic downturn hurts all of us, and so I was surprised to learn the scouts sold more than 100 boxes at four bucks a pop. Were the girls so busy finalizing deals they missed the itchy fingers making off with their till?

The cops came and interviewed the girls and their parents, minus the skinny mom. During the sale, she kept going outside to smoke. Around noon, she left for a meeting and told her daughter that grandma would give her a ride home.

Grandma had a different spin: "A meeting with oxycodone is more like it."

Everyone says skinny mom took the money, but I don't know if she's been caught. *The Riverside Gazette* hasn't published a police report, maybe a good thing, as it spares her daughter further shame. How could a mom steal from her kid's scout troop?

We pull into the parking lot, empty except for a security vehicle and minivan. "They're waiting outside," says Colleen. "But there's just three girls."

I stare through the windshield at the entrance where security lights illuminate them. They wear the same hoodies and jeans from last night. I guess scouts don't require uniforms anymore. Maybe it's a money thing. Of varying heights, the girls cluster side by side and peer at us. Their arms hang limply in front of their bodies, yellow bags by their feet. "They look like meerkats."

"Huh?"

"You know, the dark-eyed critters that stand upright and get featured on *Animal Planet*."

"You're comparing them with cats?"

I cut the ignition. "It's Earth Day. We're supposed to connect with the natural world."

Colleen taps the St. Christopher statue on the dash, a quick gesture from her index finger, just like always, and reaches for the door handle. She lumbers out, closing the door so forcefully, Big Blue shudders.

I step onto the asphalt and lock the door. The scouts wave and grab their yellow bags, different from what stores use for merchandise. I wonder where they got them. Leader Deb, a foot taller than the girls, widens her stance and bends down. Her awkward position makes my back twinge. She speaks at their eye level, probably giving orders to behave. Her sweatshirt hood flops over her face, and the girls laugh, shrill sounds that vibrate against Big Blue.

The clamor intensifies. "ECHO!" booms a girl. More whoops

ricochet off the mall's brick siding. I'd forgotten the giddy screech of tweens.

"HOOT! HOOT!" calls Colleen.

"Are you encouraging them?" The sky, bruised purple and black, swells with a pink blush. Visibility increases, and I see the girls smile.

"ECHO!"

Colleen yells over the din: "Hurry up and get the rest of your troop. We have to hustle for sunrise."

Doesn't Colleen realize we can walk to the top in thirty minutes? Yet moving the group uphill could be like herding cats, and I'm glad Colleen wants them to hurry.

Leader Deb lopes beside us and raises her right hand over her head. The girls raise their hands, too. Mouths stop. Leader Deb speaks softly to us: "The others in the troop went home around 2:00 a.m." With no further explanation, she lowers her hand: "Scouts, let's have quickie intros, and then, we go."

The tallest girl stretches her neck. Her head moves forward: "I'm Mikayla. Those other girls went home because they got scared, but my mom said we had to stay."

Leader Deb stretches her neck, too. I should have noticed the mother-daughter resemblance. She sighs: "The cotton candy machine played a saccharine tune all night long. I called security, and they unplugged it, but there was a backup battery that couldn't be removed. The song played every fifteen minutes."

"It was creepy," lisps the girl with purple braces. She slides her tongue over the bands. "I'm Rennie."

The smallest one says, "My real name is Jessica, but my grandma calls me Bit, you know, for Little Bit." She tugs at her brown hair. "They said the machine was haunted, but I wasn't afraid."

How young they are, I think, to be away from home for a night, sleeping at the mall. No wonder they got scared.

"My mom let us have free cotton candy," brags Mikayla.

"It got stuck in my braces." Rennie curls her lips in a funnel shape.

Bit combs fingers through her snarled bangs. "Some got in my hair."

Colleen claps loudly: "Can you walk fast?"

The girls shrug.

Colleen fails to register their lack of enthusiasm. She raises her left arm and clenches her fist. The girls stare quizzically. I'm thankful they don't ask what the gesture means, for Colleen will crank out a whopper. "I'll let you in on a secret," she says. "When the Boy Scouts hiked this trail, they were slow. I bet we get there before they did."

What Boy Scouts? I elbow Colleen, but the girls are hooked, and they fall in beside her. We traipse across the parking lot, dimly lit from towering lights that fade as we step onto the hard-packed dirt.

"We don't need flashlights," says Mikayla. "I can see."

Bit extends her right arm and waggles her fingers. "Yeah, like opening your eyes under water."

I blink as if looking through cellophane and step tentatively, same as the others.

"Keep your flashlights ready," commands Leader Deb.

"Always prepared," says Colleen. "The scouting motto, right?"

The girls laugh and scurry ahead. Light filters through a gray scrim unlike the black velvet cloaking the valley below us. I recall how our troop began its trek down by the river, and by the time we reached this plateau, most of us had blisters. We never imagined a mall being built on the hillside, any more than we could have envisioned the Agnes Flood or the recovery money that funded construction hundreds of feet above the water. Now bankruptcy looms large, another sign of the times.

"This trail's a mess," sneers Mikayla. She lengthens her stride to avoid paper cups, snack wraps, and beer cans.

"We'll pick up trash on our way out," says Colleen. "Good thing you have your bags."

Rennie disagrees, "I'm using mine for arrowheads."

Arrowheads? Where did she get that idea? My eyes fix on Colleen.

"Everybody picks up trash for Earth Day," reminds Coleen.

Leader Deb arches her spine: "I don't recall you saying anything about that."

Colleen murmurs: "Lack of sleep impairs memory."

Leader Deb laughs, and the group walks on. I grip Colleen's arm and hiss, "You can't have them pick up trash. We don't have any gloves. And what about the custodial crew?" After Colleen organized the First Annual Mall Parking Lot Cleanup Day, the crew got pissed off, saying it made them look bad, and worse, they could get fired. Colleen, stunned by their accusations, yammered about the value of community service and how one person's involvement can make a huge difference. The custodians felt otherwise, grinding their teeth until Colleen promised: "No more."

Colleen snaps at me, "We'll be finished before those guys get to work. The girls need to understand they can create change. You too."

I balk, having endured many of her taunts, totally unfounded. In fact, I drive her in Big Blue whenever she launches a new cause. I've told her to focus on one issue, rather than bounce like a ping-pong ball, but my reality checks have yet to settle her. A few days ago, she was rabid, foaming about climate change and how people need to look beyond themselves. Ha, Colleen should know.

The trail climbs gently, and to the north, we view tailings, deposits of rock and aggregate dug from mines. The treeless gaps lack the pattern of farm fields, yet the zigzags shine as if sewn with galvanized ribbon. Only the trick of dawn's light could provide synchronicity, for the old roads that used to haul coal, remnants of anthracite mining, have permanently scarred the terrain.

Colleen notices my gaze: "From a distance, the hills look pretty, huh?"

I nod, and Colleen uses my silence to blather about her supposed book. Even though I try to tune her out, she always finds a reason to mention it: "This area could be part of my new chapter. I'd use photos if I had my camera."

She expects me to ask for details. No way. Bit overhears and points her finger skyward: "Look, the clouds are pink. Put them in your book."

"Makes me think of cotton candy," grumbles Leader Deb.

Rennie says: "Who has a cell phone? Take a picture."

Mikayla pouts: "I told you, Mom. I need a phone."

"The clouds are nice," murmurs Bit.

I smile, and Colleen says, "Admit it MK, you feel good out here."

Pressing my lips tight, lest she think I agree with her, I stare at the ground. Gravel mixes with the dirt and makes for unsure footing. The walk may take longer than we figured. Plus, Colleen wheezes and moves slowly. She pauses to tell the girls, "We'll be at the ridge just as the sun crests. Who wants the prize of seeing it first?"

"Me! I love winning stuff." Mikayla breaks into a trot. Rennie matches her pace. Bit follows them.

"Careful," calls Leader Deb. Her caution proves unnecessary. The girls get winded within 200 yards.

"You said it would be easy," complains Mikayla. "These rocks are ugly."

"I want breakfast," says Rennie.

"Donuts at the top," reminds Leader Deb. "Chocolate milk after we get back."

My teeth hurt from the thought of so much sugar, but the girls trill happily.

"Is that when we get the makeup?" asks Mikayla. "I want sparkle stuff."

"I want purple mascara," says Rennie.

"What's with makeup?" asks Colleen. "You're too young."

The girls aren't much past the age of making mud pies, yet they burst into laughter as if Colleen told a joke.

"The kiosk is opening early, just for us. Before any shoppers get there," says Mikayla.

"We get lots of free samples."

"And this is for your Journey Badge?"

"No, our Grooming Badge."

"What?"

Leader Deb lengthens her neck. "They promised us an Earth Day makeup class."

"Everything is free," says Bit. "They'll give us stuff to take home."

"Coupons too," adds Rennie.

Leader Deb explains, "The products are organic, no testing on animals."

Colleen walks with a labored gait, and like me, she must be wrangling with the new trends for scouts.

"Gross," yelps Mikayla.

"That's for sure," says Colleen.

"My shoes. Gross."

"You stepped in dog poop," screams Rennie.

"Gross!" holler the girls until Leader Deb raises her arm for quiet. Then we all check our shoes. Thankfully they're clean.

Mikayla twists to scour her waffle soles and stamps her feet. "Race you to the top," she whinnies to Rennie. They thrust their bags at Leader Deb and shift to a canter, arms bent, hands holding invisible reins.

"Stay clear of the rocks, could be copperheads," calls Leader Deb.

"Too early in the season for snakes," says Colleen. She and Leader Deb disappear beyond the bend where scruffy bushes flank the trail.

Bit lags by me. I offer to take her bag, and wordlessly, she hands it over. She breathes like a steam engine, and her short legs work double-time. I trudge along, feeling the strain that comes from infrequent exercise. Colleen and I used to walk mall laps on our breaks, but we quit after losing a few pounds. I vow to resume the workouts and try to muster encouraging words for Bit. Then I chide myself: Why did I let Colleen drag us out here? Most people will celebrate Earth Day at a festival in Riverside Park. Bands play folk music. Concessions sell veggie burgers and tofu-on-a-stick, served with recycled paper products. The Luzerne-Wyoming Counties Department of Conservation distributes free tree seedlings, but few survive. People leave their little baggies on porches where the seedlings shrivel up, and that's why Colleen says incentives are needed to get them planted. Then I have a brain jolt: What about trees up here? I glance at the hardscrabble ground, so barren, it probably requires topsoil. Undoubtedly, I learned such details in earth science, but I don't recall.

Bit slows. Her voice is squeaky: "I've never seen a sunrise. What if we're too far away?"

"You can't miss it," I assure her, glancing at the clouds, now splashed with grenadine. If Colleen notices, she'll start crooning: *Just another tequila sunrise.*

"What if we're not there in time?" worries Bit.

"The sun comes up no matter where we are."

She jerks her head right, and then left. Does she think the sun will sneak past us? Bit reaches for my hand, and I almost yank it away, so startled by her gesture. I'd expect a much younger child to hold hands, and even though she's tiny, she must be about eleven. "Your skin feels like my mom's."

What an odd comment. Maybe the mall campout was her first night away from home? A drum beats in my chest: how I missed my mother when we were apart.

"But the thing is, you look kind of like my grandma."

I stumble on loose rock yet recover quickly. Have I aged so much? My daughter is grown, living halfway across the country, but I'm not a granny yet, and only recently colored gray roots. Then I brighten. Around here, many women become grandmothers in their thirties, and as I'm way beyond there, Bit might be complimenting me. I smile at her.

"I'm staying with my grandma," she says, and swallows hard. "My mom stole the money and can't show her face."

I grasp her hand more firmly and process how her mom is the skinny oxycodone mom. Then I share what I rarely tell others, "When I was your age, I stayed with my grandmother, too."

"Your mom do drugs?"

Breath catches in my throat. I hesitate to dredge the memory, still raw after decades. What words can explain how meds and chemo made her a stranger? My voice goes flat: "My mom was in the hospital."

"Did that work?" she asks in a high pitch. "Every night I pray really hard."

"HURRY!" bellows Colleen. "The sun won't wait."

We jog, no longer holding hands, owing to our mismatched sizes. Bit gasps from the exertion, yet she keeps three steps in front of me. Occasionally she glances over her shoulder and blinks. Her mouth hangs open.

"We're getting closer," I say. Up ahead, Mikayla and Rennie leap, waving.

Abruptly Bit stops and squares-off to face me. She extends her arms like a crossing guard, so I can't get past. "Right there," she says, chin thrust forward.

"What?" I pivot and squint at the opposite hill where an amber rim peeks over the dark tips. Within seconds, a butter-scotch disc takes shape.

"Sunrise, I can't believe it!" Bit cups her hands to her forehead like a visor and surveys the horizon, spiked red, purple, and orange. "I love this."

The golden orb ascends, casting its pristine hue on landscape ravaged by mines. For a moment, the whole world glistens. "Make a wish," I prompt.

"Will you make one, too?"

"Sure," I agree, wondering what possessed me to talk of wishes. Colleen is the one to encourage playful exchange. I turn and scan the expanse for her and the rest of the group. The white light exposes a harsh underbelly: mine tailings. Never has the abandoned landscape looked so bleak. Perhaps Colleen could spin a positive yarn, expecting me to say something nice, but I lack the words.

Bit follows my gaze and lowers her hands. Her eyes narrow to mere slits.

I sigh, and then remember a feature in *The Riverside Gazette* about land reclamation programs near Pittsburgh, the other side of the state. The place was an armpit, but trees and vegetation made it beautiful, and it has become a tourist destination. Now the local conservation department wants to jump on the bandwagon, holding public meetings to initiate similar efforts.

Wyoming and Luzerne counties are trying to combine resources like they do for the Departments of Mental Health and Aging.

"Did you make your wish?" asks Bit.

"I have to think." This area, so scalped by mining, makes me question if improvements are even possible. The counties have little money for new endeavors, and I'm not sure people care about the mines that closed years ago. I can hear Colleen: *Out of sight. Out of mind.* Yet I suppose attitudes could change.

"Awesome!" calls Mikayla.

"We saw it first," brags Rennie.

Bit, hands on her waist, whispers to me, "If they find out I saw it before them, they won't believe me. They'll say I was too slow—or too little." She shifts from foot to foot. "I don't have to tell them I saw it first. It can be our secret."

"Okay."

She rolls back her shoulders and grows taller. Her voice is strong, "I want to come here next year. Maybe I'll bring my mom. The whole troop can come with us."

"Sounds like a plan," I say and make my wish. Then I try to picture the hillside with greenery, certain we deserve more than forsaken blight. The Girl Scouts would welcome a service project, and I smile with thoughts of them planting trees. Yet I know better than to say anything to Colleen when I reach her, or pronto, she'll have us charging down the trail so I can drive her to Riverside Park for the free seedlings. I won't mention anything until we get back to the mall.

Bit marches, knees pumped high: "The sun makes me feel good."

"Me, too." Beams of light spread warmth as I envision baby Christmas trees, young shoots of maple and oak. The prime time for planting will begin in a few weeks after the danger of frost gets lifted. Surely the scouts can earn a badge for their efforts. Even better, Colleen can exult with the focus she needs and claim the tree planting project as her own idea.

The sun climbs bright and promising as we join the group. What will Colleen say when I offer to drive her in Big Blue?

DAMN STITCH

TIFFANY stood behind the crowd of runners, arms at her side, and hoped to appear less awkward than she felt. Ahead of her, participants in bright athletic gear clustered shoulder to shoulder, scuffling their feet as they established position. Did they stand close to ward off the cold? Many wore shorts or cropped leggings, hardly suitable for Thanksgiving in Northeast Pennsylvania, yet Tiffany guessed they'd warm up once they got moving.

"Twenty minutes to blast off," bellowed the announcer into a microphone. Danny "Downbeat" Brown, a DJ from radio station Froggy 101, croaked his signature *Ribbet-Ribbet*. The runners laughed as he danced atop a flatbed truck parked in front of them.

Tiffany rocked on her heels and scanned the bobbing heads. Where were Colleen and MK, her coworkers from the mall? They'd signed up together as a group. Maybe they tried to call her? Tiffany's sweatpants didn't have pockets, so she left her cell phone in the car. Surely, they'd look for her back here. No way would they expect to find her up front with the elite runners. Tiffany was lean enough to fit in with the athletes, but she lacked their enthusiasm. She had avoided exercise since childhood, begging off on tag or kickball, games that made her sticky, snot bubbling from her nose. Why had Colleen and MK talked her into this? She curled her hands inside her sleeves, warming her fingers, and inhaled sharply. Ugh: the muddy stench. Water View Park, the staging area for the Turkey Trot, butted smack up to the Susquehanna River.

More runners pressed in beside her. Some were draped with plastic trash bags like ponchos, undoubtedly to ward off the chill. Not a bad idea, thought Tiffany, assuming they'd discard the bags after they started the race. She considered moving behind them, so they wouldn't notice she didn't have a trash bag but feared drawing attention to herself. Tiffany wasn't the type to get up early for a fundraiser. Yet part of her welcomed the event, and that's what she had to remember.

"Get the blood pumping!" announced Downbeat. He cranked up the volume on huge, black speakers, the size of refrigerators. Piano riffs mixed with swirling guitar chords. Tiffany wanted to cover her ears. She had expected to hear something country, not some oldies tune that still got played for pep rallies and high school graduations. The crowd cheered and sang along to "Don't Stop Believin'." Tiffany balked at their singing. They droned on and on like karaoke gone bad.

A commotion up front disrupted the momentum. Tiffany rose on tiptoe and spied a big, red-haired woman rocking her hips to the heavy bass. Only Colleen would dare to rump-bump through the crowd. Hand held high, she waved in Tiffany's direction. Her other arm, bending and rowing like it was a paddle, forced runners to step aside.

"Why are you way back here?" laughed Colleen as she reached Tiffany. "You look stiff enough to walk the plank."

Tiffany widened her eyes. Colleen, of considerable girth and older than her mother, wore a neon yellow sport shirt with Lycra tights.

"I got these at a closeout sale at Lady Footlocker," bragged Colleen. She smoothed her palms from her ribs to waist, coming to rest on her hips. "Feels good, like I've got on Spanx, holds everything nice and firm."

Tiffany glanced down at her own navy-blue sweats, worn throughout high school for gym class. She planned to throw them away after graduation last year, but now was glad she'd kept them.

"Where's MK?" asked Colleen.

Tiffany liked MK and how she drove that big old blue car like it was something special. She gave Tiffany unsold issues of *People* and *Cosmopolitan*, the covers ripped off as required by publishers. "I thought MK was giving you a ride."

Colleen extended her chest and grinned, "Klooch drove me here. He's at the registration tent, signing up as a late entry. He said he'd find us."

"Oh," said Tiffany. She'd seen Colleen line dancing with Klooch at Riverbed Tavern. He was built like a football player, a good size for Colleen, who'd been married when she was young, but never talked about those days or her divorce.

The singing continued and thundered more loudly, distorted by echoes reverberating from boulders on the other side of the river. Colleen whirly-gigged her hips and elbowed Tiffany, an attempt to get her shaking, too. "Warms you up."

"I did my stretching," said Tiffany.

The song ended. Colleen exhaled thoughtfully. "What's taking Klooch so long? Where's MK? We should have planned a meeting spot. They must be looking for us."

Tiffany nodded despite a sense of relief. It might be best if they didn't show. That way, no one would notice if she snuck off after the starting gun sounded. Tiffany figured she'd keep pace with the crowd until they rounded the parking lot, but when they came to the hill, where willow bushes flanked the road, she could pretend her shoelaces needed tightening, and then, as soon as she stepped away from everyone else, she'd steal back to her car.

"What's got you smiling? That funky chicken dude?" asked Colleen.

"Gobble, gobble," chortled a man in a fuzzy, yellow chicken suit, offset by knee-length red and white striped stockings, complete with a beak-shaped head piece and a dangling, red comb. He flapped his arms and jogged along the sidelines. "Gobble, gobble."

"Does he think he's wearing a turkey costume?" snorted Colleen.

Tiffany was relieved she didn't call him over or gobble back at him. Colleen had convinced her and MK to enter the Turkey Trot. Hardly athletic, all three had spent the past month walking laps at the mall during their breaks. Colleen would meet them at the food court and they'd circle out past American Eagle and Sears, both now closed along with JC Penney. Colleen said leases weren't offered for the empty retail spaces, unlike Borders, which had closed and reopened as Books-a-Million.

Each time they walked, Tiffany speculated which store would pull out next. She repeated the rumors that percolated while she was serving customers at the Java Bean: *The entire mall could be closing. Some investor in China wants the place as a trucking depot for Marcellus Shale.* But Colleen said not to worry yet. The deal could take months, maybe a year. Her assertion did little to brighten Tiffany's view. "I can't blow twenty bucks for a race when I might be out of a job."

"That kind of thinking gets you nowhere," warned Colleen.

"Hmmm," muttered Tiffany, her brain bogged down with uncertainty: Would she need food stamps? Assisted housing? As Tiffany imagined the worst, Colleen had blustered about the power of positive thinking, claiming the Turkey Trot promoted a good cause. To prove her point, she paid Tiffany's entry fee. The fundraiser benefitted Santa Fest, held at the Our Lady of Perpetual Help Outreach Center. This past Christmas, it became obvious that the number of needy kids had increased well beyond the supply of donated clothes and toys. Raising money for holiday gifts would prevent children from leaving empty-handed.

Tiffany cringed at the thought of poor kids not having presents, and for the first time all morning, looked with pride at the swell of participants. The economic downturn hurt many, yet these people had pledged donations and then gotten up early on their day off. They revealed a generosity she failed to consider. Or maybe they just wanted to eat second helpings of pumpkin pie minus a concern for calories? She bent from the waist and touched her toes, mimicking the motions of those near her. After resuming an upright position, she placed her hands on her hips and twisted from side to side. Tiffany wanted to extend her arms to stake her personal space, but she knew she couldn't.

"Don't you love this? All these people," said Colleen. "There's way more than I expected. What do you think, a few hundred?"

"Hard to guess," said Tiffany.

Colleen tugged on the participation number pinned to her chest. "Mine says 272. I got it last night with my registration packet." She squinted at Tiffany's sweatshirt. "Where's your number bib?"

"I didn't think I needed one if I'm not running. We're walkers, right?"

"It doesn't matter if you run or walk," sighed Colleen. "You're supposed to wear a number bib."

"No one told me."

"If we had more time, we could get you one at the registration tent."

Her comment affirmed Tiffany's sense that she didn't belong here. But she couldn't leave now that Colleen had found her. Or at least until Tiffany ditched her and the others after the race started.

"Fifteen minutes," roared Downbeat. He played a new tune,

rollicking with an accordion's oom-pahs and da-da-da. The crowd laughed.

"Not the chicken song," moaned Tiffany. Da-da-da-da-da-da drummed vigorously as people raised their arms and formed bird beaks with their hands. They tapped their fingers four times, and then flapped their arms another four beats, whereupon they wriggled down, shaking backsides like tail feathers. Spare me, thought Tiffany.

Downbeat chased the chick-a-turkey across the flatbed truck. The tempo increased. People flapped arms like poultry on steroids. Colleen gyrated and wing-elbowed Tiffany. More runners flapped with the brood. Where had they come from? A woman wheezing to Tiffany's right bumped against her. She had the orange frizz of a bad perm, not so different from Tiffany's mom. Last year for Thanksgiving, her mom went to the Mohegan Sun Casino with her new boyfriend, Alex. He said there was an all-you-can-eat-buffet for fifteen bucks. Her mom had whispered, "I'll bring you a doggie bag if I can."

Now her mom lived five hours northwest of here, in Warren, where Alex had a job driving a water truck for Marcellus Shale drilling. Her mom worked at the 7–11, easy walking distance from the trailer park where she and Alex had a doublewide with all the other newcomers in the fracking boom. Right before her mom left, she told Tiffany the rent was paid through December for the apartment they had lived in for the past three years, the longest Tiffany had ever stayed in the same place. Her mom smiled like she'd given Tiffany a winning lottery ticket. "When I was your age, I had a kid, you, and we lived in a basement with Brian at his parents' house. We didn't have a car. You're lucky. You can go places. You got a high school diploma."

What good was that? Tiffany grimaced. Having opted to finish high school rather than drop out like most of her friends, she had also worked part-time, saving money for a move to the Jersey Shore, where she believed her diploma would get her a decent job. Yet, so far, nothing had come together like she envisioned.

"Are you okay?" asked Colleen as the chicken song ended.

"Too early to be outside," said Tiffany. The last thing she needed was for Colleen to promote the bright side of life in a voice that made Tiffany want to puke. All the same, she was glad Colleen had made her promise to attend the post-race Thanksgiving dinner at the outreach center. No way could she drive ten hours roundtrip to her mom's place, especially since staying the night was out of the question. Tiffany needed to be at the Java Bean by 6:00 a.m. because the mall opened early on Black Friday.

Plus, her mom hadn't invited her. "Alex is taking me to Presque Isle Casino," she'd said.

Colleen waved at a group of men, most with gray hair, and beckoned for them to squeeze in close. Tiffany recognized the Wednesday mall walkers, their red jackets embossed with the word PUMPERS.

As the men jostled beside her, Tiffany heard Colleen tell the woman with the orange frizz, "They had heart bypass surgery. Mercy Hospital gives them the jackets if they keep to their exercise program."

"Ten minutes!" roared Downbeat.

Tiffany sniffed Aqua Velva aftershave. The scent tickled her nostrils, and she remembered watching her granddad dab it against his cheeks. After he retired from Penn Electric, he moved to Florida, but Tiffany hadn't visited. She lacked the cash, and his girlfriend didn't like company.

Downbeat's tunes went from bad to worse as he played "We Are the Champions." What kind of people liked oldies?

"Here! We're here!" screamed Colleen, jumping up and down like a cheerleader.

Klooch smiled broadly, growing larger as he moved toward them. The long sleeves of his black technical shirt emphasized thick muscles. "Excuse me . . . Excuse me," he said as people moved out of his way. Tiffany was certain he'd crush toes if he stepped on them. Maybe that's why no one complained about having to move aside?

MK followed behind Klooch, brown hair pulled into a ponytail with a green bow like a kid rather than a middle-aged woman. "I couldn't find you until I saw Klooch," she panted. Beside her was Tad Hajduk with a camera suspended from a strap around his neck.

Colleen arched her eyebrows like crescent moons. She whispered to Tiffany, "MK's hanging out with Hottie, but she doesn't want me to know it yet—being as he could have had a thing for me. But I think they're good together."

"Right," said Tiffany. Last month, Colleen and MK had dragged her along to his photography exhibit at the Downtown Arts, a dusty brick building near the railroad tracks. The area was so dreary it made her want to leave, and if she had driven her own car, rather than ridden with them in Big Blue, she'd have gotten the hell out of there, for sure. Yet after Tiffany walked inside, the sunflowers painted at the entrance surprised her, as did his photos. Hottie, as Colleen called him—but not to his face—had assembled a montage with the theme of Unexpected Wonder. Tiffany recognized that many of the scenes in the images had been shot near Tunkhannock and Wilkes-Barre and was amazed at how his depictions roused feelings of respect. The barns, lumber mills, and coal breakers stood proud, a reminder of long ago prosperity. But his best photos showed elderly ladies outside Golden Touch Beauty Shop, their hands cupped like sugar scoops as they smiled and patted their freshly coifed poufs.

"Five minutes and counting," cried Downbeat.

"Good to see you," said Hottie, radiating charm. "I'm not running the 5K, just taking photos at the finish line."

Tiffany gulped. 5K? Colleen said they were doing a 3K. He must be mistaken.

Hottie removed the lens cap from his camera. "I want to take a group shot before the race starts."

"Thought you'd never ask," laughed Colleen, insisting they all link arms.

"Victory," cheered Klooch.

Hottie clicked the shutter.

"TWO MINUTES!"

Before Hottie left, he brushed the back of his hand to MK's cheek. She reached up and laced her fingers with his.

Colleen nudged Tiffany. "See what I mean?"

Whatever, shrugged Tiffany. The air swooshed as runners shook to keep warm. All breathed deeply. How much longer did they have to wait? Tiffany raised her arms above her head, reaching in the air and pretended to climb a ladder.

The bald pumper with liver spots flecking his cheeks and neck winked at her. "Breakfast at Tiffany's," he joked, same as when she served him at the Java Bean. Tiffany could never remember his name, but he always tipped her a quarter, and she thanked him, unlike Shayna, the other employee, who flared her nostrils and hissed that he was cheap.

"Colleen says you want to move to the Shore," he said.

"Wish I could. But before I can leave here, I need to find a job at the beach."

He patted his heart, "If you're at the Shore, no more breakfast at Tiffany's."

"Like that's going to happen."

"You and me," he said, crooking his finger. "We need to talk after the race."

"Don't tell me the mall is closing. Everybody's talking about it."

He shook his head no, pink from the cold. "My son owns a gelato shop at Secret Harbor. Not some dump like those joints in Atlantic City. It's nice, three blocks from the ocean. His wife works there too, but she's having a baby. Come spring, they'll need to hire a good server."

"You serious?"

"There's an apartment up top. Just right for somebody starting out."

She tried to process what he told her.

"COUNTDOWN TIME!"

Colleen grinned. She and Klooch gave Tiffany a thumbs-up. Electricity charged the air. In the distance, past the ocean of heads, and well beyond the river, puffy clouds floated in the sky. The sun pierced their gray undersides, sending forth rays like striated magnets, and they pulled at Tiffany with a strange gravitational force.

"Twenty . . . Nineteen . . . Eighteen . . ." The crowd undulated in waves of a fervent sea. She pivoted right, then left, noting how faces looked pensive. She wondered if she mirrored the same expression. Did she appear as out of sync as she felt?

"Ten . . . Nine . . ."

People breathed in rhythmic unison. Tiffany could almost hear their muscles ready to burst. She swallowed fast. What am I doing here? Could I really move to the Shore?

"Five . . . Four . . ." The crowd chanted with Downbeat.

"Get ready to go," said the bald man.

"Three . . . Two."

The starting gun exploded. Tiffany shot forward. "Celtic warrior!" screamed Colleen.

Hard sounds meshed with pounding feet on asphalt. Spectators blew horns and yelled: "Go! Go!" Their words hammered at

Tiffany's brain. Her rib cage expanded, making her chest lunge out as her legs demanded: GO.

From behind her, she heard Colleen, "Hold up, we're walkers."

Tiffany had never been competitive, never participated in school sports; but now, as she dashed with those beside her, she wanted to go fast, faster than any of them. Tiffany didn't care about her time. She just wanted to go, get out ahead, away from the roiling crowd, the good causes, the thunderous motorcycles leading the way.

The group charged past the parking lot where she planned to stop. Tiffany laughed, but the panting, the rapid breaths almost choked her. She coughed, and then inhaled carefully, concentrating on each breath, knowing she could move on her own. How she placed didn't matter. Her enthusiasm surged: charging, charging. Delight bubbled from within, and she laughed again, grinning at how she must look like she was meant for this. The feeling grew stronger. Then, like a gong sounding in her ear, she heard: *Secret Harbor, Secret Harbor.* Tiffany had hope: Go. Go.

The road ascended from the park with a steady climb. Her lungs ached. She plodded on as sleek-bodied runners wove past her. Tiffany urged her feet to continue and noted how the spectators had thinned out. Leafless trees stood like watchmen. There were no cars. Tiffany figured traffic had been blocked off for the race, yet not many people drove on the road anyway, other than fishermen or hunters. Why hadn't Tiffany seen the race volunteers? During the warm-up, Downbeat announced they'd be placed every quarter mile. Had thinking about that gelato shop caused her to miss them? Could she make a home at the Jersey Shore?

The pavement leveled off at the T-stop where runners bounded across River Road. Tiffany saw an orange cone. Was this only a quarter mile? A man in a plaid jacket stood beside the cone. "Looking good," he yelled. She felt relieved, knowing the course would shift down to the flats. Energy steamed her muscles. An adrenaline high took over. She wanted to hold hands with the people around her, singing, running, celebrating. She seemed to light an internal firecracker.

Warmth spread through her core. She shook her arms and tried to cool off, but the action made her hotter. Her temperature soared. She needed to take off her sweatshirt. How to remove it without stopping? First, she wriggled her right arm from the sleeve, then her left. She felt cocooned with her arms pressed inside the pullover. Her fingers stretched below to the hem, where she grabbed material, yanked it up, and swooped the sweatshirt over her head. She tossed it to the gravel berm and hailed her success. Yet her tank top, wet with perspiration, made her falter from the cold. She shivered, and then exhaled with a sharp huff that stopped her teeth from chattering. If she moved to the Shore, could she run near the ocean before going to work?

"You can do it," cheered a woman in a fluorescent green jacket. Beside her, two toddlers waved RUN DAD posters, almost as big as they were.

Why had Tiffany hated the mile run in gym class? As a senior, she feigned menstrual cramps, earning an excuse to skip the run and sit on the sideline bench with the other girls who did not participate. Now exhilaration whistled her on. Her feet zipped along the ground despite the annoying song that played in her brain. She tried to get it out of her head, but the tune had slow-burn intensity: "Don't Stop Believin'."

Up ahead, she saw a man wave a red flag back and forth. Was she approaching the mile marker? Had she missed a cone? As she got closer, she heard the flag man yell: "Walkers to the left. Runners to the right." Tiffany noticed yellow tape wrapped around the trees, same for the pole topped by a street sign. It was the kind of tape used at crime scenes. "Walkers to the left. Runners to the right," repeated the man. Then she realized the tape indicated separate course routes. Why the split? What was the difference?

She thought about slowing to ask the flag man but decided to keep with the pack. They turned to the right where River Road curved upward. Hemlock trees paralleled the road, dwarfing the runners as they plodded up, up, up. Feet thumped against the asphalt. Tiffany's thighs felt heavy, her tongue thick from breathing hard. How could she be so hot when it was cold outside?

They passed the abandoned state hospital grounds, built far from town. The place had closed before Tiffany was born, yet it still seemed creepy. The sprawling acres, littered with weeds and leaves, housed a three-story stucco building, its windows broken, probably shot out by drunks.

Onward, whispered Tiffany, eager to join the runners where the road leveled off. Her feet welcomed the even keel, and she gloried for the length of a football field. All too soon, the road dipped and veered south. Runners galloped downhill. Tiffany increased her gait, motored by the urge to clap. She pranced and edged closer to the man in front of her. His yellow shirt flashed in the sun, luring her to greater speeds. They ran in syncopation, and she could almost taste the saltiness of his sweat. It made her think of ocean swells, the pounding surf. The runners shifted together, powered by gravity, faster, faster. Tiffany shook her fingers. Then, without warning, the man slowed: "Stitch!" he yelped.

He clutched his stomach, and Tiffany, unable to stop, rammed into his backside. The woman behind Tiffany plowed into them, and they all tumbled over, thudding onto the road. Other runners went down. A woman with wet, slippery skin slid on top of Tiffany. For a moment, Tiffany couldn't breathe. She squirmed to the left, wormlike, and got kicked in the head, her skull grinding against the asphalt. She closed her eyes. A shoe stomped onto her cheek. Tiffany was caught by a trap of bodies. People yelled, static commands. Then someone, a woman, grabbed Tiffany's arm, dragging her out of the pile, away from the runners who arose and surged forward. The woman, with a gray frosted perm, appeared sprightly as she reached under Tiffany's armpits and hoisted her upright. "Are you hurt?"

Tiffany opened and closed her mouth like a fish. She watched as the man in the yellow shirt hobbled back onto the course.

"Does anything feel broken?" Thin lines etched the woman's cheeks, and they deepened as she questioned Tiffany. "Is your head okay?"

"Yeah," said Tiffany, a quiver in the back of her throat.

"Let's get you over to the side." The woman guided Tiffany toward a baby-sized Christmas tree, the kind that filled the woodlands, but never got big. "I'm Pat. I'm a volunteer."

"Like Colleen?"

"Colleen?" Pat tilted her head, eyebrows pinched.

"You know, with the walkers," murmured Tiffany as runners sailed by them. Could she catch up?

Pat kept a firm hold on Tiffany's arm. "Why don't you sit down, and I'll get you some water."

Yes, water is what Tiffany needed. She bent from the waist, pressed her hands to the ground, and lowered to a kneeling position. Then she pushed back to sit cross-legged on the hard turf. Only a few stragglers ran by them. How far were they from the finish line? Did a crowd await them at the outreach center?

"What's your name, dear?" asked Pat, handing Tiffany a plastic bottle of water.

Tiffany took a long drink and flinched when a few drops fell from her lips to her chest.

"What's your name?" Pat had a take-charge voice like a teacher.

Blinking, Tiffany kept the bottle to her lips, and blocked the spout with her tongue.

"I'll call for some help." From her jacket pocket, Pat retrieved a flip-top phone with huge buttons on the face, the kind used by senior citizens.

Tiffany watched for more runners, but none appeared. Could the entire group have passed by without her realizing it?

Pat spoke softly into the phone. "To look at her, she seems okay. But she may have hit her head. She hasn't told me her name. If she had a bib with a number, we could check with registration, but it must have fallen off."

Tiffany strained her ears for sounds of the pack. She was alone, left behind.

"To be safe, send the ambulance."

"No! I don't need an ambulance," shouted Tiffany. She tossed the water bottle and pushed up into a standing position.

"Whoa," said Pat, grabbing hold of Tiffany's elbow.

"I'm supposed to be with the walkers."

"She doesn't want the ambulance."

Tiffany shifted from foot to foot.

"I'll ask her." Pat peered at Tiffany. "Can we give you a ride in our van? There's no charge."

Tiffany shrugged.

"I think she'll take it. See you in a few minutes." Pat returned the phone to her pocket and took Tiffany's hand in hers. "Do you have any pain?"

"Nu-uh." Nothing hurt. Tiffany didn't feel much of anything. Yet as Pat kneaded her palm, she was soothed by the woman's gentle touch. How odd to be so comforted by a stranger. The sensation made Tiffany smile.

"That's a good sign," said Pat.

The Luzerne-Wyoming Counties senior citizen van, an old, half-sized school bus painted cobalt, sped into view. Tiffany laughed: "Breakfast at Tiffany's."

Pat laughed, too. "Do you feel well enough to take a few steps?"

Tiffany padded forward. The van's muffler drummed with the echo of the long-gone runners. She could go after them if she wanted. And then she thought about moving to the Shore. Was Secret Harbor the place for her? Maybe yes, she thought, and stepped forward.

"Very good," said Pat.

A stinging sensation prickled Tiffany's face. She rubbed her cheek and watched the van ease to the side of the road. A man wearing a baseball cap got out and waited by the open door. He waved for them to come over.

Had the runners crossed the finish line? Tiffany imagined the sound of applause and took giant strides toward the van.

"You made it." He smiled at Tiffany. She glanced in the side mirror, certain to find the waffle print of a shoe stamped on her cheek, but her skin just looked pink. Her face seemed frightened.

Pat touched her shoulder. "Should we take you home?"

Breathing slowly, Tiffany nodded and moistened her lips.

Pat's eyes shone, black, like polished coal. "Let's go."

Tiffany grabbed the safety-grip and stepped into the van that smelled of pine air freshener. Then she noticed a St. Christopher statue, no taller than a clothespin, displayed on the dash. Lots of old people put them in their cars, even MK, on the dash of Big Blue. Did they really believe the statue could protect them? Tiffany slumped against the seat bench, yearning to curl into a ball and hug herself.

"Where to?" called the driver as he started the ignition.

Pat turned from the front passenger seat and squinted, "Tell us your address."

Tiffany kept her hands at waist level, folding and unfolding them.

"Where should we go?"

"Home," whispered Tiffany, shrinking away from the woman, her questions, and the scent of fake pine. She felt like she could mold into the seat and never move.

"Yes, dear, but where?"

"I want to go home," blurted Tiffany. She bit the inside of her lip, making fists as she punched at the seat. "I want to go home."

But she couldn't think of where to tell them to take her.

LIQUIDATE

COLLEEN sits in the passenger seat of Big Blue, rattling a key chain like she's the Salvation Army bell ringer. "Bet you're wondering how I got these keys?"

I shrug, figuring she'll blab no matter what.

Jangle-jangle.

The car echoes with her clanking as I turn the steering wheel and guide Big Blue into a parking space near the food court's main entrance. In the past, these spots were prime real estate. Rarely could I snag one when racing to my shift at the bookstore. But today the entire lot is up for grabs, not even a security vehicle graces the expanse. The mall closed eight weeks ago. After months of blitzkrieg liquidation, Colleen and I said goodbye to the jobs we'd known for years. Yet Colleen, ever primed by her routine at the Hallmark store, maintains a daily greeting. She texted me early this morning, using all capitals: GOT SURPRISE 4 U.

I've made a rule against responding to Colleen before 10:00 a.m., especially with us not working.

But Colleen, never one to hold off, texted again: R U OK?

I placed the phone face-down on the kitchen table and debated drinking another cup of coffee. My nerves get jittery from too much caffeine, and I am trying to scale back. Plus, rising coffee prices along with my unemployment meant a budget constraint of no more than two cups.

The phone vibrated with yet another message. I peeked: I COME 2 U.

My abs tensed. Colleen doesn't have a car, and if someone gives her a ride, she might stay all day. I'd never get rid of her. With that disturbing realization, I called her number. She answered on the first ring. "What took you so long?"

"I was trying to meditate. The quiet clears my head."

She exhaled into the mouthpiece, creating a distortion that prevented me from clarifying her tone. Exasperation? Camaraderie? Or worse—concern for my well-being? Her voice revved, "You won't believe what I have to show you. We need to drive out to the mall."

"What for? There's nothing there."

Colleen laughed, "You'll understand when I show you."

How could I beg off? My non-schedule robbed me of excuses, and I feared she might find a way to come and get me. "I'll pick you up in an hour," I said flatly, lest she think I was too interested. Then I showered and put on jeans and a blue sweater so Colleen couldn't grouse about the gray sweats I'd slept in the night before and worn for the past two days.

Colleen leans across the passenger seat, shaking the key chain like a tambourine. She raises her hand to shoulder level and twists her wrist back and forth to jiggle the keys. Then she stops so abruptly, I speculate about the dramatic intent.

"It's natural to feel depressed," says Colleen. "But you have to stay positive. We're hardly down-and-outers. Think of us as between economic opportunities."

I cut the ignition. Big Blue sighs. The front end vibrates ominously, forcing me to tune out Colleen with reminders the mechanic gave me at a recent oil change. With his left eye going around and round, the mechanic said the pistons and compression rings were on borrowed time, and the repairs, if he could even get parts for the old engine, would far exceed its worth. Head bowed, I left there certain of one thing: no way would Big Blue ever go to a junk yard in Northeast Pennsylvania rusting with other cars on slag heaps at abandoned coal mines. My grandmother would never forgive me.

Colleen pats my arm: "Insomnia can be awful."

"What do you mean? I'm getting sleep." I don't tell her I wake up every few hours; that's nothing new, since I have handled interruptions in my sleep ever since I had a baby who didn't sleep through the night. So what if Jenna is grown and living in Chicago? The skill of plodding on after poor sleep is like riding a bicycle—once mastered, you can always pedal, though you may be wobbly if you're out of practice.

"Maybe you need Ambien, or some other drug?"

I grunt, "Like I can afford to see a doc."

"If you ask me, red wine is the best prescription for a good night's sleep."

"Spoken like an expert."

Colleen laughs, opens the passenger door, and then leans forward to tap the head of the St. Christopher statue on the dash. "Amazing how you keep this."

"Tradition," I say, recalling how my grandmother positioned the clothespin-sized figure with Peel-n-Stick, certain of St. Christopher's protection as she drove on roads that brought her perilously close to the Susquehanna River. She claimed he saved her from skidding out of control, ever proud of her driving record, save for a few fender benders she didn't like to mention. That's part of the reason I glue the statue back on whenever it comes loose. Thankfully my grandmother passed away before the church demoted him to non-sainthood. By maintaining his presence, I grant St. Christopher renegade status. Who knows? His spirit may keep me afloat.

"You're thinking negative again, aren't you?" scolds Colleen.

Before I can protest, she gets out, lumbers over to my side of Big Blue, and yanks open the door. She stands, arms crossed over a black fuzzy jacket. The key chain dangles from her ring finger as she taps her foot. I glance down at her leggings, tucked into boots, everything black. The faux suede boots muffle her show-off *thwomp thwomp* on the asphalt.

"You like my boots? I got them for a steal at Payless," she says. "They practically gave them to me."

Blowout sales punctuated the mall's final days. Professional liquidators, contracted at higher pay than we ever received, facilitated the disbursement of all merchandise, even the fixtures, lighting, shelves. I felt like we were in the vortex of a locust feeding frenzy. How could Colleen exult over getting a deal? Her boots are the clumsy kind worn by teenagers, and the foot part seems too short, making me wonder if her toes are scrunched up inside. On red-haired Colleen, the boots look like cast-offs from a Viking, the loot of a paltry raid.

I get out and lock Big Blue, force of habit, even though we're the only people in view. The cold air stings my nostrils. I scan the lot, noting how ice rims the perimeter. This is standard for March when humidity rises, promising warmth, only to disappoint after dark with temps that dip below freezing. All too often, black ice mars the roadways, and we were fortunate not to encounter any on our drive over.

"I can't imagine what this place will look like by summer," says Colleen.

I nod, strangely comforted by the familiar surroundings. The vacant mall is supposed to be converted into a massive depot, a staging area for Marcellus Shale drilling equipment: huge cranes, pipes, trucks, fencing and other kinds of machinery needed to extract natural gas from below the earth's surface. The fracking boom has scarred the northwest part of the state, and Colleen says the same will happen in Luzerne and Wyoming counties. The mall, with its proximity to I-81, has been heralded as an ideal location for setting up logistics.

"Turn off your brain," says Colleen. She positions her green, quilted purse higher on her shoulder. The bag is big enough to carry a bowling ball, which makes me wonder about the contents. I'm sure Colleen got it on sale and wants to show it off, though I pretend not to notice when it brushes against my elbow. Maybe she has notions of filling her bag with stuff that's been left behind? She'll be disappointed, for I've heard there's nothing left to take.

She links her right arm through mine and tugs me to the main door. The oversized monitor that welcomed us each day, its lights flashing with markdowns and special events, remains blank. Odd that it wasn't sold with everything else. I'd think it would have been taken for some sort of scrap value, rather than get left here and smashed to bits along with the walls destined for deconstruction—necessary measures so the trucks can pull up to the loading docks.

Colleen steps ahead of me, shakes the key chain, and then, one by one, inserts keys into two separate locks on the door's aluminum frame. "I know you're still wondering how I got these keys."

I clench my jaw, refusing to take the bait.

She can't hold off and turns to face me: "Klooch got them. He's friends with a guy who worked mall security. The dude was smart enough to keep the keys, knowing better than to hand them over before he got his last paycheck."

"If he hasn't gotten paid by now, he'll never get a dime."

Colleen sucks the back of her teeth.

Then I ask the question she has been waiting for: "Why did Klooch get those keys for you?"

"The man aims to please." Her voice is so smarmy I gag. Colleen has been hanging out with Klooch ever since he and another township-worker built sidewalk ramps for her nephew, Brandon, so he could maneuver his wheelchair to the high school. Brandon says Klooch is a nice guy, and I guess I agree. Klooch, a big man, looks good with Colleen when they whoop it up and dance at Riverbed Tavern. "He wanted to come with us. But with his job, he can't take the risk."

Risk? An alarm triggers in my brain. I step away from the door. "I don't need any trouble."

"Not to worry. They haven't posted No Trespassing signs. We're good to go."

She pulls open the heavy glass door, and against my better judgment, I follow her through the entrance to another glass door that she unlocks. As I step into the food court atrium, I expect to sniff coffee, but instead, my nose twitches from the dank odor. I feel like we've gone underground even though sun filters through the skylight. I stare ahead to the store fronts, eerily dark with their tomblike presence. "What the hell are we doing here?"

"A surprise," she reminds, all smiles like it's my birthday. She pounds her chest: "Change keeps us young."

"Say that when the unemployment runs out."

"Can't you understand? Life is most vital when we're at the edge of our comfort zone. That's when we refigure the essential plan."

Colleen must be reading self-help books again. If she spews more inspirational crap, I'll turn and march away.

She reaches into her bag and pulls out two skinny flashlights, the size of ballpoint pens. She hands me the red one and then shines her green light against the empty garage of storefronts. "Can you remember when this place opened?"

I sigh loudly, so she can't drag me down memory lane.

Colleen laughs: "*The Riverside Gazette* called it the Shoppers Cathedral."

Shopping had never interested me, and yet I was thrilled to get hired by Waldenbooks. When Borders bought them out, I was kept on, and after they went bankrupt, Books-a-Million took over. Best of all, they made me a manager. "My job was a godsend."

"Yeah," agrees Colleen. "Status."

"I don't know about that. I was just glad for a paycheck and shifts that let me off before Jenna got home from school."

Colleen turns in a circle, wielding her light like a wand. "Funny to think how you and I connected right here in the food court."

I click my flashlight on and off, making polka dots in space. "At first, we acted like we didn't know each other since we didn't hang out in high school," I remind her. "So much time had passed after we lost touch that when we got jobs at the mall, it was like we were new people."

"At midlife, no less," laughs Colleen.

My brain uploads a sequence of turning points: school, marriage, child, divorce, moving, job, and reconnecting with Colleen. Engrossed by those images, I plod along in semi-darkness, following Colleen past vacant store fronts. I shine my light into the former JC Penney, considered an anchor store, yet it was among the first to pull out as sales and profits tanked. Then my thoughts grind to a halt. No job.

Colleen picks up the pace, yet I hold back. The musky odor gets more intense, undoubtedly due to the filtration system not running without electricity. My flashlight casts a powerful beam despite its small size and it shines across the metal grates covering the entries where signs for retailers no longer appear. I visualize Bath & Body Shop, Lady Footlocker, and American Eagle. All gone.

"Pick up the pace," trumpets Colleen.

Is she rallying a Tour de Mall? The smell worsens. It's like a mausoleum. My throat constricts, same as when I enter a funeral home, wary that the sight of the deceased will create a final imprint. I prefer portraits of the living. "Wait up," I call.

Colleen pauses, and I reach her side. She holds her light under her chin and grimaces like kids do on Halloween, but this is not a fun house.

"Have you ever smelled the inside of a casket?" I ask.

"Stuffier in here than I thought it would be," she rasps.

I shine my light toward more storefront grates. They resemble the teeth of rats, sharks, menacing animals. A thud makes my ears strain.

Colleen hears it too. She steps closer to me.

Thud. Thud.

"What's that?"

"Probably nothing," she says. But she doesn't walk any further.

"Maybe somebody's here," I whisper, picturing crackheads or escapees from the Frackville Prison.

"There's no power. Who'd come in here?"

"My point exactly. Let's go."

Colleen gets my gist, and we turn around, seeking the dim light of the food court. "I wanted to give you my surprise at the Galleria," she says.

"They gutted it."

"The ceremonial effect would have been nice. But you're right, we should get out of here." She wheezes as we hustle through the ghostlike atrium, lunging for the glass doors to freedom. We step double-time, my arm out, right hand holding the key to Big Blue. Without speaking, we get in the car, hoisting our hips onto the seat.

I clip my seatbelt, turn on the ignition, and crank up the heat with an uncomfortable realization, "You didn't lock the doors."

Both of us stare through the windshield as if expecting to see someone.

Colleen takes a long cleansing breath. "I've never liked what locked doors represent—the shortcomings of humanity."

I laugh and she laughs with me. Buoyed by the sensibility that bonds us as friends, I shift from park to drive. Next thing, Big Blue stalls out. "I guess I turned on everything too fast," I say. "We'll have to wait a few minutes. Don't want to flood it."

She nods and takes another long breath. "Let me give you the surprise while we're sitting in here. It probably makes more sense anyhow." She fiddles with her bag and extracts a manila folder jammed with papers, a couple of inches thick. All smiles, she uses both hands and holds it high like a religious offering.

I press my palms against the steering wheel, expecting her to wax eloquent with some nonsense, but she shoves the folder at me, knocking my forearm. Lips pursed, I take the folder and open to a bunch of typed pages.

"It's my novel. What I sent with my application."

"All this typing came from you?" I am aghast. For years, Colleen has yammered about her supposed book, but I never thought she put anything to paper.

Colleen continues, "After Hottie got his job teaching photography at Anthracite University, he told me about their writing program and helped me to apply."

"You?"

"I didn't say anything in case I didn't get accepted."

"Makes sense, what with your age."

Colleen's voice gets high like she inhaled helium. "The director uses the term 'late bloomers' and says I'm perfect for their program."

What can I do but smile? I thumb through the folder. The type is blurry, owing to the fact that I forgot to bring my reading glasses. Somehow, my inability to discern what's printed seems a metaphor for Colleen's plan. Surely, she hasn't thought through the details. "How will you get there for class? It's not like you have money to buy a car. And what about tuition?"

"I got a partial scholarship, and the government gives grants for displaced workers."

Leave it to Colleen to wrangle a freebie.

"Guess what else? Mrs. Pavinsky says I can have her car in exchange for cleaning her house and driving her to Bingo."

"What about Carlos and Rosalina?" They moved next door to Mrs. Pavinsky, and I often see the whole bunch piled into her old Chrysler.

"They made enough money to fix their van," says Colleen. "Now with my help, they can have some free time, too. But Mrs. Pavinsky wants to keep watching their kids."

Ever a proponent of the barter system, Colleen employs an exchange mode learned from her way-back days of crochet vests and long, patchwork skirts. Maybe she's doing a good thing? Mrs. Pavinsky told us her son in Scranton wants to get rid of her car and put her in assisted living. Now, I guess, the help from Colleen, Rosalina, and Carlos allows Mrs. Pavinsky to stay in her home. Yet Colleen hasn't had her own vehicle for ages, and is clueless about the price of maintenance and gas. Besides, it's a long haul to the university. "It won't be cheap driving to class," I remind her.

"That's the best part. The program is low residency, meaning I go to campus for a couple of weeks in the summer, and the rest of the time, I work online. My nephew gave me his extra laptop."

"Am I the only one who didn't know about this plan?"

"Adaptation and change. It's the story of how people survive."

I lean forward to start Big Blue. Colleen puts her hand on my elbow. Her face is aglow, skin reflecting the red tinge of her hair, colored by Heather, her niece who graduated at the top of her high school class. Even though everyone expected her to attend Penn State like her older brother, she is enrolled at Empire Beauty School. "I haven't given my manuscript to anyone but you," says Colleen. Then she corrects herself, "Except the draft I sent to the university."

"What about Hottie?"

"He read a couple of chapters, and then he got too busy. Someone told me he's been hanging out with you."

My cheeks grow warm. I volunteer at the downtown arts center where Hottie has a studio, but I haven't told Colleen, wary she'll want to make something of it, especially since he's cooked me dinner a few times. He comes over to my place, too.

Colleen puts on her sing-song voice: "Klooch called me when he was driving to work yesterday morning. He said he saw Hottie come out of your house like he'd spent the night."

I blink and stare ahead.

Colleen laughs. "You can tell me what's going on when you're ready. No worries. I just wanted you to be the first to get this draft. You've been with me through most of it."

I should feel honored, but my emotions, too snarled for explanation, prompt me to restart the ignition. "I'll let it idle a bit, so we don't stall out again."

Colleen nods and turns on the radio. All we hear is static. She shuts it off, says nothing, and kneads her hands together. Her silence unsettles me. She sniffles and stares out at the mall-no-more. Her chest lifts as she rubs her eyes. Is Colleen getting maudlin? No. I want her to rant, pound her chest, rail about us getting laid off, about the businesses that went bankrupt after easy loans from banks, and about how the bailout smacked of economic collapse. But Colleen says zip. Her failure to respond does not bode well. Where's the Celtic warrior when I need her?

Then I get a brilliant idea. "How's about I treat you to lunch? Might be the last time I can afford it," I joke.

"It's kind of early for lunch."

Now I'm worried. Colleen never passes on a free meal. She looks at me, her lips turned down, and she speaks haltingly, "We'll always stay in touch, right?"

Perhaps I should share what I've reconciled, for she has listened to my dream of moving to an ocean town. I chose Point Pleasant for the happy-sounding name, certain I could wake up smiling. I even had a lead for a job at a gift shop. "I'm not going to Point Pleasant," I blurt. "Hurricane Sandy destroyed the place. It will take years to rebuild."

"I figured as much," says Colleen.

Same old know-it-all. Yet I'm relieved. "The engine's warm," I say, shifting Big Blue into drive. "The more I thought about leaving here, the more I realized, I didn't want to go. I've got roots here."

"You need to recognize what's really important in life," says Colleen.

We motor down the long driveway from the mall, looking out over the valley, where beyond, the hills rise to silver peaks. Usually by noon, the icy glaze has melted, so I'm surprised to see the glistening sheen.

"Nice to have clear skies for a change," she observes.

It is pretty, and I figure we should take advantage. "Let's take River Road," I tell her, making Big Blue purr. The route was my grandmother's favorite, mine too, despite the lack of guardrails. Much of the road parallels the river, and whenever I drive beside the Mighty Susquehanna, I'm soothed by something magical.

"Just watch out for black ice," she says.

"Now that's a switch. You're warning me about danger."

"Well, you have to admit, the weather's been unusual."

"Hmm," I say, hoping she doesn't start her crap about climate change and global weirding. At the end of the drive, I pull to the T-stop. My foot eases onto the brake. I look both ways before turning left. White crinkles of ice, as delicate as pralines, have formed on the roadside berm, same for the drainage ditch adjacent to the river. Surprised the ice hasn't melted, I keep to the posted speed of 40 miles per hour, glad to have enough time to savor the moment. All too often I've rushed past, failing to appreciate the glimmering water, its wide expanse. I stare across to the opposite shore where rocks sprout like mushrooms.

"Did you know Hottie wants to talk with you about his grant from the Humanities Council?" asks Colleen.

I keep mum about being with him when he got the award letter. He was ecstatic to receive the funds for expanding the arts center, and he insisted we celebrate at the Riverbed Tavern.

Colleen's voice speeds up. "With his job at the university, he needs to hire a site manager to register people for classes, arrange showings, handle publicity, and do sales for the gallery."

"A lot of that gallery stuff is kitsch," I say.

"I told Hottie you'd be perfect for the job."

This surprises me. "Oh."

"He agrees but thought you might be moving to the shore."

I press down on the gas pedal. Big Blue rumbles ahead. What would Colleen say if she knew Hottie and I had stayed at the bar for last call two nights ago? We realized the extra drinks meant we couldn't chance driving, so he walked me all the way back to my place. How we had laughed, feeling good. When we got to my front door, he said, "You make me realize what I've been looking for is right here."

"Want to come in?" I murmured.

My heart still races with thoughts of that night. Without realizing what I'm doing, I press harder on the gas. Big Blue charges ahead. Next thing I know, the tires lose traction, causing us to swerve left, then right, and we slide onto the berm.

"Black ice!" yells Colleen.

I turn into the skid, just like Triple A recommends. Or maybe it's the opposite? Frozen turf crunches below the tires. Colleen screams. I grip the steering wheel, frantically turning us in the other direction. Big Blue fails to respond. We careen down, scratching against bushes, nose edging toward the riverbank. Our speed increases. Fast. Faster. I hear Colleen gulp, or maybe it's me? Then we both scream as a magnetic force pulls Big Blue into the watery expanse.

Splash. Swoosh. Big Blue bucks up. We rock, sway, tack back and forth. I blink. Are we afloat?

"Get out," yells Colleen, kicking open her door. Big Blue lists to the driver's side. My head hits against the door frame, a dizzying whack, making my eyes flutter like I'm a kid on the Flume Ride. Everything gets fuzzy. What's going on? Why do my feet feel wet? Water seeps inside, rising past my ankles, my calves, with the cold so numbing, I can't move.

The river belches mud. The stench constricts my airways like a noose, and I gag, lungs tightening with thoughts of my grandmother and how she sprayed us with her Chanel perfume during cleanup from the Agnes Flood. Then I see her sitting beside me. How can this be? She is wedged between my hip and the driver's door, wearing her favorite blue pants suit, the one she had on when she bought Big Blue decades ago. I want to reach over and hug her, but my arms feel paralyzed. Even worse, she is kicking me away to the middle of the seat. I turn my head and spy the St. Christopher statue, appearing larger than ever. St. Christopher holds out his staff, and Jesus on his shoulder points for me to take it.

"Celtic warrior!" bellows Colleen as she scrambles back into Big Blue. She kneels on the passenger seat and grabs my arm, pulling and yanking. She's rough and tugs me forcefully as I try to shake her off. Can't she see I'm with my grandmother?

"Stop it. Leave me alone," I mumble.

Colleen digs her nails into my arm and crabs backward, dragging me across the seat and out of the passenger side. The water, waist deep, whips with a current that robs us of our footing. She puts her arm around my shoulders, and we pause, trying to maintain balance. Then, by taking baby steps, we pad against the bedrock, knees bent, genuflecting like we are schoolgirls at Our Lady of Perpetual Help Church.

The water is freezing, and each step gets harder. I fear going under to the menacing troughs below. Can I move my arms enough to swim? My breath comes in short, rapid gasps. We don't speak, mustering all energy to reach land. Why does the shoreline look closer than it is?

My feet are numb. A rock bangs against my ankle bone. I feel like we're plowing against an incoming tide.

"Not much further," pants Colleen.

I grind my teeth to keep them from chattering. We traverse a rocky ledge, then sink into mud. I worry the sticky gunge will yank off my shoes, but Colleen won't let me bend over to check them.

"We can't stop. We've got to keep going," she huffs.

The wind whistles, spraying water. My nostrils quiver.

"So close."

Do my eyes play tricks? Is Colleen correct that we're almost there? We slog up to the bank, tottering like babies learning to walk. Colleen's upper boot shafts have slipped down, bunched around her ankles like baggy socks, yet the water-logged foot beds adhere tightly, making wet smooches against the dirt. The sound starts me giggling. Or maybe I'm shivering.

Too shocked to do anything but stand there on the bank, we turn and look out at Big Blue, filled with water up to the windows. I've never considered the river as being particularly deep, but it might swallow Big Blue. Yet ever stalwart, Big Blue refuses to go down. Perhaps a rock anchors the chassis in place?

"Big Blue," sighs Colleen.

Winds unfurl with a mighty force and spin the front end so that Big Blue faces us. The clouds part, and a shaft of white light pierces the windshield, illuminating the dash. I spy St. Christopher, his halo ablaze in glory. On his shoulder sits the child Jesus, clapping his hands. My grandmother sits at the steering wheel. She smiles, and I remember how she said church funerals were no fun. She wanted a burial at sea. When I laughed, she rasped, "Someday you'll understand."

Why hadn't I realized she wanted Big Blue to go with her?

Tree branches clatter. The wind quickens. From above us, we hear a truck grind gears and stop. A door opens, and a man yells: "Are you okay?"

A gust slams against Big Blue, setting the chassis free. My grandmother waves, and then spins the wheel to catch the current. St. Christopher raises his staff, shaking it victoriously. The child Jesus holds his nose, ready to go under.

Am I laughing or crying? Colleen makes the same weird sound.

I know there are bridges and sandbars downstream that can ground them. But maybe not. Surely, they could sail along to the Chesapeake Bay, arriving as the dogwoods bloom, their pink and white flowers urging them onward to the Atlantic.

Big Blue surfs to the river bend, navigates the curve, and then disappears.

ACKNOWLEDGMENTS

THE SEEDS of *St. Christopher on Pluto* took years to germinate, and I am thankful for the friends and colleagues who helped with the process.

I am indebted to Wilkes University's Maslow Family Graduate Program in Creative Writing for its ethos of writers helping writers. Director Bonnie Culver and cofounder J. Michael Lennon, along with fellow faculty members and graduate students, provided laughter, energy, and support. I am grateful to Sara Pritchard, my literary matchmaker, for her thoughtful response; to Taylor Polites for humor and perception; to Christine Gelineau for reminders to stay the course; to Bev Donofrio for her astute comments, and to Kaylie Jones, Jean Klein, Laurie Lowenstein, Rashidah Ismaili Abu Bakr, Lenore Hart, John Bowers, Nina Solomon, Greg Fletcher, David Poyer, Jeff Talarico, Ross Klavan, Joyce Anzalone, and Bill Schneider for their insight and encouragement.

I am thankful for the critique and enthusiasm of a spot-on writing group: Gale Martin, Mary Beth Matteo, Richard Fellinger, Donna Talarico-Berman, and Lori Cramer.

I am thankful for the camaraderie and feedback from the Den Mother writing group: Justin Kassab, Nina Long, Krista Harner, Catherine Donges, and William Donges.

I have much appreciation for the Indian Creek Neighborhood for expanding my writer's eye with the wellspring of community. Heartfelt thanks to Janeal and Jack Jaroh for laughter, walks-n-talks, and many turns of phrase, and to Lesley Simko, for calls and texts: *Look out your window. There's a car floating downstream.*

Special thanks to my sister, Marcy McKinley, for uplifting chats and for sharing my fiction with the Island Ladies Book Group. To Nancy Flynn, for her exceptional evaluation and response. To Tracey Pawelski for promo points. To Cale Kenney for sharing details. To Deb and Pat Heffernan, for soup dumplings and dialogue. To Amye Archer and Jim Warner for inviting me to read at Prose in Pubs, in Scranton, PA, and to the Mulberry Poets and Writers for inviting me to read at Keystone College, in La Plume, PA.

I am thankful to Diane Donnelly McKinley and Gale Brown Donnelly who weeded the garden in Danville, PA, and helped me to unearth the title.

How can I ever thank my many teachers over the years? Steven Schwartz, Wayne Ude, and Bill Tremblay at Colorado State University, and Jack Vernon at State University of New York–Binghamton taught me so much about form and technique.

My deepest thanks to West Virginia University Press for their support and guidance, especially Abby Freeland, Charlotte Vester, Sara N. Ash Georgi, and Rebecca Rider, who is an outstanding copy editor.

I thank my mother, Constance, for cultivating my appreciation for story. I wish I could present her with my first copy of the book, for her spirit resides in the pages.

Finally, and most importantly, I am grateful to Mike Lester, my best friend for life, who gave love from the get go, and to our daughters, the female warriors Darcy, Kelsi, and Hali—ever accepting of the writing life, they are a continual source of joy.